Donnie Baseball

A Novel

Tom Gresham

Donnie Baseball

A Novel

Tom Gresham

Tom Gresham

ISBN 9798787350937

Cover design by Thomas Mervenne

To Shannon, Elise, and Luke

Tom Gresham

Now the trouble with turtles is that they believe all things come to him who will but struggle. There's always room at the top for one more, they think. And in this strange faith the snapping kind is of all the most devout. For it's precisely that that makes them the snapping kind. Though the way be steep and bloody, that doesn't matter so long as you reach the top of the bleeding heap.

Nelson Algren, *A Walk on the Wild Side*

Chapter One

Donnie Wilson's professional baseball career ended the day he realized he did not know where he was. It was a hot afternoon game and the small, ragged ballpark where he found himself was more than half empty and nearly hushed, so absent of enthusiasm that he could hear murmurs of lazy conversation from the stands as he dug his back foot into the batter's box. He paused, lining up his fingers just right on his bat and staring out toward yet another anonymous pitcher, and it occurred to him that he couldn't name the city where this little head-to-head matchup—one of the thousands in his unstoried career— was about to happen. He stood there, his legs spread, one foot in the box and one still out, and worked his brain over this puzzle.

He knew he played for the St. Paul Saints of the Northern League, but this game wasn't in St. Paul, which had a rowdy, circus-like atmosphere that rang with all the noisiest minor-league bells and whistles—goofy fan promotions, ear-splitting music, wacky mascots, partying crowds that barely noticed the game on the field. This place inhabited the other, less lively pole of minor league ball. It was bored, dozing.

It was also a mystery. He'd slept on the trip in, waking only in time to stumble from the bus steps through the locker room door, and could not now recall any useful clues. He'd been daydreaming through the first five innings, which had never been a problem before this season, and he wasn't sure if he'd once known this city and forgotten it or had simply never cared enough to be aware.

The pitcher, a lefty, wore a white jersey with red cursive "Red Hawks" across the front. Donnie vaguely remembered Red Hawks from somewhere. Where, though? Old, nondescript warehouses peeked above the outfield fence, which was covered in advertisements for chain restaurants and local businesses Donnie had never heard of. He'd always imagined he'd one day play in large, raucous ballparks where the fans were intense, the players were famous, and the views were of bold, distinctive city skylines. Instead, he'd spent fifteen years on forgettable fields like this one.

"Wilson, you hitting today?"

Donnie snapped to attention and discovered the umpire and catcher watching him.

"It's hot as balls out here," said the ump, a gray-haired veteran who had removed his mask. His face was pink and sweating. "Let's keep it moving."

Donnie nodded, brought his front foot into the box, and settled into his stance. A left-handed hitter, he wrapped his bat parallel to the ground over his left shoulder. He felt it wavering languidly by his ear.

"Red Hawks," he thought as the pitcher peered past him to the catcher, taking his sign. "Who the hell are the Red Hawks?"

When the pitch came, Donnie barely registered its presence. So relaxed was he, though, and so instinctive was hitting a baseball to him, that his bat swung almost without his knowledge, a quick, direct jolt through the air that connected squarely with a tailing, inside fastball. That ideal connection with the fat part of the bat so clean and true that you can barely tell you've hit the ball at all. Donnie was the most surprised person in attendance to discover that a line drive was curling down the first base line, headed for the corner.

He jerked into action, racing toward first, taking a wide turn, hitting the bag hard and heading for second. He was thinking triple, knowing the right fielder had a long way to run, and he looked toward the third base coach for direction. The coach, a young, heavy guy everybody called Chubs, was waving his arm frantically in a wind-milling motion, telling him to keep moving. Donnie obeyed, motoring through second and pushing for third.

As he grew closer, he saw Chubs on his knees behind the bag, fanning his hands toward the ground and begging Donnie to slide. A third baseman crouched with his glove out, awaiting the throw. Donnie launched himself headfirst into the air, his arms extended in front of him like a gliding superhero, and slid violently into the bag. His arms crumpled at impact and his helmet slid down over his eyes. He felt the tag come down hard on his back—too late, asshole, he thought—and heard an umpire shout, "Safe!"

He pulled himself upright, wiped at the dirt on his uniform front. He felt his already sore body complain. Chubs slapped him on the ass. "Attaboy, Pops," he said. "Who said old men couldn't fly? That was some serious giddy-up there." Donnie adjusted his helmet, looked at the coach.

"Chubs," he said. "Where the hell are we?"

Chubs grinned broadly. Then he realized Donnie's seriousness and a look of confusion crossed his wide face.

"Third base. You OK? You hit your head?"

"I know third base. What city?"

"Damn, Pops," Chubs said, laughing. "Are you old enough for Alzheimer's?"

Donnie stared at him, waiting.

Chubs lost his grin.

"Fargo," he said. "In America."

That was it. Fargo. He'd once known that.

Donnie reached down and scooped dirt into both hands, something he had done every time he had reached base safely over the past twenty-five years. He proudly went without batting gloves and holding the dirt kept his hands clasped into fists so that if he did a feet-first slide he would instinctively hold his hands up and closed, instead of open and dragging on the ground. His Dad had taught him the trick after he had sprained his wrist in Little League when he was eleven years old.

He thought of Max, his nine-year-old son, who was now a veteran Little Leaguer. Donnie hadn't seen him play a game yet. His wife, Amy, said the kid was right good. "A little Donnie," she told him. They were across the country in Richmond, Virginia. Since Donnie was gone every spring and summer, he had barely taught Max a thing about the sport that was his livelihood. The kid probably wore batting gloves.

Chubs sidled up behind him. He was sweating profusely and smelled like the bottom of a locker. "One down, Pops. And there's a big arm in right."

Shit. Fargo. How many times had he stooped to pick up dirt on one of these fields, running through the game situation—the outs, the score, the pitcher, the batter, the arms in the outfield—and prepared himself for action? All to try to do well in some nothing game everyone would forget the moment it was over.

He'd talked with Max on the phone not long ago, and the kid, who wasn't the affectionate type, had said for the first time that he missed him. Donnie had been shocked into some muttering reply, later wishing he'd said something more.

The opposing catcher approached the mound to confer with his pitcher. Donnie rolled his right shoulder, grimacing at a grinding sensation he'd been feeling lately. He turned and studied Chubs.

"How old are you, Chubs?" he asked.

"Thirty," he said. "I'm a baby next to you."

Being older than some of the coaches was all part of not being on a big-league team at his age or even in Double or Triple A, but on an independent outfit that wasn't affiliated with a major league squad. At the very bottom of the ladder, as if he was starting over, unable to identify his surroundings they were so obscure.

He'd occasionally felt ridiculous since the start of the season. His attention would wander in new ways, pulling him away from the game in front of him. For the first time, he wondered what he was doing. What did he even hope for? He was thirty-six, a wreck of a career behind him. Most guys his age—the ones who never made it to the top—had seen the path ahead and retired five years ago at least. He was still one of the best two or three hitters on the Saints, but that wasn't good enough to provide any real hope for more. His current teammates, rambunctious guys in their twenties, called him Pops, directed a torrent of old fogey jokes at him, and sought out his advice like he was some elder statesman, a role he neither liked nor wanted. He wanted to be the guy the other players envied and secretly hated for his sure future. He had once been that guy.

11

He'd tinkered with his stance in the spring, hoping to unlock some brilliant thing inside him that had been slumbering. Every spring he went through this now. And every summer was the same. He was no better than he'd been the year before—a productive, unremarkable player in a country teeming with them.

A smattering of halfhearted, vaguely directed boos drifted onto the field. The Fargo manager had used the catcher's visit to buy some time and now trudged to the mound to switch pitchers. A new reliever trotted in from the bullpen in foul territory. Chubs spoke in Donnie's ear, "This guy's got a big splitter. Be ready to go on a wild pitch." He paused, patted him earnestly on the shoulder. "Just don't hurt yourself, OK, Pops?" Chubs laughed hard and backed away. "And don't get your ass lost."

All his work had resulted in this: He was a punch line. Donnie suddenly felt very strongly that he never wanted to be called Pops again. He didn't want to be the source of any more chuckles for idiot coaches and shitty players. He was exhausted, tired of fighting without reward, and he wanted off that base and out of that ballpark. He wanted to leave Fargo and never set foot in the city again, nor in St. Paul or Binghamton or Toledo or Modesto or Winnipeg or Kingsport or in any of the other dozens of cities where he had once stood, clutching dirt and imagining something grander. He wanted to sit in the stands at some slapstick kids' game, laugh with Amy and watch Max play ball.

He took an aggressive lead off third base. The next batter, Javier, a scrawny middle infielder with a loose, weak swing, popped a shallow fly ball into right. Donnie dropped back to the base to tag up.

"No, you're staying, you're staying, you're staying," Chubs said, steps ahead of him down the line in foul territory, his hands in the air to halt him.

But Donnie could not stay a moment longer. As soon as the ball plopped into the right fielder's glove, Donnie pushed off the bag with a grunt, his surgically repaired left knee—injured one night years ago when he ran into a wall in Toledo—groaning at the pressure, and raced with everything he had for home plate. Chubs' voice rang in his ear, "No, no, no!"

The catcher in all his gear waited impatiently at home, his feet bouncing, his masked face toward right field. Donnie saw him drift up the line toward him, meaning the throw was off target, leading into Donnie. The ball arrived on a skip into the waiting catcher's mitt when Donnie was still two steps away. Without slowing, he rammed into the catcher's chest as hard as he could. He lifted his arms in front of him and pushed up. He'd been taught in high school football to run through someone on impact—to hit him as if he wasn't there. He felt the catcher loosen sickeningly, felt the guy's feet give way.

Donnie tumbled across home plate, the catcher somewhere down behind and beneath him. The ball rolled away harmlessly toward the backstop. Donnie's helmet spun in mad circles beside him. The crowd woke with gasps.

The old ump spread his arms wide, indicating Donnie was safe, but he said nothing. His weary green eyes were on the fallen catcher.

Donnie looked back at the guy, too, and he saw that he lay flat and still. Donnie rose to his feet and watched him for several worried beats, until the guy exhaled dramatically and lifted himself to a sitting position. Dazed and slow, he searched for the ball in his mitt and appeared dumbfounded to find it missing.

Donnie pivoted, a final responsibility cleared, and left the field. He ran with his head down past his teammates, ignoring their back pats and raised hands, and then continued without breaking stride through the dugout and into the tunnel that led to the visitors' clubhouse. The clanging of his spikes as he jogged across the tunnel's concrete floor reminded him of the steady, tick-tock score of a thriller as the suspense builds. He burst through the clubhouse door and dropped onto the bench in front of his locker for the day. He struggled to catch his breath. He looked down and realized his hands were still clenched tight and full of dirt. He opened his hands and watched the dirt fall to the floor.

When he got back to his tiny St. Paul apartment, Donnie slumped into his twin bed, kicked off his shoes, and slept entombed in his silent, windowless room for twelve hours, out cold from eight p.m. to eight a.m. He slept as though submerged, held down in unconsciousness. Once before, when his father had died, he'd slept the same way, his body shutting down on him while his brother and mother handled the immediate aftermath without him. He'd felt guilty about it then, and he felt guilty when he awoke this time, too. He tried to convince himself that it was OK to rest now. He could skip his run, his pushups, his crunches. He didn't need to start the day with one-hundred swings of the bat. He lay in bed, telling himself this, until he found himself shooting to his feet and cranking through the swings, spraying imaginary line drives all over his bedroom. He craved the motion and was itchy and antsy without it. The single goal that had animated and occupied him for as long as he could remember was a thing of the past, and the rhythm of his days was about to change, but his body didn't know it yet.

He packed quickly and efficiently and headed for the airport. He didn't bother saying goodbye to any of his teammates.

As the plane prepared to land in Richmond, Donnie searched through the window for landmarks below. He counted four baseball fields with their lights on, a warm, welcoming glow in the dark night, and he reflexively shut the shade.

Donnie fell asleep in the back of a cab and was startled to find himself suddenly in front of his house, a well-kept three-bedroom colonial in the suburbs of Henrico County, near the Richmond city line. The street was decently lit, a gauntlet of exterior lights dutifully on in front of the houses that lined the road in even spaces. Their house was neither the largest nor the smallest on the block, certainly nothing like the Tennysons' place across the street—a goliath for the block after a large addition the year before. Max's best friend, Lucas, lived there, though Donnie wasn't sure how much longer the neighborhood could contain the boy's father, Foster.

At the front door, as Donnie fished for his key—one he hadn't grasped in months—he wished he'd called first.

Amy will take this hard, he thought. She will be devastated for sure.

He wondered why this had not occurred to him before—why she hadn't occurred to him before. It was one thing to quit and somehow another to say it aloud. To admit it.

The first thing he registered in his house was the surprising sound of music. It was dizzy pop, something candy-flavored and familiar from the clubhouse. A male voice at a high pitch, altered with machines and backed with an insistent beat.

It's a Javier song, he thought. One of those songs we always hear when Javier's in control of the stereo.

Heard, he corrected himself. One of those songs we always heard.

He called for Amy, but he did not get a response. He followed the music toward the kitchen. He pushed through the swinging door.

Amy screamed, her eyes round with terror, and shot to her feet from her seat at the kitchen table, where she'd been on her laptop. A bottle of beer slipped from her hand and smashed and scattered on the floor. Donnie put his arms up high. "I'm sorry, I'm sorry. It's me, It's me."

Amy put her hand to her chest and took two steps back. "Dammit, Donnie. What the hell?"

"I'm sorry," he said, slowly making his way into the room. He moved toward her hesitantly, his hands raised as if to show her he meant no harm. "I'm sorry."

Amy was trembling but then she exhaled, closed her eyes, and shook her head twice. She took two steps toward Donnie and hugged him hard, her head buried into his chest. "You asshole."

He hugged her hard in return. She kissed him on the chest and backed up, looking at him with concern. "They let you go? I thought you were hitting well."

Donnie walked across the kitchen to a closet, opened it and grabbed a mop and a bucket. "I let myself go. It's over. I'm done." He avoided her eyes.

Amy followed him to the closet and grabbed a dustpan. "Honey, I'm sorry. Did something happen?"

"I was standing on third and I just all of a sudden knew it was time to stop pretending."

"Just like that?"

"Just like that."

"I really am sorry. You had a hell of a run, kid."

Donnie didn't answer. He filled up the bucket with water and floor cleaner and mopped where the bottle had broken, pushing the loose glass into a pile. Amy picked up the mouth of the bottle and used a broom to push the broken bits in the pile into the dustpan.

"I know it sucks, babe, but Max and I are going to love having you around."

The sound of footsteps came from upstairs, and Amy looked at Donnie with a cocked eyebrow. "Speak of the little devil," she said.

"I'm on the case," Donnie said.

Donnie returned to the foyer and caught a movement on the stairs out of the corner of his eye. He looked up to discover Max lying on his belly, peering around the turn in the stairs. Donnie had been debating Amy over the phone recently about how to handle Max's night-wandering ways, which had developed soon after Donnie left for spring training when Max saw some scary movie at a friend's house. He would not fall asleep upstairs alone anymore. Amy had taken to getting in bed with him and staying there until he drifted off. Donnie thought this was silly coddling and told Amy so. "He's too old for that kind of thing," he said. She said that was easy to say when you weren't there dealing with it every night, hoping like hell for a few minutes of peace before the day ended. You become willing to do whatever it takes to get those precious quiet moments to yourself, she said. Believe me. Plus, she went on, the little guy really is scared. You can tell by his heartbeat. It's fast as raindrops in a storm. There's no faking that.

"Hiya, Max," Donnie said. "What you up to, buddy?"

Max stood and slumped down the stairs, pausing on each step, his eyes cast down. He stopped at the bottom step and folded half his body over the railing. Not the kind of emphatic welcome Donnie wanted, but that wasn't the boy's style and his attempt at nonchalance at least amused Donnie. The kid didn't understand his parents could see right through him.

"It's good to see you, but you gotta get some sleep," Donnie said. "You're up way too late."

Max straightened and looked at him. His worry was obvious.

"Will you come up too?" he asked.

Donnie put his hand on his son's chest and immediately felt what Amy was talking about. Raindrops in a storm. Max watched him, confused.

"Just this once, OK?" Donnie said. "Just because I've been gone. We're not doing this tomorrow."

Max's face filled with relief.

Donnie picked his boy up and started to climb the stairs. Max let his chin rest on Donnie's shoulder.

"When are you going back?" Max asked.

"I'm not. I'm here for good. No more summers away."

Max pulled back and studied his father, apparently trying to determine whether this was good or bad news. Donnie didn't give him a hint in either direction.

Ten minutes later, Donnie lay awake on his back in Max's room, his sleeping son's head resting on his arm. Max had crashed almost immediately.

Donnie scanned the posters of pro athletes on Max's wall, including one of Donnie's buddy Stubs Woodson, a second baseman for the Reds. Next to Stubs was a crudely colored homemade poster. The image was of a lefthanded batter standing at the plate in an awkward stance, his one eye looking off the page, apparently toward a pitcher. His feet were arranged at an impossible angle. He had a thin, toothless smile on an egg-shaped head. There was no clever detail to make it distinctly Donnie—no recognizable form to the face, no familiar shape to the torso—but his name was there across the top, the letters in "Wilson" scrunched together where Max had begun to run out of room on the poster board. Smartly, the young artist had left a team name and logo off the uniform and cap, a nod to Donnie's fitful, nomadic passage through teams and cities.

Donnie stared at this vision of himself and wondered how it could have been different. He wished like hell, of course, that his son could have a real poster of him on his wall, but it was more than that. He also wished the poster didn't stir such regret in him. He tried to step back and appreciate what the act meant—what it said about the way Max felt about him—but he got nowhere. The poster felt like an insult, and that's all that Donnie was capable of feeling.

When Donnie returned downstairs, he and Amy sat at the kitchen table and talked well into the morning hours. They drank beer and talked about baseball—first about the end of the career that had always been central to their lives together and then with nostalgia about the beginning, when they were young and didn't know what lay ahead. Then they talked about Richmond and home and Max.

"I don't know what I'm going to do with myself now," Donnie said. "Playing baseball is all I've cared about my whole life."

Amy shook her head. "It was never going to be the only thing, though. It was always going to end at some point, and you were always going to be here figuring out what was next. It was just a matter of when."

"But it's not the ending I wanted. It's not the ending I was supposed to get."

"That's like bitching about not winning the lottery."

Donnie pointed his beer at his wife. "You're not being supportive."

Amy smiled. "Yes, I am. In my own way. You just don't know it yet."

Donnie nodded. "Every once in a while, you could coddle me, you know? Treat me like I was someone who needed that kind of thing."

Amy stood up, walked behind Donnie, and wrapped her arms around him. "I literally wouldn't know how to do that, and you'd hate it if I did." She leaned over and kissed him on the mouth, then straightened and took the bottles from the table and dropped them in the recycling container under the sink. "I do love you, though, and I am happy to see you."

"I guess I'm happy to see you, too."

Amy returned to the table, stopped next to Donnie, and gave him an artful caress on the shoulder. "Let's go upstairs and you can prove it to me."

Donnie sighed and stood. "If you say so."

Amy took his hand, something he couldn't recall her doing even when they were young and walked him toward the stairs. "It's not all bad," she said. "You won't have to miss me anymore."

Chapter Two

Five years later

The Canterbury Youth Baseball complex in western Henrico County was a gem, a bejeweled stunner of a facility readily accessible from bristling Patterson Avenue, which cut past when running west to east in a determined path from the snoozing outer reaches of laconic, exurban Goochland County toward the steel, metal, and glass of downtown Richmond, a forever-striving, mid-sized city that continued to contend with the damning, misleading, and wholly fair title of the Capital of the Confederacy. Canterbury still felt new and fresh after three short years in existence and the players and parents who spent hours of their spring, summer, and autumn lives there—under a stiff sun, at humid dusk, under bright-white lights—felt blessed by its immaculateness. The manicured fields without the slightest spot of clover, the clean, unwavering lines on the basepaths, the wide, spacious dugouts with water fountains and bat racks and white boards. In the swept and swiped bleachers, fans snacked on hot dogs, chicken sandwiches, and nachos while breezing the Internet on the park's free Wi-Fi. Bored siblings could expend their jittery energy at the massive playground. Parents stopped at the snack bar for iced coffee.

In the parking lot, Donnie checked his pockets twice to make sure his keys were there. Then he locked his car, a thoroughly used Honda sedan with splotches of white delamination across the top of its otherwise navy-blue roof. He wore an orange Clemson ballcap, a T-shirt for the Easton bat company, and knee-length cargo shorts. His face was covered in a two-day growth of stubble that was grayer than he was ready to see during his rare glances into a mirror.

He walked with an easy, limber gait across the scorched blacktop, the bald sun seeming to hit him from different angles, toward the array of adult regulation fields on the complex's west side. He lowered his eyes as he walked, wishing he'd remembered some sunglasses, and so he was too distracted and mentally adrift to notice his son until he was almost upon him at the edge of the parking lot. He only recognized Max, finally, when he heard his voice, sullen and annoyed, say, "Don't you have to work?"

Max had a peevish look on his face. He was wearing his uniform, though he hadn't put his hat on yet, and was carrying the equipment bag Donnie had given him the year before on his thirteenth birthday. He was walking alongside his best friend, Lucas.

"Got out early," Donnie said. "Hey, Lucas, how you doing?"

"Alright, Mr. Wilson. We'll see how things go today, I guess."

"You pitching, Max?"

"I told you this morning I was."

Donnie could see the tension in his son's shoulders. "Just wanted to make sure. You gonna keep that front shoulder tucked this time?"

He shrugged. "I don't know."

Donnie felt a familiar irritation growing. "Get your hat on, boy. How many times have I told you your hat's as much a part of the uniform as your pants? You wouldn't show up to a game without your pants, would you?"

Max stopped, unzipped his bag, pulled out his hat and put it on slightly askew—a small act of rebellion—without a word. They walked in silence on the concrete path until they reached Max's field. At the gate, Donnie said, "Remember that shoulder, buddy." But Max simply kept walking onto the field, where his teammates were stretching and gabbing in the grass. Lucas turned and waved. "See ya, Coach."

Donnie lifted his hand and gave a brisk wave to Lucas and his son's retreating back, and then walked down the third base line, clear of the bleachers to his preferred viewing spot. He liked to be on Max's open side when he pitched, so he could get the best possible sight line on his son's delivery. He always stood out there alone.

Things didn't go well from the start. Max was lit up for three runs in the first and two in the second. Donnie couldn't believe how disconnected his son's delivery seemed, how unprepared he appeared to be. He looked as though he had picked up pitching that morning. In the third, he walked the first two batters on nine pitches. Donnie felt a helplessness darkening all his very best intentions.

"Wake up, Max," he said, wrestling to keep his voice low. "Wake the hell up."

On the mound, Max stared in at Chuck Slater's catcher's mitt and wished the whole thing would be over already. His command was shit, every pitch a struggle, and he knew he wasn't going to get any better before his day was through. He wanted out of there.

He nodded at Chuck's signal, a single finger stretched toward the ground, feeling ridiculous about it. He had only the fastball, but his coach made him take signs as though a curve or anything else was possible. He made him nod, too. Sometimes, Max would shake his head instead as though there were other pitches to choose from and he wanted his catcher to call for something else, but everybody knew what was coming. Players on other teams had taken to making loud jokes about it from their bench. "Oh, God, look out for the splitter!" they'd cry, gripping each other for support.

Max stepped gently back and entered his windup, a classic, tight, controlled motion that his dad had drilled into him. He delivered his pitch. It darted into the dirt in front of the plate and slipped beneath Chuck's dropped glove, scooting away to the backstop. The batter watched without flinching. Chuck ambled resentfully back to retrieve the ball, his armor appearing to weigh heavily on him, while the baserunners jogged to second and third.

To his right, Max heard Dad mutter curses. Although Max didn't look his way, he saw him as clearly as if they were standing nose-to-nose. He knew Dad's jaw was pushed forward in anger, and his fists were bouncing rhythmically off his thighs. He knew he was pacing in his customary spot down the third-base line behind the chain-link fence, away from the stands and the other parents.

"Slow down, Max. Slow the hell down," Dad shouted. "You're getting out front of yourself. Slow it down."

Dad thought this was helping, this tossed-out advice, but Max was exhausted from all the teaching, the instruction, the lessons, and tips that were always coming his way. A curveball is what he needed, but his dad wouldn't allow it yet. Dad had taught him a changeup, but Max could barely throw that pitch in the direction of the plate. He was too humiliated to even consider throwing it in a game.

One year before, it had been different. He'd been thirteen, playing his last year of Little League, just under the cutoff with an April 30th birthday that made him the oldest kid in the league, and the mound had still been only forty-five feet from home plate, the same distance it had been his whole life. He'd been a monster, firing fastballs past everyone at will, setting down every overmatched kid who creeped into the batter's box with a worried look and a tense hold on his bat. This year, though, he'd moved up to the full-sized field and the mound had moved back. Sixty feet, six inches, just like the big leagues. He couldn't believe what a difference that short stretch had made in his world. And other kids seemed to be growing much faster than he was. Kids he'd looked down on before had somehow passed him when he wasn't paying attention. Now hitters seemed unconcerned when they faced him. Eager even, their bats waving with menace and their swings assured, powerful flashes that sent line drives all over the field.

His parents had enjoyed all of it the spring before—his dad rooted down the line by himself, his mother clapping in the stands with the rest of the parents. And when the game ended, they would come together from their three separate spots and leave as one unit, side by side, and go out for burgers or pizza.

That wasn't going to happen again. One night in October, his mother had gone to bed late, taking a mix of pills meant to help her sleep. She'd never woken up. As sudden and simple and final as that.

The infield chatter behind him had subsided to a halfhearted murmur. Donnie could hear the frustration in the voices of the teammates who bothered to say anything. Lucas, who was over at shortstop, begged him to throw strikes.

"C'mon, let him hit it, Max. We got nothing else to do out here. We don't mind helping."

He thought of his father's advice as he nodded again. He entered his delivery, slowing down this time, and reached back for yet another fastball. It sailed above the head of the batter. He'd slowed down too much. Chuck sagged and dropped his head before shuffling toward the backstop again.

Hoots came from the other team's dugout. The hitter flipped aside his bat and started for first base as his teammate on third trotted home. Max took two steps as though he would cover the plate, but he saw that it was too late and stopped, deciding not to pretend. "Dammit," his dad shouted, kicking at the dirt with such gusto that Max involuntarily shot a glance in that direction.

He felt not only Dad's gaze now but Mom's too. She was leaned forward, her elbows on her knees, eyes on him as she cupped her hands and yelled reassuring words of encouragement. Only she wasn't there. No matter how long he searched the stands, he wouldn't find her. Never again.

Max's coach approached the mound—an agent of mercy. As Max shuffled off the mound and headed for the dugout, he felt his father's frustration as though it was his own and it filled him with rage. Screw that miserable man. Max took off his hat and walked with it by his side—just like taking off your pants, Dad had said. Max may as well have flipped him the bird.

Donnie wasn't sure what made him angrier: his son's brooding or the way Greg Hall's kid started carving up hitters with his lollipop curveball as soon as Max settled into the dugout.

He was sickened to see his boy responding to adversity the way he was, going quiet and separating from his teammates. He'd always hated guys like that. They were frontrunners, alive and part of the team only when things were going well for them. He'd never guessed his kid would turn into one. For years, people had told him that Max looked like "Little Donnie" out there, and he'd always silently agreed with them. He didn't see it anymore, though. The resemblance was gone, and it wasn't just the way he played. His looks were changing, and Donnie no longer saw a younger version of himself in the boy. He was losing that kid.

Jay Hall was having a big time up there. He had a large, looping curve for a fourteen-year-old, and he was chucking one after the other, showing some swagger as hitters flailed at them. Donnie spotted him holster an imaginary gun after one strikeout. He remembered how Max used to pump his fist toward him on the mound, as though seeking confirmation he'd done as well as he thought he had. Donnie would pump his fist right back at him, and he'd feel a surge between them, his strength there for his son to use.

21

Donnie had played against Greg in high school, outdone him more than once on the field, and he had no respect for the guy then or now. Greg wasn't a fan of his either. He was bellowing from the stands. After one strikeout, the kid's fourth in two innings, Greg said loudly enough for Donnie to hear from his post, "Maybe they shoulda started him, huh?"

Donnie wondered what would happen if he climbed into the stands and beat the guy.

Instead, he worked to calm himself down, employing a strategy Amy had suggested years ago and he'd adopted only now in her painful absence. He imagined how unhappy Greg might be, how his life might not be so great. It was not difficult. Jay would be worthless in high school ball. Not only did Donnie believe the curves were hurting the kid's elbow, wearing it down toward early surgery and taking miles per hour off his future fastballs—his delivery was too open coming home, overtaxing the arm—but he was developing bad habits. He wasn't learning how to pitch, how to work fastballs around the strike zone. He was just flipping a trick pitch at a bunch of kids who still don't know how to hit it. Next year, they'd be a bit better at it. The year after that even better. Pretty soon, if all Jay had to offer was a soft curve—and it would be—then he might struggle to make a varsity roster, let alone attract college interest.

Greg approached between innings, looking ridiculous in coaches' shorts and wraparound Oakley sunglasses. He played on some traveling slow-pitch softball team, one of these outfits stuffed with oversized men who could barely move except to muscle monstrous home runs. The team name, "XXL," was on the front of his too-tight T-shirt. The thing was that Greg wasn't one of the big guys. He was a yappy little guy with a snub nose and uneven goatee. He also was the pitcher, and he was always trying to explain to people how it was more complicated than lobbing the ball up there. There was a skill and an art to it.

"Donnie Baseball, looking good," Greg said. "Max, though, not his day, huh?"

"His head's up his ass lately is all."

Greg laughed. "Jay's coming along. He keeps getting better and better."

"Yeah, sure."

"Some kids are like that. Other kids are more throwers than pitchers. They get away from Little League and they can't survive just winging it anymore. The big boy field's a whole new ballgame." Greg stopped, shook his head in unconvincing sympathy. "Jay's suited to it, though. He's got a maturity to him."

A pinch-hitter strode to the plate. He was taking Max's place in the lineup. The kid held his hands too low for Donnie's liking.

Most days, Donnie would have let fly with all the ways that Greg was wrong, but he felt such warmth in the assurance he had in his imagining of Jay's career arc. He liked knowing these things, revealed to him on baseball fields as though he was privy to some private wellspring of knowledge. He found he could feel sorry for mouthy, pathetic Greg, looking dumb as shit in his costume, holding onto this moment of his boy's success and thinking it meant anything. It wasn't shit. Poor Greg and Jay were going to look back on these days and wonder why there couldn't have been more of them.

"He's a nice little player," Donnie said. "Good curve."

The pinch-hitter was late on a fastball and dribbled a weak ground ball to second. He was thrown out by three steps. All that wasted motion, Donnie thought with pride at being right.

Greg chuckled.

"What about that Cole McGuire?" he said. He exhaled and shook his head with embellished astonishment. "Two-and-a-half million is a hell of a lot of money. Wish he'd share some with me."

Donnie stiffened. Cole, who was all of eighteen, had recently signed a pro contract with the Pittsburgh Pirates. First-round dollars. Donnie had schooled Cole closely on the finer points of pitching, only for Cole to leave him for the Woodson Baseball Academy. In the paper that morning, Cole had credited WBA and its director Stubs Woodson, who had once been Donnie's best friend, for getting him ready for pro ball. Donnie hadn't been mentioned.

"The money is so good for these kids now," Greg said. "They get a great nest egg right away and then if things don't turn out they still got that big check to lean on. What'd you get in your day?"

"Too long ago to remember."

"I bet it's all gone now anyways."

Donnie felt his newfound resolve unravel. "More than you ever made playing ball."

Greg grinned a malicious grin. "And I guess I spent just as much time in the majors."

Donnie took two steps and shoved Greg hard in the chest. The guy fell over too easily, his head snapping back when he landed and his hat and expensive sunglasses flying off. Donnie caught the look of childish fear on his face as he dropped. Donnie felt as though he'd pushed over some shrimp kid on a playground somewhere. He took two steps back as though he could retreat from what he'd done.

Greg clambered to his feet and scooped up his precious shades, and then he was all flustered, macho anger.

"You goddamned has-been," he shouted. "Grow the hell up."

Greg turned and hurried to the stands, shaking his hat out and inspecting his sunglasses. Donnie watched him go and felt defeated. The crowd had turned to him, rows of blank, questioning faces wondering what the hell they were seeing. He looked toward the dugout and saw that Max had finally raised his head and he too was staring at him.

Of course, Donnie thought. Of fucking course.

When the game ended, Max appeared on the field for the handshake with his uniform unbuttoned and untucked, his hand limp and low by his thigh. His hat off. Donnie waited at his spot for Max to come see him for the walk back to the car, as he usually did, but the boy bolted for the parking lot with Lucas. He'd be heading for the Tennysons again. Donnie didn't bother trying to stop him.

Chapter Three

Donnie was into his second beer, his notebook open before him on the kitchen table, when his brother, Joe, opened the back door without knocking. Baxter, an aging beagle, woke briefly from napping by Donnie's feet before returning to a contented curl.

The kitchen was a wide-open room with natural light flooding in from the back of the house and stainless-steel appliances Amy had picked out. The stylishly rustic table was restored wood from an old barn. The floor tile formed an elegant pattern that reminded Donnie of a stained-glass window. Amy had overseen all of it. She'd also paid for it out of the income she'd earned as a partner at a boutique PR firm.

Joe walked straight to the fridge and retrieved a beer for himself. He joined Donnie at the table. Donnie kept his focus on a chapter on basic mechanics for outfielders. He was breaking down the proper way to catch a fly ball when a runner on base was tagging up. He was finding it difficult. It was easy to show someone the correct way, but tricky to explain it with only written words.

Joe opened a magazine. "You walk Baxter?"

Donnie lifted his pen and dropped it to the table with an emphatic, annoyed clatter. "You see I'm working, right?"

"Just worried about your dog."

"Don't be. We went on a good long one. He's exhausted."

Joe nodded. "Glad you guys are getting your exercise."

Donnie picked his pen back up and shook his head. "Shit."

"What about Max? He around?"

"At the Tennysons."

"Good lord, he got his own room there now? Foster can probably claim him as a dependent on his taxes this year. How'd he pitch?"

"Like shit. He gave up when things didn't go right for him. Just fell apart."

Joe shook his head. "Poor kid. You better not have given him a hard time. He's been through enough as it is."

Physically, Joe bore an uncanny resemblance to their father, a short man with a thick neck and forearms and a broad chest. However, he acted more like their mother, a friendly woman who was also forever in her family's business. She'd had the instincts of a micromanager, but she'd lacked the control of one. She was always urging her sons and her husband to do things, but never forcefully enough to be convincing. She'd died ten years ago—five years after Donnie's father. It had been just Donnie and Joe since.

Donnie knew the words on the page weren't working. He aimed for clarity as a coach. He prided himself on it. Coaches were always talking too long, saying more than they needed to, because they were so impressed with their own wisdom, and they didn't trust the intelligence of their charges. Donnie, though, understood that the simplest directive was the most effective one, and it wouldn't get lost in the noise of coach-speak if it was delivered alone. But Donnie had two paragraphs of winding sentences even he couldn't follow. He sifted through the words and tried to will them into better shape.

"So, I've got a favor to ask you," Joe said.

Donnie dropped the pen again, this time without any fanfare, and leaned back in his chair. He found he appreciated an excuse to look up from the page. "Yeah?"

"I'm helping organize this softball home run derby for the foundation," Joe said. Joe volunteered extensively for a foundation that raised money for fighting heart disease, which is what had gotten both of their parents. "Got a bunch of sponsors, lots of people coming."

"Why would anyone go to that?"

"The foundation's powerful, man, and a couple of companies have made it a community engagement thing and they're going to have prizes and food trucks and games and bouncy houses and all kinds of stuff for the kids. Companies are sponsoring players. It's gotten out of control. It's going to be a wild scene."

"Sounds ridiculous."

"I wanted to see if you'd help out."

"Nah."

Joe acted as though he was confused. "But you've got no game that night. No practice. Hmmm. No excuses. Seems like a great fit for you?"

"Man, you're into my business."

Joe crossed his fingers on both hands and held them toward Donnie, his face full of phony pleading. "It'd be a big help."

"I'll think about it. I might be doing something with Max."

"Yeah?"

"Yeah."

"Bring him along then."

Donnie closed the notebook. He had no idea of plans with Max, but maybe he'd be able to make some. The boy really was spending more time with the Tennysons than he was with Donnie.

Joe reached down and scratched Baxter beneath the ear. "Also, Stubs called this morning. Asked you to call him back."

"Called you?"

"That's right. I'll text you his number to make sure you got it."

"No need."

Joe frowned. "Seems silly not to call him back."

"Enough, Joe."

Joe's phone chirped, and he checked it obediently. "Don't get too lit," he said, rising from the table and nodding toward Donnie's beer. "We're going out."

"The hell you talking about?" Donnie said. "I'm not going anywhere. I'm working."

"Oh, right," Joe said, pausing and looking at the notebook as though it hadn't been there before. "How's that going?"

"Good. I'm just in a dicey part."

"I'll just tell Otis and Ricky you got homework."

Joe watched him. Donnie considered the beer in his hand. "I guess I could use a break."

The arrival of WBA had put Donnie in a tough spot. His coaching work had dried up so thoroughly that his income was almost nothing to speak of. He caught the odd team coaching job—American Legion in the summers, head coach of the JV team at Deep Creek High School. He'd gone from a full schedule of pupils, filling his evenings and weekends, to a slim roster of kids who would meet with him only from time to time, either at Deep Creek or in Donnie's backyard, where he'd set up a batting cage and pitcher's mound—neither of which saw much action anymore. He had little to do with himself. Somehow, though, his lack of earning power hadn't been clear to him until Amy had died. Suddenly, he was staring down a life without a job and without income, unable to pay the bills and forced to move with Max out of the house the boy had grown up in, and he got scared. He'd be failing not only his son but his late wife and all the work she'd done. He went to Otis and Ricky, who he'd known since he was a kid, and asked for a job on their maintenance crew at Deep Creek. They jointly oversaw the grounds there. He'd worked for them a couple of summers when he was a student. They'd hired him right away. It wasn't much money, but at least something was coming in again and he wasn't just draining what Amy had left behind.

Donnie and Joe found Otis and Ricky at a corner booth at O'Charley's, a nachos and chicken fingers chain with wood paneling everywhere. Televisions hung from the ceiling in every corner and were splayed beyond the bar, showing baseball games. The crowd was mostly families and old folks. Joe hated the place and every other strip-mall franchise in the world, and he had complained the entire drive there, but if they wanted to drink with Otis and Ricky this is where they had to go. Both lived within a couple of minutes of the place, and they refused to go to any of the "snobby" places Joe preferred.

Otis and Ricky had chosen to sit next to each other in the booth, leaving the other side of the table open. They looked ridiculous crammed together as they argued about something. Their relationship was shaped by their unending bickering, though Donnie had long ago understood that they loved the bickering—

27

there was rarely anything angry about it. They were both in their early fifties. Otis was a wiry white man with thick gray hair and the hardened, sunburned look of someone who had spent his life working outdoors. Ricky was black but in some ways his mirror image, tough and weather-worn and lean as a line.

As Donnie and Joe approached, Otis glanced at them and grabbed the last of the mozzarella sticks from a crumb-strewn plastic basket, while Ricky got the message and topped his glass with the final splashes of a pitcher of beer.

"Hiya, lovebirds," Donnie said, letting Joe sit on the inside. "Interesting seating arrangement. It's suspicious that I can't see your hands."

Otis flipped him off with both hands, while Ricky lifted one hand, and kept his left, the one closest to Otis, below the table, and acted embarrassed. Donnie pointed accusingly at him, but Ricky then lifted the hand and hailed at a waitress, while Joe perused the menu as though it might have changed.

"Who you putting your money on this year, Donnie?" Ricky said. "Chicken shit"—he thumbed toward Otis and made a disgusted face, then smiled and pointed toward himself and grinned broadly— "or chicken salad?" He puffed up his chest.

"I'm going to see if I can get odds on a double heart attack."

Joe chuckled, "You might have a hard time finding someone who'll take that one."

Years before, after the death of their beloved mentor, Samuel Jones, Otis and Ricky had been named to run the facilities and grounds together, but they'd argued immediately over who got the grounds and who got the buildings. Their preferences depended on the season. They both liked outdoors in the fall and spring and indoors in the winter and summer. So, once a year, in the middle of the summer, they held a triathlon to determine who had the year's choice. The selected events were a 400-meter run, a tennis match, and a wrestling match. The competition always attracted a small but drunkenly feverish crowd of those in the know.

The older Otis and Ricky got the more entertaining it became. They liked to compete throughout the year, too. Otis kept a duffel bag of whiffle balls and bats in his office, just so he could stage the occasional impromptu staff game at work. Donnie never understood the point of it and always declined to join them. Inevitably, Otis would reply, "To hell with you then."

The next triathlon was coming up fast and Otis and Ricky couldn't talk about anything else at the table, but Donnie and Joe didn't mind. Winding those two up and watching them go was well worth a night out. They argued about whose serve was better and who was in better shape and who was going to kick whose ass. After dinner came, Ricky provided an in-depth moment-by-moment recap of the previous year's wrestling match, which he'd won to snap a 1-1 triathlon tie, while Otis interrupted routinely to disagree with his friend's colorful version of events.

They drifted off the subject for a while after dinner, through another round of beer, to talk about the school principal, who they were sure was having an affair with one of the guidance counselors, but then circled back when Otis bragged about keeping a recording of the NCAA wrestling championships and studying the moves. This prompted Ricky to hop out of the booth and start cranking out pushups, drawing the attention of everybody in the place.

Otis leaned from the booth, crying at him. "You're cheating. You're cheating. Chin's got to touch the ground." He looked to Joe and Donnie for support, but they just smiled back at him. "Those are BS." He spilled off the bench and dropped onto the floor, where he faced Ricky and started pumping up and down, doing his own pushups as they glowered at each other.

Donnie and Joe commented on the action and enjoyed their beers.

A waitress approached and waited, watching with a tired expression on her face. All at once, Otis and Ricky collapsed onto their chests in relief, breathing in heavy, gasping breaths.

"Do I need to cut y'all off?" the waitress asked, her hands on her hips in a bored, resigned disapproval.

"Ma'am, could someone who was drunk do what they just did?" Joe asked. "These are very old men."

"You ever hear of drunk muscles?" she said.

"C'mon, girl, give us a break," Otis said from the floor, resting his chin in his hand and looking up at her pitifully. "We're still thirsty."

Donnie gave her a broad smile. She was young and pretty, with blonde hair tied behind her head in a ponytail and an appealing way of crinkling her nose in frustration. "How about one more round and we're gone? One more and I'll clear these jerks out of here. Promise."

She held up a single finger in the stern style of an elementary school teacher. "One more. And you stay in your seats like big boys."

As she left, Otis and Ricky fell heavily into the booth.

"I didn't agree to just one more round," Ricky said. "I'm only getting started."

"We all got jobs," Donnie said. "Right?"

Otis and Ricky gawked blankly at him, though Joe was nodding.

"Look," Donnie said. "I been getting up early to get some work done. I need my rest."

Otis studied his empty glass. "Your supervisor's unaware of any early work."

"I told you last week," Donnie said. "It's this book I'm writing."

"A book?" Otis said, arching an eyebrow. "Hell, I didn't know you could write your name."

Donnie saw Ricky's elbow jerk beneath the table and nail Otis in the side. Otis grunted.

"It's really good. I'm not kidding. And it will go great with the instructional video I got started on with Max, too," Donnie said. "In fact, I haven't seen a book as good as mine on the fundamentals. They'll publish it if they're smart."

"Who's they?" Otis said.

"The publishing people," Donnie said.

"They will for sure," Ricky said.

Donnie recognized the trumped-up enthusiasm in Ricky's voice, and the silent way Otis and Joe let the topic die without further comment.

"Hey," Joe said, breaking the rare moment of quiet. He pointed back and forth between Otis and Ricky. "Which of you can do the most sit-ups?"

Chapter Four

The Tennysons' basement was just about Max's favorite place in the world. Four years earlier, Lucas and his family had uprooted from the house across the street from Max and his parents. Max had been upset at the time, sure he would see much less of his best friend. However, that had not been the case, and Max had come to love the new house, his home away from home. It didn't hurt that it was massive, with wonders in every room. The basement was the highlight for Max. It was what Mrs. Tennyson called an English basement, below ground on the front half of the family's stately Georgian house and above ground on the back. The back half had large floor-to-ceiling sliding doors, so that you could simply open them to step onto the back terrace. The terrace overlooked a long, lush lawn and then beyond it the equally lush golf course of the Tennysons' country club. Inside the basement were a large-screen television, two large sofas, a ping pong table, a pool table, and a set of free weights. It was a place to spend hours without ever getting bored.

A full-sized refrigerator was reliably stocked with snacks, sodas, and sports drinks—and beer. Max now watched as Lucas, his best friend, filled a grocery bag with cans of Stella Artois from the fridge's lower shelves. Max wasn't worried about getting caught at the moment—Lucas's mom was a powerfully strong sleeper, and his father was out of town—but he had concerns about down the road.

"That's way too much," Max said. "There's no way your dad's not going to notice."

"He's been gone a week," Lucas said. "He's not going to remember. He'll just tell Mom he's getting low."

"I don't know," Max said. "Seems like a lot."

Lucas lifted the bag from the floor to test its weight. He added one more beer and closed the door. He was a broad-shouldered guy with muscles forged on his father's weights. The varsity football coach at his school had already called him about attending summer practice in August, though he was only going to be a freshman. "Look," Lucas said. "You don't have to drink any if you don't want."

"I just don't want to get busted."

"We're good. Dad's gone, Mom's knocked out, and we can slip in and out of here however we want. Now you ready?"

Lucas cradled the bag against his chest, and they walked through the sliding doors, crossed the terrace and the backyard, and climbed a ranch fence—Lucas slipping the beer beneath its bottom rung—onto the slumbering golf course. They didn't talk as they walked, and Max swiftly became transfixed by the summer night. It was slow and dark and wide open on the course, and he felt his nerves calm. They could hear girls' bright, enticing voices ahead of them, chatting and laughing

31

and giddy. They followed a golf cart path down a sharp, long dip typical for the rolling back-half of the course, and then climbed to a shelter near the tenth tee, which was the layout's high point. From there, they could see much of the front nine and part of the back. To the south was the distant hum of traffic and blinking lights, the Huguenot Bridge, and the black, hushed gulf that was the James River.

Three girls—Liz, Whitney, and Caroline—waited patiently on a bench in the shelter, pressed close together. Caroline, a pretty brunette with a perpetual smirk that showcased her dimples, held Max's eye just a moment past normal— from what he could tell in the moonlight, at least. On a separate bench, a boy named Fletcher lay with his arms over his eyes.

"Beverages have arrived," Lucas said. "Nice and cold." He lifted the top off a water cooler, glanced inside to confirm it was empty, and placed the bag of beer in the cooler.

The girls acted excited with the arrival of the beer and grabbed cans and then broke off on their own, moving a short distance from the shelter away from the boys.

Fletcher was a sly little guy, dressed in a polo shirt, khaki shorts, and docksiders with no socks. He kept sliding his hand through his thick, blonde hair, or flipping it off his brow, and running his mouth at the girls, who didn't pay attention to him. He and the girls attended Carrington Prep with Lucas, while Max went to public school and was headed to Deep Creek in the fall.

The girls ignored them. They were singing in low voices while attempting to arrange an elaborate dance routine. Max didn't recognize the song. The girls kept screwing up and falling all over themselves with laughter.

The boys watched, clutching and sipping their beers as they'd seen others do. Max had downed a handful of beers already that summer, no more than one at a time, always in the Tennysons' basement. They had been his first.

Max finished his first beer, drinking faster than he ever had before, and went automatically for his second. He recognized a lightness and fogginess he'd felt before in the basement and wondered if that was technically being drunk. It was seductive, whatever it was.

"Yeah, boy," Fletcher called after him. "Max's getting messed up."

Max shrugged, popping the top on the beer as offhandedly as possible. The girls broke from their pack, and Caroline approached Max at the beers while the others visited Lucas and Fletcher. She dropped her empty into the cooler, grabbed a new one and opened it. She held it out wordlessly to Max, and he bumped it with the can in his hand. They both sipped.

"The others are dragging you down," Max said. "You're an all-star among scrubs."

Caroline laughed and gave him a short, knowing push in the chest, holding her hand there a fraction longer than necessary. "Don't make fun. We're really working hard."

"You're talented. No use hiding it. You should be on tour with Beyonce or somebody instead of slumming around with us."

She pushed him again and laughed. He was a head taller than she was, and it was enough to make him feel towering. "You have any particular talents I should know about?" she asked.

Max felt staggered by good fortune. "I don't know," he said. "Hopefully."

Fletcher and Lucas approached together, and Caroline backed ever so slightly from Max, so that he could feel the gravitational pull between them go limp.

"What're you dopes talking about?" Fletcher said. "Politics? International affairs?"

"I was just asking if Max could dance or had some other talent," Caroline said.

"Actually, you know Max is really good at piano," Lucas said. "He still does lessons with a little old lady and everything."

Max grunted. "My dad makes me." He felt guilty as he uttered the lie. It was his mom who had always enforced the lessons, and she wasn't around anymore to play that role.

Fletcher laughed. "Damn, man, my parents stopped making me take lessons a long time ago. You get a sticker if you do good?"

Max noticed Caroline didn't say anything. She looked toward the other girls. They were taking pictures of each other with their phones and laughing. "You jerks! Don't take anymore without me," she said toward them, skipping away.

Fletcher watched her leave, then shrugged. "I am feeling good right now," he said. "Really damn good."

"Yeah, it's alright," Lucas said.

"What about you, Max?" Fletcher said. "These beers treating you good?"

"They ain't treating me bad."

Fletcher and Lucas laughed.

Suddenly, Whitney shrieked, "It's Mad Dog."

The boys looked where she was pointing. Out beyond the girls, snaking its way toward them from the direction of the clubhouse, were the headlights of a souped-up golf cart. The driver, they knew, was "Mad Dog" Carlyle, the night security guy famous for breaking up fun.

"Time to bolt," Fletcher said.

Lucas moved to the shelter. He replaced the top on the water cooler, sealing their supply and the empties out of sight. It was critical not to get caught with the goods. Then everyone ran, each with a partly filled beer can in hand that

33

could be easily disposed in a pinch—Fletcher and the girls in one direction, toward where he lived, and Lucas and Max heading for Lucas' house. Max felt like a top-flight sprinter as he and Lucas flew through the grass, tossed themselves over the fence—carefully holding their beers upright—and burst laughing into the unimpeachable sanctuary of the basement.

Later, after a couple of games of pool, Max and Lucas returned to the course with utmost care and fetched Mr. Tennyson's remaining beers. Max felt better once they were safely resting in the fridge.

Chapter Five

B ailiwick Publishers' office was a stale and stolid building on a street of nearly windowless warehouses in an old industrial area in the city. As Donnie drove through it, he found himself wondering how he'd lived in Richmond much of his life without passing through it. It was a compact area laid out in jigsaw puzzle random plots, tucked off two densely trafficked roads that linked suburbs to city. Everything was built low and large, but it was quiet, too, so that despite the canyons of warehouses—and the commerce they suggested—there was an eeriness to it. There didn't seem to be enough people for all the square footage.

Uptight already, Donnie felt even more out of his element, confused by this niche of the world.

Bailiwick's lobby area was modest and occupied only by a bored-looking receptionist with unnaturally red hair. Donnie settled in a chair in the small reception area. He'd taken the morning off from his job, and he felt strangely as though he was playing hooky. He opened his folder—one he'd swiped from Max's school supplies—and studied his handwritten notes and printed excerpts.

Andy Liu came out grinning to fetch him and escort him back to his office. He was bald, except for a few strands of black hair that crossed the top of his head, and wore a tie with a short-sleeved white shirt that reminded Donnie of his father, right down to the pens in his chest pocket.

"I'm so sorry about Amy," Andy said as he settled into a chair at the table in the corner of his office. "She was the best publicist I've ever been around. She sold a ton of books for us. And, of course, she was a wonderful person, too."

Donnie smiled with practiced appreciation. "I agree."

"She wouldn't accept no as an answer from anybody. Rejections were like fuel to her." Andy shook his head. "Such a tragedy. I hope you and your son are doing OK."

Donnie knew full honesty was not required or expected.

"Thank you," he said. "We're hanging in there." He paused and held up his notebook. "I'm actually here today because of her. She's the one who pushed me to write this. She used to say I needed to share what I knew and pass it on to people." Donnie opened his notebook to the sketch he'd done of a cover, *The Fundamentals of Baseball from A to Z*, showing a bat with a single baseball on each side of it, near the handle. Then, and only then, did he realize its resemblance to a dirty drawing. Hurriedly, he flipped the page and began to explain his idea for the book: An A-to-Z explanation of the correct way to play the game of baseball, covering every aspect of the sport, from pitching and fielding to hitting and baserunning. He handed Andy a preliminary list of the chapters he had in mind and how they would fit together.

Andy nodded politely throughout, often filling spaces in Donnie's presentation with "Good, good" or "I see." When Donnie finished, Andy leaned back in his chair and pressed a finger to his lips. He appeared to be thinking deeply, somehow in a room apart from Donnie.

"OK, here's what I like," he said. "You know your stuff, baseball instruction's booming, as are all these travel teams, and parents will look for this kind of thing as a matter of course when their kids really get into it. Also, I know the A-to-Z thing's been done to death, but that's because it works. I like that structure for this."

Donnie felt his hopes rising, even as he knew a "but" was coming.

"There are some, uh, obstacles, though. One, you can't do a baseball book of fundamentals that is just words. You need lots of images, graphics, illustrations. That means we'll need some artists, photographers, models working on this, and that's going to be expensive. You haven't been in touch with any, have you?"

"No. I thought if the words were right that would be enough."

Andy yawned and ran his fingers through his thin hair. He picked up a broad paperback book on his desk called *Horse Care 101* and flipped through the pages as if considering it at a store. Then he slid it across to Donnie. "Check this one out."

Donnie leaned forward and opened the book. Inside were full-color images and expertly done drawings. The book seemed lively, smart, and professional. He felt embarrassed about the pages he'd brought.

Andy said, "The words may be perfect, but which book are you going to buy if you're at a rack of baseball how-to books? One with a bunch of pictures or one that's just page after page of words. And some people really need pictures to learn and understand things, no matter how good the words are. Ideally, we'd have great pieces of both."

"Sounds good to me. I'd have a lot of ideas for the right images."

Andy didn't appear to hear him. He was considering something else. "Now you were a pro for a while?"

"Fifteen years."

"But never at the tip top level?"

Donnie sighed. "I hurt my knee in Triple A. I was weeks away from a call-up. Wasn't quite the same after that. I use that as a lesson actually."

"Really. Why don't you tell me about it?"

Donnie rolled his neck. "I was playing for Rochester in the Orioles' system. I'd turned twenty-five, so I was a bit behind what they had in mind for me. I got drafted in the first round, you see. Comes with a lot of expectations."

"I can imagine."

"I hadn't come out of the gates in the pros hitting on all cylinders, but I'd started to figure it out. By late July, I was leading the league in hitting, up around .340, and had thirty-some steals and fifteen or so homers. And playing the best goddamned centerfield anyone probably ever played anywhere. Some folks around the team began telling me that I was close to a call-up. Could happen any day at that point. So, I started to have a hard time sleeping. You know? Just from the excitement."

"Yes, it must have been very exciting."

Donnie studied Andy—he couldn't tell if he was being patronizing. "Anyway, after a bus trip to Toledo, I was desperate for some rest. Instead of going out and shagging flies at the ballpark the way I normally would do—getting the feel of the place, testing out the warning track, the way the ball carried, that sort of thing—I decided to take a nap in the training room. What happens in the first inning of the game that night? Long drive to centerfield, straight over my head. Chasing it didn't feel right, like I wasn't quite sure where I was the way I should have, and I got my steps wrong, jammed my leg into the base of the wall and tore up my knee."

"That's terrible."

"Brutal. Not only didn't I get my call-up that year, but I missed the entire next season because of the injury. Next thing you know I'm a washed-up twenty-seven-year-old who has lost a step and can't drive off his back leg in the batter's box the way he used to. My swing was never quite right after that, and I wasn't flying around the bases the same way. Bounced around too many places to name the next eight or nine years and never got as close again. I tell you if I hadn't taken that nap, I'd have been an everyday major leaguer. No question in my mind."

Andy nodded. "That's a tough break. And I can see how a story like that can, uh, enliven a book. But you see that a key biographical bullet point is missing on your resume? For the cover?"

Donnie sagged, partly out of embarrassment for telling his story. He knew it sounded like excuses, like some sad, pitiful tale. "That doesn't mean I don't know my stuff."

"Of course, of course, but the problem isn't what you know but what possible readers know. Right? You're not a name. You don't have anything attached to your name that makes it stand out from any other name. I apologize for my frankness, but what separates you from the thousands of others like you?"

"What I know. The way I can teach it."

Andy waved his hand in frustration. "You're missing the point. People have to buy the book before they can read it and see how good it is."

Donnie instinct was to feel insulted, but Andy's bearing was blunt and plainspoken. He was being analytical.

"Look, Donnie, I would like to find a way to make this work because I think the potential is good for us. However, before I even read what you've got there, I would need to silence my doubts on several fronts. Our business is a low-margin one, and we can't afford mistakes." He paused, looking at Donnie with scrutiny, as though he wasn't sure Donnie was following him. "You understand? You need to give me a reason to publish this beyond what you've given me so far."

"Beyond that it's good?"

"Correct. Have you thought about a co-author? Perhaps one of your teammates from your playing days whose name has a bit more cachet? Come back to me with something like that, and we can start drilling into the rest of it. Any ideas?"

Donnie caught an expletive in his throat before it could escape. He'd taken a roundabout way of getting to it, but Andy had gotten there alright. Co-author. Former teammate.

"You're talking about Stubs."

Andy held up his hands in mock defense. "I'm not talking about anyone in particular. I know you played with Stubs, and he'd be a good fit for sure. Or someone like him."

Donnie gathered his stuff and stood up. "Thanks for your time."

Every fall, Donnie and Amy would take a trip to Death Valley for a Clemson football game. Donnie always grew excited to be back on campus, returning to the place where he'd peaked. People revered him for what he'd done there. The only three-time All-American in school baseball history, NCAA player of the year his junior season, and the College World Series MVP when the Tigers won the national championship. They didn't care that he hadn't gone on to better things. They didn't ask him about his pro career. It was a sanctuary from all that.

Amy and Donnie would arrive hours early and get swept up in the gameday madness that had transformed the town. The six home games each fall were the six biggest days of the year.

The last trip together had been the best. Grills were already smoking, cars crawled in near standstill traffic, and tiger paw purple-and-orange flags fluttered in front of businesses and houses up and down the roads near campus. Students—the girls in sundresses, the guys in orange polos and T-shirts—were everywhere, the envy of the adults who never wanted to be too far out of sight of those days.

A tailgate near the Shoeboxes, the arrangement of squat dorms near the stadium, was their first stop, and Amy soon found herself drinking a beer next to her old Civil War history teacher, Dr. Hootie Anderson. Between bites of a fried chicken biscuit, Dr. Anderson halfheartedly apologized for not remembering her. He seemed unimpressed when Amy told him he'd been one of her favorite teachers, and he didn't ask about her line of work or what she'd been up to. Her breathless enthusiasm for what his lectures had meant to her received the most halfhearted of nods, as though he'd heard the same lines from a million half-drunk alumni before.

However, when she introduced Donnie, Dr. Anderson's mood underwent a transformation. Suddenly, he took on the wide-eyed, fixed-grinned expression of a fan. "Donnie Baseball?" he said. "You were a hell of a player, son." He wanted to talk about this game and that one, about the time he saw Donnie scale the fence in center field to take away a home run and the now-iconic moment in the College World Series when Donnie had scored from first on a single in the ninth inning, catching UCLA's whole team off guard with his hustle and daring. He'd been such a bold and thrilling player, Dr. Anderson had said.

Donnie was in heaven with her old teacher, providing context to these moments as he typically did when in the presence of Clemson folks. He explained what he was thinking, why he'd done what he'd done. He talked about the work that had gone into a particular play or the reaction from his teammates and coaches. Of the baserunning magic against UCLA, he detailed his relationship with his father and all the time he spent working with him on the fundamentals of the game. He said that his dad had always preached that he should be pushing, pushing, pushing on the basepaths, forever looking for a way to use surprise to find an advantage.

"All that work was the foundation," Donnie said, tilting his beer bottle toward the professor for emphasis. "That way when I got out there I could just follow my instincts."

Dr. Anderson nodded intently, as though Donnie was opening new worlds to him. After they'd bid the professor goodbye to head to the game—the smile on his face still bright and youthful—Amy had playfully punched Donnie on the arm.

"I wanted someone to be impressed by me down here for a change," she said.

Donnie smiled. "You're a washed-up ballplayer's wife. What's more impressive than that?"

Donnie always found the trip to Clemson thrilling. There was something about being back on campus with Amy and covering the same ground they'd once covered together when they were young. They were giddy and relaxed, transported in time. They would get drunk at a bevy of tailgates, cheer feverishly for the Tigers in the orange wash of the stadium crowd, wander postgame through the row of bars on College Avenue. Late night they'd hit the Tiger Town Tavern for greasy burgers and then they'd return to the hotel, the night's stand-in for a gritty apartment near campus. There, they'd start fumbling with their clothes before they'd even reached their room, giggling and whispering, unaware of anything else in the world. Inside, they'd have hungry, exhilarating sex that was more restless and unrestrained than the well-mapped event they scheduled at home. In the frantic bumping and catching of bodies, they'd remember what it had been like when they'd first found each other.

Afterward, though, on the drive home, Donnie would find new depths of depression. It could endure for weeks. All that youth was long gone and so was the promise of it. When they'd fallen in love, Donnie had been brimming with possibility. With potential. He was what he could become. Everything he did in college was geared to his future. His pre-dawn workouts, his light-as-possible class schedule, his summers away from her at the Cape Cod League. His commitment never cooled in those days. He never paused or groaned when the alarm went off at six a.m. He just kissed the top of her head and disappeared.

He used to carry a bat around with him all the time, tinkering with his swing fretfully, as though it wasn't already perfect. He couldn't sit still. If they watched TV together, he'd rise from the sofa to take pitches—not swinging, just keenly following an imaginary ball's path as it traveled from a pitcher's hand to the catcher's mitt behind him. He'd lived with a single-mindedness in those days that had made it seem to him as though success was a fixed and certain thing. He knew it had seemed that way to Amy, too.

Amy died the week after that last visit to Clemson. She probably shouldn't have made the trip. She had the business pitch meeting of her life coming up. A national trucking company with its headquarters in Richmond was ready to put Amy's company, Advantage PR, on a hefty retainer. Amy had joined Advantage as a part-time assistant while Donnie was still playing ball. She didn't have a background in PR, but it didn't matter. Within a year, she was full-time. Within two, she was running campaigns. She was a partner and the unofficial company rainmaker by the time she died.

Amy should have spent that last weekend working, but Donnie was convinced she went because she knew how important the trip was to him. She worked her ass off when she returned—desperately, urgently. She had been taking an assortment of pills for both sleep and back pain for a while. She hated to feel restrained or limited in any way, and Donnie had told her he thought she was too quick to take meds as a solution. She couldn't let anything slow her down, though. Still, he thought she understood what she was doing. She'd messed up, though, exhausted and anxious and her back probably hurting from the car ride, and she had taken too many of a mix she was supposed to avoid—Adderall, oxycodone, something else maybe, Donnie couldn't remember them—and there had been a heart condition that nobody had known about. That heart had stopped working suddenly before morning. When Donnie awoke, he'd somehow known right away that the woman beside him was gone. Every single morning he'd opened his eyes since that day he had flashed back to that moment. He wondered if he'd ever have another morning without that immediate jolt of pain. That horrific sudden recognition.

Donnie had parked a block away from Bailiwick. As he strolled to his car, he noticed a "For Lease" sign in front of a barren one-story warehouse building that looked as though it hadn't been in use for decades, with boarded windows, metal sheet roofing battered into irregular waves, and almost completely peeled red paint on the large weathered double doors at the front.

Donnie climbed the concrete loading ramp and peered through a windowpane with no board covering it. The inside was dark and dusty with open space everywhere over a concrete floor. No offices, no supporting columns, nothing to get in the way. It was perfect. Donnie pictured three pitching mounds on the left—he'd haul in the dirt and build them himself—and two batting cages arranged neatly alongside each other on the right. He'd lay some artificial turf down, hang a few lights. He saw young hitters getting their swings in the cages off pitching machines. He saw Max on one of the mounds, firing fastballs to a masked catcher.

It was a grim place, but it seemed purposeful and properly severe to Donnie. It reminded him of a boxing gym—a no-nonsense, fuss-free hole in the wall attractive only to people serious about their business. It was exactly what Donnie wanted. His ideal place in the world.

He wrote down the phone number on the sign before he got in his car to leave.

Chapter Six

Max woke late, having stayed up into the early morning hours shuffling between the pool and ping pong tables with Lucas. The twin bed next to the one he occupied was abandoned and the sheets scattered. Lucas, a poor sleeper, likely had been up for hours. Max stood and stretched lavishly. The clock on the table between the beds read 11:02.

He found Lucas downstairs in the den, nestled deep among pillows in a large, cushioned chair, playing Tiger Woods PGA Tour and throwing expletive-filled trash talk at the screen. The one thing the Tennysons didn't have was a piano. Max loved to play right when he awoke. It perked him up. He craved it like adults crave their morning cup of coffee. He was working on a piece now, Franz Liszt's Liebestraum No. 3, that his teacher had assigned, and it was following him around. He would hum it, imagine his fingers skipping across the keys to keep up with its demands. The notes always landed cleanly and crisply in his head. He felt frustrated not to have an outlet for it at the Tennysons, some piano or keyboard where he could help the sounds materialize the way he felt them.

Max flopped onto a cloud-soft sectional sofa that matched Lucas's chair.

"You eat yet?" Max asked.

Without looking up, Lucas promptly shouted toward the kitchen, "Ma, get us some breakfast."

Max sat up just in time to see Mrs. Tennyson enter with a flourish, speaking on the phone. She was a blonde fantasy in tennis whites, apparently just back from the courts, her flouncy skirt covering only the remotest tops of her tanned and toned legs. Max knew how embarrassed Lucas was about his mom, and Max had never said the smallest word about her out of loyalty, but he was pretty much alone among their friends. Every year they got older and every year the stuff they said got more direct and filthier. Max assumed that was why Lucas seemed to hate her now.

"Good morning, Max," she said, smiling and pressing the phone against the blessed "V" where her polo shirt had gone unbuttoned. "Will waffles work?"

"Absolutely, Mrs. T."

When the food was ready, they ate under the awning on the Tennysons' back brick terrace that overlooked the fourteenth green. The temperature was already past ninety, and the traffic of players on the course was light and sluggish.

"Got anything going on today?" Lucas asked with what Max thought seemed like strained casualness.

"Nah," he answered, studying his friend with suspicion. Lucas was watching a foursome of stooped old men waddle around the green, painstakingly measuring their putts out of either extreme care or failing eyesight. Lucas seemed engrossed.

"Want to tag along for the lesson I got in an hour?" Lucas asked.

"What, baseball?"

"Yeah."

"Pass. Dad's pissing me off."

"It's not with him," Lucas said. He paused. "I actually got one with Stubs over at WBA."

Max dropped his fork and stared at Lucas, who was working hard to get his shoes tied just right. When his friend wouldn't look up, Max slammed the table and Lucas's head shot up.

"You're going behind my dad's back?" Max said, nearly shouting. "After all he's done for you?"

Lucas looked sick. "It's nothing like that. Dad just thought that … I mean, I'm still going –"

"Do you even know what loyalty means?"

"I know. I'm sorry. Damn, I knew it."

Max collected himself and stabbed at a slab of waffle. "Easy, man, I'm just screwing with you." He stuffed the waffle into his mouth and spoke between bites. "I'll go. I don't give a shit."

Max had passed the Woodson Baseball Academy facility many times, but he'd never been inside. It was a massive, windowless warehouse facility set back off Broad Street in the sprawling suburbs of western Henrico County. A dull block of steel. It blended in with a series of nearby big box stores—Babies R Us, Home Depot, Target—that were all fronted by acres of parking lots. Tightly packed cars jostled past on Broad in fits and starts. Twice Max had been in the passenger seat of his father's beater when they'd passed the place and twice his dad had spat theatrically out the window.

Mrs. Tennyson dropped them off out front and split to run some errands. Max didn't know what the errands were, but he understood that when he saw her again she'd have some sandwiches or burgers, anticipating their next need and meeting it. His mother had never done those things. She was busy, she was anxious, she was exhausted, she was forever on the phone. Typically, she was a step behind. It had bothered him in those days, even pushing him to whine at her a few times. He hated to think about that now.

As he approached the wide automatic doors, Max spun around once and searched for any sign of his father, just in case. He felt guilty as he crossed the threshold.

Chapter Seven

Joe was pleading with Donnie. Donnie stood in Otis' office, a modest, neat nook without walls in a corner of the maintenance shop at Deep Creek, and held the phone to his ear, feeling bored with Joe's spiel. Joe was still pushing him about shagging balls at the heart organization home run derby fundraiser. It seemed like a job anyone could handle, but Joe was treating it like sophisticated skilled labor. Donnie was suspicious. His brother was belaboring points and making arguments he clearly didn't believe in. He was leaving something out.

"C'mon, man, I need your help for this," Joe said. "It was a disaster last year."

Otis entered, sat in his swivel chair, and put his boots on the metal desk where two stacks of paper sat. He acted as if he was alone, never looking toward Donnie or otherwise acknowledging another presence. He frowned, appearing deep in thought, opened a drawer and pulled out a *Tennis* magazine. He began leafing through the pages with the distracted air of a farmer perusing a seed catalogue for the umpteenth time.

"Give me a break, Joe," Donnie said, turning his back on Otis and his distractions. "That can't be true. Throw a bunch of kids out there and you're set."

"They'll be in the outfield, dummy," Joe said. "I'm not talking about that. I'm talking about beyond the fence. We lost a bunch of balls last year because we put some kids back there for the homers and they couldn't handle it. The balls kept bouncing into the woods and we couldn't find half of 'em again. One kid busted his face running into a tree. I thought his mom was going to sue."

"I'm a grown man. I'll feel ridiculous."

"Come on. For Mom and Dad."

Donnie had wondered if it was going to go this far. What a strange brother he had. "Alright, alright," Donnie said. "You're a shameless bastard."

"I don't know what you mean."

When Donnie hung up the phone, Otis grunted at him.

"This is my personal space," Otis said.

"I find that disturbing. I forgot my phone."

Otis nodded. "What you got left this afternoon?"

"I gotta line the baseball field. That's it. Everything else is trimmed and pretty."

Otis turned his magazine sideways, studying something. "I'm thinking I'm going to hit that old man Ricky with a lot of drop shots and lobs this year—really mess with his head. Get him frustrated going back and forth. Rope that Dope."

Donnie shook his head and grinned helplessly. "Maybe just try getting it over the net whenever you can. It's not exactly Federer against Nadal when you two get together."

"Not exactly, but it's kind of funny to think it's the same sport, isn't it?" He looked up. "On the same size court with the same types of tennis balls, keeping score the same way? Federer-Nadal or Otis-Ricky."

"You don't get enough credit for being a deep thinker, Otis. I really believe that."

"Thank you much," he said, giving him a wink. "Tell every woman you know." He paused and shrugged toward a plastic bat and a mesh bag of whiffle balls propped against his wall. "We're thinking of having a little staff game this afternoon. Want to join?"

"You serious?"

"About whiffle ball? You bet your ass."

Donnie took off his hat and thoughtfully scratched his head. "I think I've got a bit too much self-respect for that."

Otis looked up and for a moment Donnie thought his friend looked hurt, but the moment passed and Otis smiled with a familiar disdain at him. "You and your pride ain't always very fun to be around, you know?"

Donnie left Otis to his magazine and went to the back of the shop. He checked the capacity on the line chalker, saw that it was nearly full, and rolled it out the back door, where he'd parked the pickup.

His job was keeping Deep Creek's fields maintained, as well as the fields at Reece Middle School next door. When he'd returned to the maintenance staff, Otis and Ricky had handed Donnie the fields duties right away, since none of their other employees liked the work and Donnie embraced it. Donnie had worked two summers with them in high school and become near-legendary for his love of cutting grass in the incapacitating summer heat.

When they were kids, Donnie and Joe had biked over to Deep Creek most days after school to watch practices, play pickup games with their friends, especially Stubs, and to visit with Otis and Ricky in their maintenance shop. Donnie and Joe got older, became students themselves, and Otis and Ricky gave them their own keys to the facilities so they could shoot hoops in the gym at any hour they wanted or grab a pitching fence and a bag of balls to hop on the baseball field on weekends. Stubs often was with them. If it was baseball, their father was, too, throwing batting practice or knocking ground balls and fly balls at them with a fungo bat. After Joe graduated and went to Washington and Lee, where he joined a frat and occasionally played third base, it was often just Donnie and Stubs and Donnie's father. Deep Creek was where Donnie had grown up more than any other place in the world, especially its baseball field, and now it was his job to care for it.

Donnie pulled the truck behind the concession stand, lifted down the line chalker, and went to work. He knew it didn't make any sense, but cutting grass in the heat, lining fields, doing anything out there in the sun reminded him of being young and playing ball. He found the discomfort of the sun comfortable. Soaking through his clothes, losing pounds of water weight each day at work, carried an echo of his prior life. He liked to be exhausted at the end of a day. It was the only way he'd ever fallen asleep since Amy's death.

Often, he would bring a notebook with him on the mower. Riding alone, the mower whirring, the grass disappearing beneath him, he would think about his book and ideas would appear from everywhere. He would let his mind relax and jot notes all day, expertly maintaining his line in the field. Today, he was thinking about a chapter on preparation. He wanted to write about the best ways to get ready to play, and all that he could think about was how devastating being unprepared had been for him that one time. That story would open the chapter, but he would leave out plenty of details—the way he'd left out details when he'd told the story to Andy Liu. It's true he'd taken to pro baseball badly, scuffling through a few mediocre seasons in the lower minors, showing only flashes of the promise that had gotten him a big bonus and swarms of attention. His pro performance had been most notable for his many game ejections, including two instances of charging the opposing pitcher, and a reputation was starting to follow him from town to town and umpire to umpire. However, he'd rallied at the end of the previous season, corralled his behavior, and earned a spot in Triple A.

They'd been in Toledo for a three-game set. Their bus had broken down on the drive from Rochester, so they'd arrived late, only about two hours from game time. He thought every day about that final step at the wall—the way his foot had crumpled and twisted, and his knee had buckled and torn. He'd rehabbed in Richmond, driving Amy crazy.

He'd told Andy Liu about the physical setback the injury had caused, but he didn't tell him about the feeling of unfairly having to start over. He felt perpetually frustrated by his place in life, impatient and antsy with every day in the minors. He felt robbed and wronged. He was supposed to be in the majors and every bit of not being there—the bus trips, the shitty crowds, the food, the pay, the fucking anonymity—drove him to distraction. He couldn't let anything go, couldn't leave a bad at-bat or game behind. He carried everything with him and let every misstep grow into something larger. He felt grudges for everyone else in the entire sport. If he had a couple of rough days, instead of staying the course he would decide he was simply doing something wrong that needed to be fixed. Consequently, he was forever uncomfortable, tinkering, trying to regain the way he felt before the injury. He didn't understand that he could never reclaim that moment and needed to find a new one. He did now, though, after years of thinking of little else. It was one of many mistakes he wouldn't make if he could go back and start again.

Soon, he wasn't in Triple A but in Double A, then out of the Orioles' organization. Then there was a whirlwind of releases and pickups, each stop less promising than the last, though he could always see a possible path—if things just broke his way for a change.

Some people close to him would favor Donnie with the knee as an excuse now, as though his failure was some sad story that wasn't his fault. He'd indulge them, nod, and give a brave spiel about the breaks of the game, and sometimes he'd lie awake at night thinking about that pre-game nap and the damage something so stupid did, but he didn't pretend to himself for long anymore that it was as simple as that. Dad had told him more than once when he was a kid, typically in reaction to one of Donnie's tantrums, that the most important thing to remember on a baseball field was that you were in control. Not God, not the umpires, not any of the other players. It was all up to you. Now, years later, Donnie couldn't shake that, no matter how much he tried to give himself a pass sometimes. He couldn't convince himself that his problems were not his own creation.

Donnie finished chalking and then walked both the right and left field lines, examining them for imperfections. He found none.

Chapter Eight

L ucas had a confounding inability to clear his hips on his swing. Since early
spring, Max had watched Dad labor over it, wracking his brain for a solution,
but nothing had worked. It was a shock to see Lucas ever pull the ball in the
air. Instead, Lucas, a righthanded batter, blocked pitch after pitch to right field.

When Max realized that Stubs Woodson was going through the same
catalogue of attempted fixes he'd seen his father try, he grew bored, knowing how
that story would end, and elected to walk a lap of the WBA palace.

It was impressive. Rows of batting cages and pitching mounds lined the
perimeter of the brightly lit interior, which was open and vast like a field house,
while the center held a practice field that surprised Max in its considerable size. The
outfield dimensions were too shallow to play a game on the field, and the ceiling
would knock down most fly balls of decent height, but it still held a regulation
infield covered in Astroturf and the outfield was deep enough for relay work and
other team drills.

Two guys not much older than Max were currently on the field, manning
the shortstop and second base positions and honing their work turning the double
play. Their swift actions and delicate footwork around the bag were mesmerizing.
Dad had told him that his favorite thing in sports was a great double-play combo,
and Max had to admit the appeal. These two were both short, compact guys with
feet that floated across the ground, gliding toward the ground balls that were lashed
toward them. When the ball arrived, they would scoop it with an unerring certainty
and flip it to their partner, who would toe-tap the bag, or straddle it and whirl,
rifling a throw to first, a resounding pop in the glove of the first baseman echoing
throughout the facility. Each of the duo appeared to anticipate the other's every
action, so that they moved in a logical, yet mysterious unison.

Max watched them and wondered how he'd fallen behind. He'd worked
hard, listened to Dad, done everything that was asked of him, but now it felt as
though other kids were moving forward and he was stuck thrashing about, going
nowhere and becoming nothing. Kids like these guys on the field were surging
somewhere special. Liszt, the composer whose piece had so gripped Max at the
moment, had been a prodigy, making a splashy public concert debut at age eleven
and publishing his first composition at twelve. What was Max doing that was
worthwhile?

"Hey, Max!"

Max turned to find his catcher, Chuck Slater, alone near a pitcher's mound,
a jumping rope limp in his hands. He was sweating and looked miserable.

"Hey, Chuck," Max answered tepidly. Chuck was a nice guy, but a bit of a
drag, too, always complaining and pulling you down with him.

"What are you doing here?" Chuck asked between deep gulps of air. "Not getting lessons, are you?"

Max felt the return of his guilt.

"Nah, I'm just here with Lucas. He's got a session." Max's expression grew amused. "What's with the jump rope?"

"Sucks, right? I'm supposed to be doing this every day at home. Coach Scott, this guy I see here, says I got heavy feet and I got to get quicker behind the plate. But I hate it so much. I mean, it's jump rope. It's hard as hell and maybe the most boring thing I've ever done in my life."

"Where's the coach?"

Chuck shook his head, a dark look of hatred crossing his face. "Snitching on me. He can tell I haven't been keeping up with it like I'm supposed to, and he's gone to rat on me to Mom." He picked resentfully where his pants had gathered in his ass. "She'll tell my dad and then I'm screwed. I've been lying about it. I'll probably lose TV and video games, and I'll have to do this in front of them now. Dad'll give me some speech about how I'm never going to get a scholarship if I don't take it seriously."

Max shook his head sympathetically. "I know that talk."

Chuck's face turned tense, and he clumsily started back in on his jump rope reps. Coach Scott arrived and put his hands on his hips, staring at Chuck as the poor kid caught his feet on the circling rope. Chuck, clearly ashamed, scrambled to get the rope moving again.

"Later, Chuck," Max said.

Chuck pretended he didn't hear him.

Several mothers sat in the snack bar near the front, sipping coffees and juices. They seemed to know each other. Max and Lucas had hung out briefly in the snack bar when they'd gotten there, having showed up thirty minutes early.

They'd also burned some time in the lobby, checking out the dozens of photos on the walls. One section was covered with head shots of select former and current WBA students. Beneath each photo was the player's name and the college where he'd signed. It was smart as hell. Every kid who walked in would dream about getting their photo up there, and so would every father. More paid lessons would result. Max couldn't get over how many local kids had found a place.

Cole McGuire's photo was about a third larger than everyone else's and was labeled "Cole McGuire, 14th Pick, Major League Draft, Pittsburgh Pirates." Cole had been nice to Max in the days when Dad worked with him on the backyard mound at their house. Max would sit quietly and watch them, absorbing the lessons, and Cole would come over and check in with him during water breaks while Dad and Cole's father conferred over Cole's progress.

49

Max hadn't talked to Cole in the two years since he'd stopped the lessons with Dad, and he'd never found out what the problem was. He guessed it was Dad's fault, though.

Cole's image was prominent in the lobby, but it was nothing like the shrine to Stubs Woodson, the WBA owner. It was the first thing you saw when you walked in the front door. A series of photos caught him in various moments of heroism with the Cincinnati Reds: finishing his swing and watching the flight of a long drive, leaping over a sliding runner at second base as he turned a double play, airborne during a headfirst slide to third base. There were posed photos of him with various stars—Ken Griffey Jr., David Ortiz, Albert Pujols—all signed by both the stars and Stubs.

Max had stopped hard at an image from Stubs' playing days at Deep Creek. Stubs was surrounded by teammates, his hat off, the front of his uniform filthy, celebrating some great moment. Among the teammates, looking young and elated, was his father, a teenage version Max had never known.

Nearly three years before, when Max was eleven, Stubs had visited Donnie one warm October afternoon, only a few days after Stubs had retired from baseball. He arrived in the late afternoon and watched Donnie work with a series of his students in the batting cage in their backyard. Each of the kids grew amped when they saw Stubs there, watching them closely, and Max could tell that they pressed just a bit harder, looking to show the big leaguer that they were capable of something.

Max and Stubs sat next to each other on patio chairs, Max pretending it wasn't a big deal to him. Stubs kept making whispering asides to him, little jokes about "your old man Donnie Baseball." He'd crowd him when he talked to him. As Dad worked with a local high school kid on the trigger in his swing, Stubs leaned toward Max, close to his face, and said, "Your dad's my favorite ballplayer of all time. You realize that? All those guys I played with in the bigs. Some were better, but none were quite so perfect as your dad was at his best. If his knee had held up, if he'd gotten a few breaks here or there, he'd have gotten the big paychecks, too." Max looked at his father with a new awe for a while after that, but he also found himself incensed in a broad, shake-your-fist-at-the-sky kind of way. He felt resentment toward all the big-league players he watched on TV, wondering how many of them were just the byproduct of the breaks his father hadn't gotten.

Stubs stayed long past the last student. He and Dad settled onto those patio chairs and rolled through beers like they were nothing, telling stories and resurrecting old, long-unuttered names, bright bursts of laughter exploding at routine intervals. Max eventually was sent up to his room. He opened the window over his bed and listened for as long as he could stay awake, though the words themselves were rarely clear, only the tenor of them.

He woke to the sound of his father shouting. Max lifted his head to the window and saw Dad and Stubs inside the batting cage. Dad was gesturing with his can of beer, calling Stubs every cuss word Max had ever heard and then some, while Stubs stood about twenty-feet away, still and calm, and absorbed it without a word in response, a bat clutched on his shoulder like he was in the on-deck circle studying a pitcher. Max could tell how this infuriated his father.

Finally, as Dad ran out of breath and energy, shouting himself into exhaustion—something about "my fucking deal, not yours"—he lifted the beer and fired it at Stubs in a desperate attempt to shake him. As though he'd been expecting it all along, Stubs swung the bat in an expert, short stroke, busting the beer in a fizzy, white cloud.

A year later, WBA opened, and the great Donnie Baseball, as far as Max knew, had never spoken to Stubs again.

When Max completed his lap of the facility and returned to the cage where Lucas labored, he could see things still weren't going well. He watched Lucas steer an inside fastball the other way, and he could see the frustration in his friend. It was a crazy thing. Nothing seemed to work. Hitting had become a mystery to him.

Stubs Woodson wasn't dejected by Lucas' struggles. In fact, he seemed energized by the challenge. No more than five-foot-nine, Stubs was an excitable guy who never quit moving or talking. He approached Lucas, who had returned to his batting stance, and kicked open the toe of Lucas' front foot. He crouched and circled Lucas, studying every inch of him.

"No stride this time," Stubs said, the veins in his neck popping as he hollered. "Not even a baby step."

Max knew this one wouldn't work either. Dad had told him it didn't make any sense the way Lucas couldn't get past this one problem. Every time he'd fix one aspect of his swing, such as a long, awkward stride toward the plate, Lucas would compensate by adding a new wrinkle that produced the same result.

And, sure enough, when the pitch came, Lucas obeyed orders and kept his feet firmly rooted to the ground, but his back shoulder plunged down instead, sending a slicing fly ball into the right side of the batting cage netting.

Stubs whooped and laughed. "Alright, alright, we gotta call it, my man."

Lucas angrily swiped his bat at a ball lying on the ground near him and got nothing but air, nearly falling and compounding his anger. "Idiot," he shouted.

"Don't sweat it, kid," Stubs said. "We're gonna get it. This damn thing ain't beating us."

As Lucas packed up his equipment, Stubs bolted for Max.

"Max Wilson, it is damn good to see you again," he said, reaching out his hand. Max took it and shook, wincing at the strength of Stubs' grip. "You were a bit little twerp the last time. I'm sorry as hell about your mom. She was a wonderful person. You doing OK?'

"Yeah," Max said, numbed to this conversation by now.

"How's your pops doing?"

"Decent."

"Good, good. I haven't seen him in a while now either, which is a shame. I'd love for him to come by here."

"Yeah, I don't know, Mr. Woodson. Seems like a long shot."

Stubs smiled as though he knew exactly what Max meant. "Stubs. Call me Stubs. I somehow got to where that's the only name I feel like answering to. How's your summer going?"

"Good, I guess."

"Oh yeah? Lucas said you were struggling with a few things."

Max looked toward Lucas, hoping to show his displeasure with him, but his friend pretended not to notice.

Stubs was bouncing from foot to foot, eager for an answer. Max couldn't understand why he cared so much how he was doing.

"It's not a big deal," Max said. "A few control things I can straighten out with my dad. It'd be nice to have a curveball like everybody else, but he wants me waiting."

"What're you, thirteen?"

"Fourteen."

"Waiting for what?"

"Few things, I guess."

"Is he one of these guys that babies kids' arms?" Stubs said, his face fixed with stunned incomprehension. "Donnie Baseball of all people? I never would have guessed it. Holy hell. I would have thought you'd have a whole arsenal of pitches at this point. Fourteen! No one waits that long. That whole thing about the curve hurting your arm is an old wives' tale anyway."

Max laughed darkly. "I got a two-seam fastball and a four-seam fastball. I can't throw a change to save my life, so I'm supposed to get by with those for now."

Stubs looked around, spotted a bucket of baseballs, and retrieved a ball. He held it in front of Max. "I'm showing you one thing, OK?" he said, his voice lowered and conspiratorial. "Knuckle curve. No twisting the arm. Great pitch, and I don't have to teach you anything but the grip. You know this pitch?"

"Heard of it. Verlander throws it, doesn't he? And Mussina did?"

"Exactly. A few other studs, too. A pain in the ass to hit."

Stubs handed the ball to Max. "Show me your four-seamer."

Max knew his father would be irate, but he was tired of being the kid that played by different rules than everyone else.

Max gripped the ball, his index and middle finger crossing the seams in four places. Stubs took the ball and rotated it in Max's hand so that those fingers now ran parallel to the seams, from the closed area of the horseshoe shape of the seams to the open area. He tucked Max's index finger so that the knuckle curled into a seam.

"Done," Stubs said.

"That's it?"

"That's it. Throw it like a fastball and try not to laugh when those jerks fall down trying to hit it."

Mrs. Tennyson was waiting in her Range Rover at the curb when Max and Lucas emerged. They piled into the AC-cooled back seat, leaving the front passenger seat empty, as though Mrs. Tennyson was a chauffeur. Burger King bags waited for them in their seats. Max reached into Lucas' equipment bag and pulled out a baseball. He tried the knuckle curve grip. It felt natural and right.

Max lifted the ball to his release point. He did as his father had taught him and imagined the pitch. He saw Chuck's catcher's mitt, felt himself let the ball go, pictured the nasty break of the pitch as it approached home plate. A batter swung and missed and nearly fell, just as Stubs had said he would.

"You gonna use it?" Lucas said. He stuffed a handful of greasy fries into his mouth.

Max moved the ball back and forth in the air, the grip relaxed. "Can't wait."

Chapter Nine

Donnie's lesson arrived just before five p.m. as he weed-wacked around the home dugout. It was his first private appointment in a week, and he was anxious for it to go smoothly. He needed to rebuild his client base. WBA was sucking up every ambitious kid—or kid with an ambitious father—in the area. His American Legion team would be following behind at six for practice. Things weren't going well with them, either, their play on the field not matching their considerable talents.

The kid came with his father, a clean-cut guy still in a tie from work.

"I'm a little surprised we're meeting here," the dad said.

"I work here. They're OK with it."

"No, I mean the guy who passed along your name said you were set up in your backyard for this."

"I am," Donnie said. "This is just easier for my schedule."

Kyle, who was twelve, had an equipment bag at his feet. He wore a little league team's hat, shiny black spikes, and a local baseball camp T-shirt tucked with care into spotless white baseball pants. The bag was huge. Donnie couldn't get over how much parents spent on the players he coached. All the kids were gear guys now, obsessed with bats made with space-age alloys and gloves with exoskeletons designed to mold to their hands. They had two or three of everything and spent more time checking out catalogues and websites than they did practicing, eventually arriving at the field as though they had spent an hour primping in the mirror.

Donnie and Kyle walked to the bullpen area down the right-field line. The father followed closely on their footsteps. They warmed up unhurriedly. Donnie liked the kid's easy motion. He was mid-sized for his age, which was ideal. The short kids never got a chance to pitch and work at it, and the big kids could just hump up and throw it past people.

Donnie had tied a red string in a square on the side of a batting fence to serve as a target for his pupils. He moved it behind the plate.

Donnie had Kyle show him his four-seam fastball grip, and then he set him on the pitching rubber he'd set up forty-five feet away from the plate for the younger kids. He told him to hit the target. It was a bit of a ruse. He knew what the kid would do wrong before he did it, and he jumped at him as soon as he budged.

"No, your arms are stiff. Relax, be loose," he said. He held Kyle's gloved hand and lowered it to his belt. "There ya go. Relax. Relaxed is powerful. Relaxed is athletic. Relaxed is quick. Stiff is stiff."

Donnie always interrupted his students before the first pitch of their first lesson. It was a way of impressing upon the kid and his parents that Donnie knew his stuff and paid attention to detail—and that their kid needed the lessons. Donnie adjusted the set of their arms and toned down that first step back, and then he targeted the pivot of their back foot over the rubber. Balance was everything, he told them as he made them pose, still as a statue, at the top of their windup, perched on one leg like a crane. That was almost always the first lesson. Some kids never got around to throwing more than a dozen pitches. The kids tended to get frustrated because they wanted to show off how good they were, but it also earned Donnie their trust. They figured he must know a lot about pitching to show them so many little things they were doing wrong.

Donnie liked Kyle. He had excellent control for a kid his age, and when Donnie showed him a proper two-seam fastball—someone had taught the kid the wrong grip—he was impressed with the running, tailing action the kid summoned immediately. That was a gift most pitchers never received. He was earnest and patient, too. It made Donnie think of Max, who had been an eager pupil, taking in everything without debate, until a few months ago.

"Do you throw the two-seamer to both sides of the plate?" Kyle asked. "Or just when you're going inside?"

Donnie was surprised by the question, a good one kids never thought to ask.

"Absolutely, both sides. You can get folks out throwing nothing but a two-seamer if you got a good one and you move it around and up and down. And you got a good one. It'll be a great one soon."

Kyle smiled for the first time. It looked as though he was trying to suppress his excitement but just couldn't.

"It's cool," he said, holding the ball in front of him and studying the grip. "It's really cool. It feels completely different, but I like it."

With every student, Donnie aimed for the same moment of transcendent understanding that would transform a player, though he knew not to expect it routinely. It often was a single thought, one simple suggestion, something tidy and positive, that would walk around with the player from that day forward. It was a different nugget for everybody—tuck your glove, quiet your body, relax your hands, balance over the rubber—and the trick was to pick the right one. It couldn't be a negative, couldn't be a "don't."

Donnie loved that some tiny adjustment could be the difference between struggling and thriving, and it was a matter for him of identifying the one that matched a particular player. There was more to coaching, of course, more gradual building and tinkering, more of the less momentous stuff that would nonetheless form into something whole and substantial. However, he'd gone through his own career convinced he was missing a critical clue, and he felt a sense of revenge and immense satisfaction when something crucial clicked suddenly into place for one of these young players. His entire purpose was now built on witnessing that sudden emergence and the disbelieving smile that would force itself onto the faces of even the sullenest kids, their thrill at an unfamiliar and profound success overtaking them.

He often would imagine a pitcher standing on the mound or a hitter fixed in the batter's box with Donnie's voice stuck in his head. Not a paragraph, not some grand, inspiring speech, just a handful of words, perfectly chosen to last. He knew it gave him a stature in these kids' lives that few were capable of. It was his chance of enduring. He'd had a coach named Scott Randolph who had spent thirty minutes with him when he was fifteen. Randolph told him one thing about his curveball—hold your shoulder on the target a split-second longer—and the impact was immediate and startling. Donnie heard Scott Randolph's voice on every single curve he threw after that.

At the end of a half-hour, the dad approached.

"That's the best I've ever seen him throw," he said. Then he smirked in a way that bugged Donnie. "Cash only, right?"

"You got it."

The man handed him a twenty and a ten. Donnie slid them into his back pocket.

"Can we get to the curveball next week?" the father asked.

Donnie stopped fiddling with the cage and looked at the man.

"I don't teach that until they're fifteen."

"All the other kids are already throwing one and they're fine."

"They're not likely to stay that way."

The father rubbed his eyes. "Isn't that a myth? That whole idea that the curve hurts kids?"

"Not to me."

"Anyway, I heard at Woodson's they teach it a way where you don't twist the arm. You know that way?"

"That B.S. knuckle curve?" Donnie said, looking at the father with disdain. "Trust me, they don't know what they're talking about. It's a gimmick. It'll just get him away from the right way of doing things. Look, a good fastball and good control are eighty-five percent of pitching. Let him focus on the other fifteen when his arm's ready."

The father toed at the dirt, considering this.

"I don't doubt you know what you're talking about, and Kyle clearly took to what you were saying. I appreciate all that. But he needs to take this step now to keep up. He's got a tryout for traveling ball coming up soon, a space opened up on one of the top teams. They're not going to take him without a good curve."

Donnie nodded, as if he'd expected this. "Way to look out for your son."

The father folded his arms and his eyes narrowed. "Excuse me?"

"You heard me."

The father stared at him in disbelief. Donnie stared back.

"We're leaving now," the guy said.

The man turned and started to walk briskly toward the parking lot. Kyle, his large equipment bag slung over his left shoulder—smart, Donnie thought, not putting that much weight on his throwing shoulder—fell in line behind him.

"Sayonara," Donnie said after them, flipping a ball in the air, though he knew they couldn't hear him. "Think of me when your kid's elbow is shredded and you're paying for surgery."

Donnie did not linger on them leaving. He'd only done that once—with Cole. That one had bugged him for a while. Instead, he packed up the chalk liner and pulled a weathered notebook out of the truck. He sat in the dugout alone, sorted through his notes for his book, and waited for practice and another chance.

Chapter Ten

Two days later, Donnie met Morris Garnett outside the old warehouse property he coveted. He was in a hurry because his team had a game, but he was eager to learn the reality of the situation—to understand what he needed to do to make that compelling space happen for him.

Morris was the commercial broker he and Amy had enlisted a couple of years before when they first explored with some seriousness the idea of a physical facility. Morris had seemed surprised to hear from him when Donnie called, possibly because Amy had managed all the contact with him before, but he warmed up. "I like your taste in neighborhoods," he'd said on the phone after Donnie identified the spot. "It's an exciting little area."

Morris was leaning on his red SUV, fiddling with his phone, when Donnie pulled to the curb. Donnie was wearing his Post 125 uniform already, since he'd be going straight to the field afterward, and he felt dopey as he shook hands with Morris, who was six-foot-four, black and, as Amy had said more than once, "gorgeous." He looked comfortable in a blue suit with no tie, and he grinned broadly with the dashing, contented smile of someone who had it all figured out. The heat didn't seem to bother him or his perfectly shaved head, which was smooth and clear of even the smallest bead of sweat. Donnie, meanwhile, mopped his forehead with a kitchen towel he'd brought along.

"Alright, Donnie Baseball," Morris said, removing a key from his pocket. "Let's see what we got here."

The right side of the double door at the front opened with some effort. Morris propped it open with a couple of broken bricks, saying, "This place could use a little fresh air." The inside was dark and suffocatingly hot. Morris removed his jacket and hooked it over his shoulder with one hand. His shoes echoed as he loped in long strides across the concrete floor. Donnie followed him and looked around, eyeballing the dimensions, and mentally moving himself in. He'd forgotten to bring a tape measure to see how a layout might work, but now that he was inside his concept seemed ever more feasible. There was plenty of room for his modest needs.

When Morris reached the center of the floor, he spun back toward Donnie, his coat flaring behind him as he turned. He held his free arm high into the air and with a sweeping gesture took in the space, as though presenting something much grander. Donnie couldn't tell if he was kidding with him.

"So, before we get into square footage and amenities and history, let's talk what you've got in mind for this place," Morris said. "This is a fixer upper for most people. It would require some serious investment to make this an office or anything that needs to be presentable. Most of that would come from the new tenant, but the landlord here knows he'd need to provide some concessions in that scenario and invest in it himself."

Donnie nodded, not sure where this windup was going. Morris pointed at him. "But you're a different animal, aren't you? You just want a space to lay out a few pitching mounds and batting cages and you're good."

"Pretty much."

"Not a lot of investment there on his part. That's a plus. On the other hand, the landlord here has been burned quite a bit lately. Several tenants—not in this space but in others nearby—just folded in the middle of leases and left him shit out of luck. And that means your financial end has got to be pristine. Understand?"

Donnie rolled his neck and considered the question. "No, I don't think I quite know what you're getting at."

"He wants assurances that the same deal's not going to happen to you. Here, for this space, that means you're going to have to pay fifteen percent of the total lease amount—and we're talking about a two-year lease—right up front. Now I think I can get that down to twelve or maybe even ten if you come in with a nice letter of credit from a bank."

"OK," Donnie said, pulling his towel off his shoulder and wiping at his slick throat. He was going to need some fans or something to make this place bearable in the dead of summer. Or maybe if he opened the windows, it wouldn't be so bad. "What're we talking about upfront?"

"Somewhere around ten grand, depending on what the bank says," he said.

Donnie could tell Morris was studying him, looking for a reaction. He nodded and walked around the space, pretending to examine it. He had money from Amy, but he was determined to ensure that money was saved to keep the house over his son's head and to help pay for college. He'd told himself that he'd only do this little clubhouse if it was with his money. He couldn't take the life insurance and savings of his dead wife and spend it on his newest pipe dream. Part of the problem is that he didn't know what money meant, how much things cost. Amy had paid the bills, managed the bank accounts, not to mention brought in the bulk of the family income. He didn't know how fast the money he had now would disappear. And how much of a difference would the twenty-five to thirty grand a year he was making even make? His take-home income was barely enough to cover the mortgage on the house.

"Tell me about this letter of credit," he said.

Morris stuck his free hand in a pocket and looked at Donnie with an expression that seemed skeptical. "Is Amy still involved in this?"

"She died last fall."

Morris flinched, if only slightly. "I'm very, very sorry to hear that. I really liked her."

"Yeah, me, too."

Morris walked toward Donnie, striding with the smooth assurance of a model in a men's clothing commercial, and stopped within an arm's length of him, as though he wanted a better look at his face. "I'm sorry," he said. "I am. But are you sure you're ready to dive into this alone? Do you have a business plan?"

"Pretty much."

"In writing? With clear financials all spelled out?"

"Not exactly."

"OK, look, I know I'm not your business adviser, but I can tell you this much: You need money, even for this simple operation you've got in mind. You might think you're not going to have many expenses, but you are. These things are never as straightforward as they seem. Stuff comes up constantly. You don't want to put all your own money up for this, and, in fact, a landlord's not going to trust you if you do. I'm guessing you're going to need a bank behind you with a loan and for that you need a business plan—a strong, detailed one—and you need to demonstrate how this business is going to allow you to pay back that loan, OK? You're going to need cash flow projections, financial statements. Hell, you're going to need an insurance policy."

Donnie held up his hand to indicate he'd gotten the point, turned and strode away, making a show of examining the space. Donnie processed all that he did not know and all that he did not have—and all that was witheringly necessary. He rubbed the towel on the back of his neck. His clothes were clinging to him. Morris was checking his phone across the room. Donnie and Amy had walked into adulthood side by side decades ago. They had helped each other navigate countless obstacles in the years since then, but only now in her absence did Donnie understand how much he'd leaned on her through each of them. It wasn't just that he missed her—it was that he didn't know how to move through the world without her. He was starting over now, and it seemed to him that he was armed with precious little wisdom to get going with.

Donnie smiled as professionally as he could at Morris. "Thanks for this. I've gotta get to the field now. I'll be in touch."

Chapter Eleven

Foster Tennyson arrived home shortly past six p.m., acting rowdy. He burst into the den, his tie loose and his suit coat over his arm, dropped his brief case with a thud and let out a piercing war yelp.

Max and Lucas were reclined on the furniture, watching TV. They didn't budge.

"Get up, you lazy asses," Mr. Tennyson shouted, tossing his suit jacket on a nearby chair. "Get up and bow to the king."

Lucas groaned. "Shut up, old man."

Mr. Tennyson cackled and leaped over the back of the sofa, landing hard on Lucas with an elbow in the kidney. They tumbled off the sofa and started to wrestle, grappling and grunting and bumping into the furniture. Mr. Tennyson was a thick-thighed former multisport athlete who still played rugby with a local club, gleefully pummeling men half his age. He was always punching and slapping at Lucas, trying to get him going.

Max slid off the chair where he was sitting and backed away to make sure he didn't catch a stray arm or leg. Lucas had no chance. At the rate he was growing, he might in a year or two, but Mr. Tennyson still had too many pounds and too much experience on him. The guy spent a lot of time on the weights in the basement, clanking iron and talking to himself.

"C'mon, Lucas, you got him," Max said. "Flip his ass."

But Mr. Tennyson pinned Lucas painfully, pulling his son's right knee across his chest and pressing both of his shoulder blades against the Persian rug beneath them.

"Call it, boy," Mr. Tennyson shouted in Lucas' face. "Call it."

"Screw you," Lucas grunted back, his face twisted in pain as he strained to break free.

Mr. Tennyson laughed, loving the response. It was exactly what he wanted.

The kitchen door swung open, and Mrs. Tennyson appeared. She wore a slinky black dress and glittering bracelets and earrings, ready for a night out. She rolled her eyes with amusement at Max.

"That's enough, Foster," she said. "You're tearing up my house."

"He won't call it," Mr. Tennyson said. "He won't tap out."

Mrs. Tennyson walked swiftly up to her boys, dropped cautiously to her knees, her legs squeezed tight together because of the dress, and slapped her palm emphatically to the floor, signaling a pin as though she'd done it a thousand times.

Lucas and Mr. Tennyson relaxed, breaking apart. Mr. Tennyson climbed to his feet and raised his hand in the air, while his son pulled himself up on a chair and tried to catch his breath.

"Still the baddest man around," Mr. Tennyson shouted. He pointed at Max. "You want a shot at the title?"

Max was ready, bouncing on his feet, considering the wisdom of the one-leg takedown technique Mr. Tennyson had taught him. He loved being part of this.

"Oh, stop it," Mrs. Tennyson said. "You can beat up your own child but not someone else's."

Mr. Tennyson laughed, kissed her on the cheek—in her high heels, she was a bit taller than he was—and slapped her on the backside loudly. She smarted in surprise and walked back toward the kitchen.

"I'll be ready in five minutes," she said.

"Whatever you say, my queen," he said. "That really means twenty minutes."

In a flash, he tucked in his shirt, tightened his tie, and pushed his short hair back into its part with a practiced brush of his hands. He appraised Max and Lucas.

"You boys look like a couple of street urchins," he said, as though noticing them for the first time. They wore T-shirts and shorts, no shoes, just like every other summer day.

"What's a street urchin?" Lucas said.

Mr. Tennyson hardened briefly, looking peeved. "Hell of an education I'm paying for at that school." He checked his watch. "You two have fifteen minutes to get dressed in something decent or you'll be eating crap nuggets for dinner rather than sitting down to a king's feast."

Mr. Tennyson loved to dine out, and Max loved to be a part of it. A trip to a restaurant was an event, and Mr. Tennyson pressed to pump it for all that he could. He favored large, loud tables, freely flowing alcohol and groaning plates of food that covered as much space as was allowed. Waitstaff were always being summoned, and dishes were ogled and praised. It was excessive and extravagant. Max found it thrilling.

Mr. Tennyson worked long hours, sometimes far from Richmond, meaning dinners out with him were rare. When it happened, though, Max was excited to be included. The Tennysons had adopted him as a near-member of the family, including him in a couple of vacations—skiing in Colorado at New Year's, the Bahamas over spring break—and spending untold amounts of money on him as he moved around by Lucas' side. Their daughter, Caitlin, was twenty-three and living in San Francisco, visiting home only for the big holidays. Lucas was the focus.

When they arrived at a private room at Chez Louis, the white-tablecloth restaurant in the fancy Madison Hotel, a large banquet table was already populated with middle-aged men and women. Max and Lucas, who were dressed now in polo shirts and long khakis, were the only kids there, but they were accustomed to it.

They'd been to a few of these celebration dinners, which occurred whenever Mr. Tennyson's company, a private equity firm he'd built, completed some big deal—a vague idea Max only understood as being a windfall for Mr. Tennyson.

Max had asked his mother once about Mr. Tennyson's work—what exactly it was he did.

"Some people think he's the devil, buying businesses just to fire people, strip the companies and turn a quick profit," she said, visibly measuring her words. "Other folks think he makes businesses better and more efficient—that he and the other people who do what he does serve an important role in the economy."

"What do you think?"

She paused, apparently caught off guard. "I think he's your best friend's father, and he's been very good to you."

Mr. Tennyson preached toughness tirelessly to the boys, telling stories about himself to illustrate his points—about the game-winning homer he hit in the playoffs in high school, the Ivy League wrestling title he won at Yale, the time he stayed up forty-eight consecutive hours laboring to outmaneuver a rival trying to buy a Midwestern baked goods company. Max's father never talked to him about his old exploits, his career, anything related to the past; he was like some old war veteran who preferred not to revisit that stuff.

The meal was fantastic, and Mr. Tennyson was on his game, ordering more of this and more of that, telling jokes loudly, hushing everyone for heartfelt, hilarious toasts. He would rise and move down the table, patting everyone on the back and checking in on them. Once, when he swung by Lucas and Max, who were tearing at crisp breasts of squab, he poured them each a bit of wine. "You boys should know what the good stuff tastes like," he said. Max saw Mrs. Tennyson across the table, looking concerned, trying to get her husband's attention. "Foster," she said. "Foster, no." Max drank it fast, in a single gulp, nervous about getting caught by a waiter, and his eyes watered and face scrunched.

Mr. Tennyson fell into shaking laughter. "That was beautiful. Beautiful," he said, ruffling Max's hair. "You'll remember that moment the rest of your life."

Lucas chugged his, too, but it didn't seem to catch him off guard, which didn't surprise Max. Lucas had proved he could work through the beers they'd had much more easily than Max could.

Dessert was a chocolate molten cake unlike anything Max had ever eaten. It had a crusty exterior and a rich, lava-like interior that arrested him, brought him into close, delicate contact with what he was putting in his mouth. He and Lucas laughed and shook their heads as they ate, not believing that anything so good existed.

"I don't want this cake to end," Max said. "I just want to keep eating it and never do anything else the rest of my life."

Lucas looked at him as though seriously considering it. "I'll ask Dad," he said. "See what he can do."

Chapter Twelve

No matter what else was happening in his life, Donnie always felt relieved to step onto a baseball field. That was true even as his thoroughly disappointing Post 125 team prepared to face the juggernaut that was Post 361. As he always did, Donnie ran the pre-game drill, dragging a fungo bat to a spot beyond the pitcher's mound and lofting high, soft fly balls to the outfielders, who never had to drift far to catch them. In those moments before each game, Donnie felt proud of the power still alive in his arms and legs, in the sudden speed of his concise, fluid swing.

None of the outfielders bothered to do things right, never using two hands or catching the ball coming forward so that they could make the catch and throw in one efficient, quick motion. Nothing bugged Donnie like an outfielder catching an easy fly ball on his heels. Cut-off men were missed, and balls bounced away carelessly into the grass where kids took their time to retrieve them.

When Donnie backed up to home plate to hit ground balls, he found that the infielders seemed reluctant to stoop to snap them up or to hustle for anything in the hole. Their throws to first were so consistently off target that he wondered if they were messing with him, pulling some prank.

He walked off the field pounding the ground with his bat in deliberate, contemplative strokes. Young kids with talent and opportunity, treating both as though they did not matter. He missed the satisfying snap of a sharp, eager team. No one still, everyone always with a purpose: moving with the crack of the bat, chattering enthusiastic nonsense, dancing on the balls of their feet. Instead, Donnie saw slack teenagers goofing off, acting as if they were on a chore they would rather skip.

Donnie had known coaching was his logical next step when his playing days ended, but he'd felt unequal to the task, despite the number of dimwitted coaches he'd suffered under over the years. Then Cole McGuire's father, Bernard, met Amy. He owned a commercial real estate firm and had hired Amy for work surrounding a controversial downtown development. Amy told Bernard about Donnie, and he grew interested, said his son seemed full of talent but wasn't getting the proper instruction. Amy told him Donnie would help.

He'd spent a year away from the sport, playing it off as spending time with the family he'd been missing so much. Amy told him he still had a lot to offer, but he wondered. He'd waited for a call from some organization offering him a coaching job, but he hadn't heard a word. That was a measure of what they thought of him. A first-round bust, one of the infamous mistakes that get dredged up from time to time. No such thing as a sure thing, they'd say. Look at a guy like Donnie Wilson.

Donnie met Cole and Bernard on a Saturday on the Deep Creek field that Donnie knew better than any other spot on earth. He couldn't believe how anxious he felt. He'd played in front of thousands, but some sleepy morning with an eighth grader and his dad had him sweating.

As he stood next to Cole on the pitching mound, he wracked his brain for what he possibly could teach this kid. He hadn't even pitched since high school.

But Cole's first pitch was a slow-motion, neon thrill, and Donnie's brain fired at what he'd seen. The kid was a mess, but only if you knew what to look for and Donnie realized with astonishment that he did. Cole looked back at him, waiting for a response, but Donnie said nothing he was so overwhelmed. Cole was an ugly kid, ungainly and large and vaguely cross-eyed with thick peach fuzz on his face. The impression he gave was of cluelessness, though soon Donnie would learn how misleading that was. He was a yes-sir, no-sir kid, accepting Donnie as an authority figure without question. The kid watched him, expecting orders. Donnie only nodded calmly and gestured with his hand toward the plate, where he'd set up a pitching screen, for another pitch.

Soon Donnie was making adjustments, barking advice, scolding. He felt such a charge of confidence that he knew he acted like an asshole. At one point, after an alteration in Cole's release point led to his best pitch of the day, Donnie said aloud, as if congratulating himself, "See, I know my shit."

Every single day since, when he stepped on a field, he felt that same insuppressible swagger. He knew it came off as cocky, but pride was not what he felt most about it. The chief thing he felt was grateful—grateful that he had a purpose and that it involved baseball, grateful that there was something he was still good at, even if not everyone would acknowledge it. He knew the game would slow down for him. He knew he would understand what he needed to understand.

That's what made the case of Eddie Barnes, his current pet project, so maddening. Eddie had three polished pitches and a great lanky pitcher's frame—6-3, 195—but his fastball was short of where it needed to be. It didn't make sense. He made throws from the outfield that would make Ichiro and Clemente envious, and no one on the team but Donnie could even play long toss with him. Yet he wasn't cracking ninety on the radar gun. Donnie saw something bigger in Eddie, and it killed him that he wasn't tapping into it.

Eddie was a jackass kind of young guy, too, which made it seem all the more wasteful. During the first practice of the season, Eddie had gotten in a fight with their shortstop, Jessie Bales, after Jessie, who played at Deep Creek, taunted Eddie, who played at Short Pump, about a long homer he'd hit off him in the spring. A week later, Eddie showed up to an afternoon game with the telltale signs of a hangover and vomited in the dugout. A few days after that, during a water break at practice, he ate a tin of dip on a dare and threw up in the dugout again. On the plus side, Eddie didn't know the whereabouts of his father and his mom didn't pay any attention to baseball. There were no private coaches, no meddling hands. He was a rare species alongside his teammates, who were as exactingly programmed as robots.

Donnie decided to start Eddie on the mound against Post 361. He wanted to see how he'd fare against the area's best lineup. He wanted to see how he'd react.

Donnie and Tag, his assistant coach, sat on overturned ball buckets just outside the head of the dugout, murmuring to each other during the game. Tag was a law student at the University of Richmond, but he didn't seem able to commit to the lawyer thing. Apparently, he'd chosen his summer internship based on finding a schedule that would allow him to coach, too. Donnie admired his assistant's position. Donnie was a full two years short of a degree, and he couldn't imagine sitting through another class, let alone the twenty or so he needed to graduate.

Donnie called pitches, signaling with a swift series of motions with his hands to Brick, a runty catcher with a shrill, peppy voice. Eddie pitched unspectacularly in the early going, giving up a run on four hits and a walk in the first three innings.

In the fourth, Eddie and Donnie had the first two batters set up perfectly. A fastball in would have locked up the leadoff guy, and a curve away would have had the second flailing. But Eddie got tight on both, his faith in his pitches failing him yet again. The fastball drifted over the center of the plate and was drilled for a double down the left-field line, and the curve rolled flat and was laced into the right-center gap for a triple. Against the third batter, he threw an 0-2 fastball chest-high over the heart of the plate—a pitch that was supposed to be up and in—and it was lined into right field for an RBI single. Donnie was jogging toward the mound before the ball was back in Eddie's glove.

"Where are your balls, Barnes?" Donnie said when he arrived. He flicked his hand toward Eddie's groin. "They still down there?"

Eddie backed up and his eyes grew wet with fury. He looked like he might punch Donnie. Eddie glanced at Brick, who had danced up to join them, and then inspected the ball in his hand, turning it over as if there was something hidden on it.

"Sorry, coach, I'm missing my spots," Eddie said with a trembling restraint.

"Don't say sorry." Donnie inched closer to Eddie and lowered his voice, noting the home-plate umpire easing out to break up the meeting. "Don't ever say sorry on a baseball field. Now pitch with some balls or I'll get someone else to."

Donnie ran off the field before the ump could say anything.

"You get him all straightened out, Coach?" Tag said, picking thoughtfully through his teeth with a toothpick as Donnie resettled on his bucket.

Donnie grunted and gave his signals to Brick.

The next pitch was a whistling four-seam fastball high and inside. The ball bounced off the ear hole of the batter's helmet with the resounding impact of a gunshot, and the kid collapsed in a lifeless heap.

Donnie dropped his head. "Good God," he said. "What an idiot."

Tag chuckled humorlessly. "That kid is just a big barrel of dumb."

Donnie spat out a mess of sunflower seeds in response. When he looked up, he saw that Eddie was looking at him from the mound. Anyone watching the kid would start drawing conclusions, assuming the pitch had come on Donnie's orders during his mound visit.

"Goddammit, don't look at me," Donnie muttered, avoiding the kid's gaze. He rose from his bucket and watched home plate with crossed arms, trying to look solemn and concerned.

The batter remained lying in the dirt motionless for a few silent moments and then jumped to his feet and took two heavy steps toward Eddie with a youthful effort at menace, trying on a pose he'd no doubt seen on TV. His coaches had rushed to check on him, and they held him back and looked in his eyes and hit him with a barrage of questions. When they were assured he was OK, they started talking to the home-plate umpire, who nodded in agreement. The ump then stepped away from them, pointing first at Eddie and then at Donnie, issuing warnings to both.

Donnie broke into a full sprint for home plate, cussing ferociously as he went. The ump, a young, crew-cutted guy named Chambers, seemed surprised to see him, which made sense because Donnie was surprised to be there.

"Screw your warnings!" Donnie said, spitting and thrusting a finger toward Chambers' face. "Take your warnings back to the cave you crawled out of."

Chambers stepped back and held up his hands as if in defense. "What the hell, Donnie? It's a warning. Settle down."

"You worm! You goddamned belong in the ground, Chambers. Let the kid pitch, you dipshit. Get back in the mud. Get back in the fucking mud."

Chambers looked baffled. "Did you say the mud?" He took another step back and shook his head and seemed to survey the figures around him. Coaches and players stood silently with open mouths. Chambers pointed off the field. "You're gone, Donnie. You know you can't talk like that."

Donnie often dreamed that he was unloading on someone. It might be Stubs or Otis or his brother. Sometimes, it was even some random man, dressed in a priest's outfit, that Donnie understood somehow to be the God who had killed Amy. He would square them up and let fly with every insult he could think of, screaming at the top of his voice, abusing them with everything he had. When he was inside the dreams, he reveled in them and the release they offered. But then he would awaken, breathing heavily, unable to settle himself down, and he would worry about their strength. Sometimes, the tantrum felt so real that weeks later he would find himself wondering if it had happened.

On the field, Donnie might as well have been dreaming for what little control he had of himself. He shouted in broken, unintelligible sentences about worms and conspiracies and caves and injustice, and he followed Chambers around home plate as if they were attached. He ripped off his hat, threw it on the ground, picked it up and threw it down again. What he said was unimportant to him, just that he was saying something and saying it loud.

Donnie eventually broke from Chambers to kick the dirt at the base of the pitcher's mound, lifting a thick cloud of dust into the air. Donnie was hard at work wearing out the toe on his right shoe when a divot in the mound caught his eye. He stopped, dumbfounded, struck silent. He put his foot down, suddenly pacified, and crouched for a closer look at the dirt. The well-worn footprint there surprised him. He looked to the top of the mound at Eddie, who was watching him with a curious expression on his face. Donnie grinned at his pupil.

Chambers eased up to his side, keeping a safe distance. "C'mon, Coach, get outta here," he said with obvious uncertainty. "We got a game to play."

Donnie stood, his eyes shifting between Eddie and the footprint in the dirt. He was still breathing hard from his efforts. "You got it, Blue," he said. "Barnes, come with me."

"He's not kicked out," Chambers said. "I only gave him a warning."

"That's OK," Donnie said. "You can't be too careful."

Donnie grabbed Eddie by the arm and walked him off the mound.

"What the hell, Coach?" Eddie said.

"You need a bullpen session," Donnie said. "Trust me."

In the dugout, Tag was red-faced with laughter. "Was that as fun as it looked?" he asked.

Donnie smirked. "Hell, yeah." He looked down the bench and spotted Adam Peters, the third-string catcher. "Let's go, Peters. Bring your mask and mitt."

Peters seemed reluctant to relinquish his spot on the bench. "What'd I do?"

"I need your glove," Donnie said. "Not your mouth."

The three of them walked past the two sets of bleachers, and Donnie ignored the rows of faces watching him, surely with judgment in their eyes. The trio walked silently across the parking lot to the adjacent Reece Middle School field, while the sounds of the game resumed in their absence behind them. At the field,

Peters dropped behind the plate while Eddie took his place over the pitching rubber. Donnie stood in front of Eddie at the bottom of the mound.

He drew a line in the dirt with his foot. "Your front foot needs to land right here," Donnie said. "Don't worry about anything else. Just give me a pitch with your front foot right here."

Eddie shook his head and scowled. "That looks way too close, Coach. I can't pitch that way."

"Just shut up and do it."

Donnie shuffled out of the way. Eddie trained a contemptuous look on him. This kid wasn't the type to take shit without pushback the way Cole was, and he was on the verge of shutting Donnie out. Donnie couldn't help it, though. He was too excited, too worried, too jumpy from waiting to see if he was right.

Eddie entered his delivery and threw. He stepped well past the line Donnie had sketched. A decent, unremarkable fastball disappeared into Peters' glove.

"What was that?" Donnie said, stepping toward Eddie. The kid was a couple of inches taller than he was. "You love losing or something? You like being no good?"

Eddie pointed his glove at him and started to say something, but he stopped and lowered the glove. He looked at Peters, who threw the ball back to him.

"It's too close," Eddie said, snapping at the ball as he caught it. "It's not going to work."

Donnie took two large, dramatic breaths, making a show of collecting himself. He thought of Max and this lethargic team and all the useless yelling he'd done lately. He'd told himself before that it had a purpose, but he knew that was pure delusion. He shouted and raged and carried on because he couldn't help it—because he had no control over the swelling frustration that filled him. He knew how to excuse it later. Tonight, for instance, he wasn't falling apart on the field. He was trying to fire up his sluggish team.

He reached down, scooped up some dirt, and rubbed his hands together.

"Look, buddy, I got an idea is all," Donnie said. "I think it'll be good for you. If it's not, ignore me. Do your own thing. I'm asking for a pitch or two."

Eddie watched him suspiciously. The kid did dumb things sometimes, but he knew how to pitch. He had a feel out there on the mound that couldn't be taught. It was unusual. He sensed the batter, felt which way he was leaning, what he was thinking. He could toy with hitters when he was on. But Donnie could sense Eddie was frustrated—the kid knew he was missing something—and Donnie understood what that was like. You kept your eyes and ears open for a solution.

"C'mon," Donnie said. "One pitch. Maybe two."

"Fine," Eddie said. He motioned with his glove to Peters, and Peters returned to his crouch.

Eddie raised his glove in front of him, eyed his target, entered his delivery. Donnie watched the line in the dirt, ignoring the rest of it. The foot landed right on the line.

Donnie didn't lift his head, but the ball produced a powerful pop in Peters' mitt. It sounded different.

Eddie kicked the dirt with displeasure and turned to face Donnie. He shook his head.

"That felt strange," he said. "Just way, way wrong. I told you, didn't I?"

Donnie smiled with a goofy helplessness. Behind Eddie, Peters was walking toward them, his mask lifted and a wide-eyed look of shock on his face. "What the hell was that?" Peters said.

Eddie sighed and faced his teammate. "What the hell was what?"

Peters flipped the ball underhand to him. "I never seen you throw like that before. That was a whole different level."

"Bullshit."

"Bullshit," Peters said. "That pitch had some serious juice."

The boys looked at Donnie, awaiting an explanation. Donnie leisurely reached into his back pocket, pulled out a handful of sunflower seeds and shoveled them into his mouth. He chewed and put his hands on his hips, taking his time to soak up the earnest attention of the two players. Was that the sudden appearance of admiration and respect on their incredulous faces?

"Your windup's so pretty that I've been missing the glitch, Barnes," Donnie said, feeling like a TV detective explaining a case at the end of an episode. "Then I saw where your front foot's been landing on that mound. You're too long on the back end. See, you're a rise-and-fall type. You get high on your kick and fall to the plate. But your final step is like a drop-and-drive guy, one of those guys with the big, low push from their legs. Neither is wrong on its own, but you got two halves that don't go together. So the delivery doesn't pop, doesn't connect. But when you shorten that step, the power stays together, nice and tight, and you get that great slingshot action. Also, now you're straighter, more in line and less across your body. Boom, there it is. There's another mile an hour or two for you."

"Shoot, that was a lot faster than that," Peters said. "It was like a different guy was throwing."

Donnie shrugged, acting as though he didn't think it was the coolest thing he'd ever seen—as though he wasn't giddy at the possibilities now occurring to him.

"It's not going to matter much if he only does it once," Donnie said.

Eddie shoved Peters harshly back toward the plate and climbed the mound. No smile, no thank you, no acknowledgement, all business. He settled over the rubber, rocked, and threw. The ball exploded into Peters' mitt.

Donnie felt a tingle on the back of his neck.

Goddamn, he thought to himself. I really do know my shit.

Chapter Thirteen

Lucas arrived ten minutes early for his lesson with Donnie. He was accompanied by his father. They were always at least ten minutes early when Foster was driving. Knowing this, Donnie was ready and waiting for them. Despite himself, he felt competitive with Foster and never wanted him to have a reason to feel superior. The guy had made a fortune doing real, adult work while Donnie's obsession over a game had culminated with him cutting grass all day and giving lessons to teenagers for sums Foster would find laughable. More than once, Amy had patted Donnie on the cheek and told him to stop taking Foster seriously.

Both Tennysons seemed unusually grim as they walked onto the field. As the father of a boy the same age, Donnie could see something in their manner that suggested a difficult car ride to get there.

"Ready to get some cuts in, Lucas?" Donnie said. "Today's the day we solve this slump."

Foster shook his head. "We didn't even bring his bat. Two errors in the last game, five in his last four. That sound like a shortstop to you, Coach?"

Donnie looked at Lucas, who lowered his eyes. Donnie nodded. "We can work on that. Both errors last game were going to your left, weren't they?"

"Yeah," Lucas said, pulling his infielder's glove out of his equipment bag and pounding the glove's well-worn pocket with a frustration that suggested he'd been mulling his mistakes over. "I don't know what happened."

"A lack of focus is what happened," Foster said. "A lack of concentration. Pure mental laziness. It seems to be infecting everything you do these days." Foster turned his attention to Donnie. "The boy doesn't listen to me, obviously, but maybe he'll listen to you. And, yeah, the last two were to his left, but the other three have been right at him."

"One was a bad hop," Lucas said.

"Excuses." Foster shook his head with a sneer. "I love excuses."

Donnie could see the way Foster's words stung Lucas, draining some blood from his face. The kid seemed embarrassed. He threw down his equipment bag with gusto and stalked toward the shortstop position in the newly groomed infield, eager to get away from his father and get to work. Donnie and Foster watched him walk away.

"I'm afraid the path has been a little too smooth for that boy," Foster said. "He expects everything to be easy, and you and I know nothing worth anything is easy."

"That's the truth. Lucas is a good boy, though, Foster, and he sure as hell works his ass off every time I see him."

"Eyewash," Foster said, waving away Donnie's words. "Phony effort. He needs to learn how to dig down deeper where it counts. He ain't hungry enough. He knows how to sweat, but sweat doesn't always mean something, does it?"

Donnie found himself thinking about his own son. Was he hungry the way he needed to be? Did he have the kind of desperation that Donnie carried with him growing up? It was a kind of itchy, gnawing urgency to succeed, a consuming fear of failing. Donnie had his doubts his boy felt anything like that. His effort was more dutiful than desperate.

Donnie walked toward the edge of the infield with a bucket of balls. Lucas waited, still looking angry. "Glove off," Donnie said. Lucas tossed his glove aside.

Donnie first took him through footwork drills. Donnie was ruthless about it. He pointed to the left and right and backward and forward, and Lucas followed the direction of his finger, moving with sliding and then chopping feet as though in pursuit of a ground ball. Donnie didn't allow for pauses—for moments to breathe. He moved Lucas until he thought the boy was going to collapse. When Lucas didn't get low enough on his side-to-side slides, he barked at him. If Lucas seemed to take a moment to gather himself before moving—to catch his breath—Donnie threw a ball at his feet and yelled at him. "Dance, baby, you gotta dance." "Heavy feet, my man, you've got heavy feet." "Get 'em up, get 'em up, get 'em up." Donnie knew plenty of kids he couldn't push like this, but Lucas wasn't one of them. He could scream and shout and give him a workout that never ended, and Lucas would never utter a single word of complaint. Was that enough though? Not for the first time, Donnie wondered if Lucas was putting on a show for his father rather than working for himself.

Donnie gave Lucas a quick water break after about fifteen minutes of unceasing action. The boy's shirt was already soaked through with sweat. Foster sat in the stands, his attention fixed on them—no phone or laptop or other distractions—though Donnie knew the man must have a million other things on his plate. Lucas returned to his spot in the field, and Donnie went to work rolling baseballs at him. Lucas scooped them up barehanded, again moving side to side, and flipped the balls back toward Donnie's bucket. Lucas was athletic and had good hands, but Donnie was convinced he was going to be too big to play shortstop. He figured he was headed to third base. Foster was insistent, though, that his boy was a shortstop.

When the bucket was empty of balls, Lucas helped Donnie refill it and then grabbed his glove and moved back to his position. Donnie backed about halfway toward home plate, grabbed his fungo bat, and began to lace groundballs at Lucas. He gave him a variety of challenges. Screaming liners that skipped close to the ground, high hoppers that Lucas charged, and awkward, in-between hops that tested the sureness of Lucas's hands. It was all about reps and intensity, ensuring

Lucas saw so many ground balls that he felt comfortable with every conceivable version that could come his way. The idea was that he eventually would be hoping every single ball came his way. He should crave to be tested over and over again. Donnie certainly had felt that way when he played. If the ball wasn't hit to him, he'd be disappointed, almost angry about it.

Lucas wasn't nearly there yet. He didn't shrink from the work. He didn't show the uncertainty that Donnie saw in many boys who were afflicted by a hesitancy that was a killer for an infielder, but he did miss more than his share of relatively routine balls. When this happened, he would cuss at himself, angrily chase after the loose ball, flip it toward Donnie, and then return to his starting spot and bounce on the balls of his feet, his glove extended in front of him, antsy and impatient for another chance.

An hour passed, and it started to get dark. Lucas never wilted, even as sweat dripped down his head and glistened his arms. Donnie told him, "Time's up, my man. You poured your guts out tonight. Well done." But Lucas motioned for him to bring it on. "Keep 'em coming, coach. I'm not tired yet." Donnie turned to look at Foster and pointed at his watch, but Foster only waved him onward. So Donnie kept hitting, even as the light faded into early evening. The field's lights weren't scheduled to come on, so they didn't, but Donnie never saw Lucas show the slightest sign that it bothered him. Donnie couldn't see him clearly after a while. Ball after ball the boy fielded or flubbed, and when he was done with each one he scooted back to his position and got ready for the next one. Donnie kept swatting grounders. The fact was there was nowhere he'd rather be. Here, on a middling summer night on a baseball field, barely anyone around, ripping ground balls into the dark. Working. Everything else in the world seemed dull. Everyone else in the world was missing out.

Finally, after two hours, Donnie understood that he was the one who needed to end this lesson, or it would go all night, father and son waiting eternally for the other to give in.

"Last ball, L Train," he said. "I've got to find myself some dinner."

He hit the ball into the night and saw Lucas's outline slide smoothly in front of the bounding ball and scoop it up. Lucas hustled in and helped Donnie collect the balls scattered around the infield.

Donnie slapped him on the back as they walked to the stands and Foster. "You, my friend, are an animal."

Lucas allowed himself a smile. "But it doesn't seem to matter how hard I work. I'm not getting any better."

Donnie nodded. "It's a slump is all. A bad stretch. Everyone goes through them. The only way to get through it—to beat it—is to outwork it. And you're doing that."

75

"Yeah, but does that always work?"

"I guess not always," Donnie said. "But doing nothing never made anyone better either."

Lucas collected his stuff and slung his bag over his shoulder. "Thanks, Coach."

Foster approached and stuck out a hand filled with more twenty-dollar bills than Donnie was owed. "Yeah, thanks, Coach. We appreciate the extra work. See ya next time."

Donnie nodded, taking the money. "Looking forward to it."

As they drove away, Donnie lugged his fungo bat and bucket of balls to his car. He was sweaty, sore, and starving but also brimming with adrenaline. He felt happier than he had all summer.

Chapter Fourteen

D onnie was early to pick Max up at his piano lesson. Max had been going to the same retired middle-school music teacher, Mrs. Davenport, since he was eight. She lived on a cul-de-sac a couple of blocks from Deep Creek. Donnie usually waited out front in the car, but this time he decided to park and walk up.

Only the glass storm door was closed, and Donnie could see inside. Max shared a padded bench in front of a piano with Mrs. Davenport, a small gray-haired woman Max already towered over. Their backs were to him, and Donnie could hear music. He didn't know whether he should knock or walk on in, and he considered returning to sit in his car until the time was up. But as he stood considering his choices, the music struck him beyond its simple noise and he realized the maturity of what was being played—like the radio, he thought—and he became curious.

He peeked in, studying his son. Max's shoulders were hunched over the keys, and his face was engrossed by the sheets before him. He looked like someone else—someone Donnie didn't know. He sure didn't look like Little Donnie anymore.

Mrs. Davenport turned and caught sight of Donnie. She beamed and silently motioned him in.

It was a well-appointed, spotless living room with subdued paintings of mountain vistas and country villages on the walls and fragile-looking vases perched on simple antique wooden tables. Donnie didn't sit down on the white sofa, knowing dirt from his job attached to everything he owned, and instead stood awkwardly in the doorway.

Max continued to play, and Donnie found he was shocked at his son's apparent skill. His hands moved with grace and precision, dancing and skimming and occasionally lingering on the keys. It was smooth and effortless looking—very different from the uncertain stabs and pauses Donnie remembered from the few times he'd watched him at recitals years before. Until recently—until he'd lost his direction—Max had played baseball with a thundering directness that overwhelmed opponents who got in his way. There was little subtlety involved. This was different. How had he gotten so good playing the piano without Donnie ever noticing? And when? Donnie remembered when Max was born and the doctor had remarked on the baby's long fingers. "A future concert pianist," he'd joked. Donnie, meanwhile, had thought about what a great curveball he'd have.

When Max finished the piece, the last note hanging in the air for a flawless moment, Max turned to his teacher and smiled, and she squeezed his arm with pride.

"Beautiful, Max," she said. "Just beautiful."

Max tapped a few random keys sheepishly in reply.

Mrs. Davenport looked toward Donnie with obvious pride on her face. "Isn't it something else?" she said.

Donnie watched Max but the boy kept his back to him. "Yes, it is."

"It's just the tip of the iceberg," she said. "I told your wife this, too. Max's talent is rare. If he decided to make a go of it, he could do big things."

Donnie blinked dumbly at her.

Max grabbed a chocolate kiss from a jewelry box atop the piano, and he and the teacher rose from the bench together. Then, much to Donnie's surprise, they hugged. Max, who had not looked his father in the eye for months, had genuine, easy affection for this little old woman who wore a sweater in the summer.

She smiled at Donnie as Max slid past him out the front door, and Donnie tried to smile back at her, but he couldn't manage it.

"Don't forget his recital's coming up," she said, as he headed for the door. "He's going to play the finale, a piece by Franz Liszt that will really wow you."

"Absolutely. I wouldn't miss it," he said, waving lamely as he slid out the door.

Max walked impatiently ahead of him and dropped into the passenger seat. He didn't say a word when Donnie got in alongside him.

As he started the car, Donnie realized he felt intimidated by his son. That music had been both impressive and foreign. He had no sense of what it meant, where it came from, how it worked, and he could not help but feel fraudulent alongside someone who did. It was like whenever he'd gotten stuck in a room with Amy and her colleagues and they started talking shop.

Once, seven years before, Amy had received a frantic phone call from Susan Tennyson, who lived across the street at the time. Max was over there with Lucas. The boys had been playing a game of home run derby with tennis balls in the spacious field behind the Tennysons' house. Lucas had defeated Max and taunted him innocently in the way that boys do. Max had gone into a fit, chasing Lucas to the house with a bat. Lucas escaped inside, locking the glass storm door behind him. When Max reached the door, he swung the bat and smashed the door to pieces.

Amy had arrived to find Max crouched behind a rose bush in a corner of the Tennysons' professionally sculpted backyard, still clutching the bat and crying feverishly, as though scared. Amy's immediate impression had been that he was terrified not at the trouble he was in but at what he'd been driven to do—at the lack of control he had over himself.

Donnie had acknowledged then that, yes, Max needed to manage his temper and that, yes, they should pay for the Tennysons' door, but, also, "that kind of fire in the belly isn't the worst thing in the world." Amy had frowned at her husband without speaking, genuinely perplexed, until he'd said, "it'll take him places one day." He felt a twinge of regret when he remembered that conversation and others like it now.

"You taking me home?" Max asked.

"We got to go to this softball home run derby thing," Donnie said. "Apple Joe needed me to help out."

Donnie hoped the mention of Joe, who Max revered and continued to call by the nickname he'd coined as a toddler, would help him buy into this plan, but Max showed no surrender at all.

"Can't you just take me home?" Max asked.

"There's no time. I'm already late."

"You gotta be kidding me. I don't want to watch a bunch of fat guys hitting moon balls. What about Lucas? They said I could spend the night there again. Mrs. Tennyson would come get me."

"Let's give the Tennysons a break, why don't we?"

Max sulked and looked out the window.

"Your playing sounded good," Donnie said.

Max let out a harsh chuckle.

"What?" Donnie said. "It sounded nice. Like a real musician. A pro."

"Come off it. You don't know the difference between good and bad. It's all a bunch of noise to you."

"Good lord, just take the compliment."

"Not it if doesn't mean anything," Max said.

Like a brick wall, Donnie thought. However, he was inspired by the calm effectiveness of Mrs. Davenport. "Your teacher clearly thinks a lot of the way you play. That should mean something."

Max shrugged. "That's just her style. She sort of puffs you up. She's always been like that."

"Maybe she means it."

Max shifted, leaning low in his seat as he considered his answer. Donnie sensed him relaxing.

"Honestly, it gets hard to tell what she really thinks after a while. She talks like I'm a genius, but I know a few kids at school who are much better than I am. She either is making stuff up or she doesn't know any better."

Donnie couldn't tell how he felt to learn Max was no master. He didn't want music competing with baseball, but he'd liked hearing Mrs. Davenport talk about his son in those lavish terms.

"She means well, though," Max said. "I'm not blaming her for anything." He paused. "I've got one of those recitals with her coming up again. I don't know if you heard that."

Donnie thought of Mrs. Davenport and her ability to motivate Max. Max may have said he didn't trust her faith in him, but he'd clearly been bothering those keys quite a bit for her.

"Tell me about it," Donnie said. "The recital."

Max shifted in his seat. "It's the same one she has every summer with all of her students. You've missed the last few," he said matter-of-factly, without any apparent intention a complaint. "I'm playing this piece, this really hard but beautiful piece. I've been working on it for a while. At home."

Donnie was surprised at his son's earnestness and knew instinctively some delicacy was required of him. "Sounds pretty great."

"It's no big deal," Max said, as though embarrassed. "You don't need to come."

"I want to, buddy," Donnie said, taking his eyes off the road as they idled at a stoplight to peek at his son, whose expression was unreadable. "I guess I haven't heard you talk about music like this before."

"Like I said, it's no big deal."

"Your mother would have loved hearing you play like that. That would have made her very proud." Donnie glanced at his son, who had slunk in his seat and was staring out the window. "You know?"

"I guess."

Donnie sighed. "Look, kid, we should talk about your mom, OK? I mean, wouldn't you like to? It could help."

Max squirmed in his seat in obvious discomfort. "Not right now, OK? Just not right now."

Donnie recently had begun to worry about how much Max would forget about Amy. He was young, and how much do you really remember about growing up? How many memories that he treasured of her now would disappear for him? How real would she remain for him when that happened?

"I think it'll help us remember her if we talk about her, buddy," Donnie said. "It's hard for me, too. Talking. But I think it'll help us."

Max's face looked hard and angry. "Not right now."

They drove in silence through Friday traffic, much of it like them pushing away from the city through thick rings of suburbs and their shopping centers, subdivisions, and schools. Donnie never ran the AC on his car, unwilling to risk putting more pressure on the old shaky thing, so they rode with the windows down.

Donnie turned on the radio. It was tuned to classic rock, where his dial always remained. He sang softly along as "Sweet Home Alabama" struggled statically from the speakers.

Max reached over and clicked it off.

Donnie felt struck. "I was listening to that."

"You're always listening to that."

"I like it. It's my music."

"How can you still stand those songs? How does that stuff not get old for you?"

Donnie reached down and turned the radio back on. "I don't understand your question."

The home run contest was set at Crooked Forest Park, a web of sports fields built where second-growth woods once had stood. The whole area had been country, but in a couple of quick decades housing developments had risen in rigorously plotted swaths through the trees and nearby farmland. A few token patches of the woods remained. Donnie remembered the area from trips through it on their way to his grandparents' house in Chesterfield County. A house had stood fifty yards off the road, tucked into the woods, and Donnie had thought of it then as *the* haunted house, a real one with boarded windows, a rotting porch, and a perpetual shadow. A massive concession stand, aflutter with sugar-fueled children, stood there now, though Donnie still detected something sinister in the spot.

In the parking lot, Donnie grabbed his glove from the back seat. He paused before closing the door and then pulled out one of the extra mitts he kept back there.

He held the glove toward Max, who was scanning his surroundings without interest. The complex was swarming with folks young and old, spread out in bleachers, leaning on chain-link fences, seated at picnic tables, waiting in line at food trucks, and, most conspicuously, playing baseball or softball on the fields.

"You want to help Joe?" Donnie asked.

Max scowled against the sun. "No."

"Suit yourself," Donnie said. "You can just chill in the stands then."

"Chill?" Max said.

"That's right. You got any money?"

"Yeah."

"Good, because I don't."

Donnie laughed. He felt himself falling into his father's old ways, telling dumb jokes and acting the boob to loosen up a churlish son. And, though Max shook his head with disapproval, a small, unlikely grin formed. Donnie saw the opening he'd sought. "When you pitching next?" he said.

"Not sure," Max said.

"You been doing your drills?"

"Off and on, I guess."

"You think again about working on that video with me? It'd only be like an hour or so."

"God, give it a rest." Max walked away, heading for the concession stand.

Donnie watched, feeling a familiar fatigue. Donnie walked toward the field, carrying the glove by his side. The stands were nearly full already. He was surprised. Like Max, he couldn't understand why anyone would come watch a bunch of big stiffs swing from their heels at little underhand tosses. Still, he detected that great old pregnant murmur in the stands that signaled people were expecting a good show and it was hard not to notice the adrenaline kicking in.

He slid on the glove and recognized a familiar lightness in his legs.

Then he spotted Joe near the first-base entrance, staring at a clipboard. He seemed aggrieved. A collection of softball players in jerseys and shorts were stretching on the field nearby, taking some nervous warm-up cuts. Little leaguers were playing grab-ass in the outfield. Everybody was waiting for things to get started. Donnie was taken aback at the sight of his brother, as he often was when he observed him at some distance. Joe looked so much more like their father than Donnie ever had. Where Donnie was lean and angular, Joe was thick and broad-chested. His hair had turned a uniform gray, the same color as Dad's, and had begun to thin in the same monkish pattern.

Donnie approached his big brother and punched him hard in the bicep. Joe flinched and stepped back. "Son of a bitch," he said, grimacing. "I'm not in the mood."

Donnie smiled, feeling rewarded. "Reporting for duty."

"Tremendous," Joe said, sarcastically. "Awesome."

"Hey, this is a favor I'm doing."

Joe looked up from his clipboard. "Things are just screwy is all."

Donnie surveyed the field and was stunned to see a familiar figure out there, dressed in an "XXL" T-shirt, shorts, stirrups, wraparound shades, and a fucking visor. "What the hell is Greg Hall doing here?" he said.

Joe smiled at Donnie. "I forgot you knew Greg. He's the pitcher for this thing. He was last year, too. Best slow-pitch pitcher around apparently. Huge reputation. Kinda funny that's a thing, heh?"

Donnie felt a sliver of embarrassment to be sharing a field with Greg. "Alright, dipshit, what am I doing here anyway? Catching the homers?"

"That's right."

Beyond the outfield fence was a spacious, open section of grass. Donnie pointed at it. "You mean out there?"

"That's where the homers go, genius."

"I gotta cover all that by myself?" Donnie asked.

"Every inch of it," Joe said with a small, barbed smile.

Joe stepped onto the field, laughing to himself, no longer showing any sign of stress. Donnie stood locked in place. He couldn't figure why his brother was screwing with him, but he knew he wasn't happy about it.

Chapter Fifteen

Max made quick work of his hot dog, then moved on to a holster of fries doused in ketchup. He sat at an empty picnic table down the right field line, just past the packed bleachers. His view of the field was blocked by spectators lined up against a chain-link fence, which rattled as kids kicked, bumped, and climbed it, but he could hear the intermittent ping of the aluminum bats as the derby contestants hacked through batting practice, grunting through all-or-nothing cuts he guessed weren't helping them calm their nerves.

Max imagined being in their place, screwing his spikes into the batter's box. Dad was always urging him to put himself on the field when they were watching ballgames together, asking him what pitch he'd throw in this spot or where he'd go with the ball if he was playing a certain position and the ball came his way. "Don't just sit there looking stupid," he'd say. "If you're always learning, you're always getting better."

The urge in a home run derby would be to swing harder. The trick, Max knew, would be to ignore that instinct and to relax past the point that felt right—to loosen your fingers so completely that you could barely hold the bat above your shoulder. "You can't tighten up if you want to get out of a tight spot," Dad would say. Or, even worse, "Stay loose and you'll never lose." His words were always there, nipping at Max in terse, impatient bursts—the delivery often fighting the message. He could hear Dad spitting out his pet sayings with an accusing edge, undone by Max's inability to hit worth a shit. Dad had all but given up on Max in that area. Now it was just pitching, pitching, pitching.

Max rose and took his fries and drink to an open spot on the fence, putting the drink at his feet. He felt a nagging embarrassment that he'd brought up the Liszt piece with his father. He'd even used the word "beautiful." On one hand, he was proud of what he'd learned on the piano—what he'd discovered there—and he was eager to try to explain to someone why it had grabbed hold of him the way it had. He couldn't wait for the recital and the opportunity to tackle the piece in a way that counted—that wasn't mere practice. Playing it for an audience was a way of staking his claim to it, nailing it down in some physical way. On the other hand, explaining this to his father undermined all that. As soon as Dad started talking, Max become itchy and desperate for him to shut up. It was the same when he tried to talk to Max about Mom. With the Liszt, Max wanted Dad to understand exactly what he meant, not just respond with a pat on the head and a few meaningless words. He had some vague hope that his performance would make it clear in a way even his father couldn't misinterpret.

Kids in Little League uniforms stood in antsy packs in the outfield. Max didn't recognize any of them, but he guessed most were two or three years younger than he was. The batter, who wore smudged eye black, skied a fly ball into the midst of them, and the kids ganged together beneath it. Several gloves reached up to snag the ball when it dropped, but they interfered with each other and it bounced off some anonymous raised glove and rolled free. They fell in a gleeful pile on top of it.

Beyond the kids and beyond the left field fence, Dad paced alone in a small, empty stretch of grass, looking like the largest kid of all. Max thought it was boredom that moved him at first, but then he picked up the purpose in his walk—the concentrated, decisive uniformity of the steps. Dad turned his back to the field and walked away from it. For a moment, Max thought he was leaving altogether. But another softball field was laid out beyond his father, its left field fence also backed up to the open green space that Dad now occupied. Dad walked all the way to the other field's fence and stopped, looking back over his shoulder toward the field where batting practice had ended and the home run derby was about to start. He seemed small and ridiculously far away. He put his right hand on the fence and lifted his gloved hand as though reaching up to catch an imaginary ball.

"Holy shit," Max blurted out.

He looked around, stunned that he'd spoken so loudly. Some middle-aged guy leaning on the fence nearby with two young boys bouncing at his sides eyed him with disapproval.

"Watch it, son," the man said. "Little kids around here."

Max nodded, chastened. Then he got a cruel smile. "Sorry, sir. I goddamned hate it when I do that."

The kids weren't paying any attention, but the man looked startled.

"You need a serious paddling," he said, shaking his head as he returned his attention to the field.

Max looked back at his dad, pleased with himself. It felt good to ignore the filter, the laws of respect that kept kids from saying what they felt. He'd only cussed in the first place inadvertently, though. He couldn't believe the levels of craziness of his father. All that pacing did have a purpose. He was getting the lay of the land, treating this event as though it meant something. He knew where the divots in the ground were now, where the topography changed.

The hitter launched a long drive in Dad's direction. He stopped walking, frozen in place, watching the path of the ball. He took two unhurried steps forward and stopped. The ball cleared the fence and landed fifteen feet in front of him. He caught the ball on a single hop and flipped it back quickly onto the field to one of the kids, as though eager to be rid of it. Then he returned to the spot he'd vacated and resumed walking.

85

The hitters retreated to the dugout and a voice came over the loudspeaker, asking the crowd to rise for the National Anthem. Max walked his fry carton to a nearby trash can, tossed it, and returned to his spot on the fence. He picked up his drink and sipped from the straw. Four old men in military uniforms gathered around a microphone at home plate and began to sing. Max sighed and took off his hat.

Donnie stood at attention, holding his battered hat over his heart and facing the giant American flag limp beyond the center field fence. He had the unnerving sense that the entire crowd was watching him, wondering what he was doing out there handling some kid's job. He focused on the flag, something he'd trained himself to do when he was a player and his mind would try to race and worry about the game ahead. No wind budged the flag, not even an innocent breeze to give it a rustle. The balls would be flying true tonight.

Donnie had been caught off guard by the initial strangeness of catching a fly ball again. During his retirement, he'd spent so much time on baseball fields, throwing batting practice and knocking the ball around the field with a fungo bat, that it had never occurred to him how far removed he was from the specific physical actions that had once occupied him. His greatest strength as a player—and, hell, probably as a person—was playing the outfield, chasing down balls that no one else imagined could possibly be caught. The first few batting practice fly balls had surprised him. He didn't gauge their paths well, and he acted dodgy, drifting toward balls rather than tearing after them.

His instincts returned with surprising swiftness, though, and soon he could feel the ball again, knowing in an instant precisely where it was going. His father used to say Donnie got such a good jump in centerfield that he was running before the ball ever even hit the bat.

By the time the derby started, Donnie felt ready. The first batter clubbed five homers with his ten swings, all of them to straightaway left or left center, and Donnie caught every single one of them. He was smooth and fast, and he knew that he looked good gliding after the ball, receiving it into his glove without any strain or obvious effort. He had a natural way of moving, even now.

The same pattern followed with the remaining hitters, and he became emboldened, no longer self-conscious about the way his job overlapped with a pack of preteens. He caught everything, no matter how challenging. He snagged several balls outstretched at full gallop, staying on his feet each time. No balls forced him backward in a hurry. There were line drives that seemed to scratch the top of the fence on their way over, and Donnie stooped to catch those as easily as flicking lint off his shoelaces. He wondered if anyone was noticing in the stands. Were they just watching the hitters, whistling and clapping for their long blasts, or did some of them appreciate the skill of what was happening beyond the fence? Donnie out there alone in the field, speeding through the grass on direct, unerring routes, catching ball after ball without fail. Did they understand how difficult that was? Or was he making it look too easy?

The announcer declared a break, marking the end of the first round. He listed the four players who remained for the finals. Donnie spat in the grass. He was sweating, feeling vigorous and light. Fast.

Max was hypnotized by his father. He'd never seen him quite like this. The man had been quietly flying across the ground, making plays Max knew to be near impossible look effortless. The area he was covering was staggering.

The man standing near Max—the one he'd cussed at out of some vague disdain that was building—seemed to be the only other person noticing it. He'd bent down to the kids with him, grabbing their shoulders and talking to them. "Boys, watch that fella beyond the fence. He's something else out there."

Max remembered the summer he was six years old, and he and Mom visited Dad in Binghamton, watching his games for a week. They had to stay in a motel because Dad didn't have enough room in the apartment he shared with a teammate. Max got to go down on the field before games to play catch with Dad and to chase fly balls in the outfield during batting practice. A couple of times he took some hacks at the plate himself. He hung out in the clubhouse, watching the players eat sandwiches and play cards in their underwear and give each other endless shit. Dad showed him off to his teammates, who were all obviously much younger than Dad was, and they were great to him. He became a kind of mascot and even got to be a bat boy for a few games, wearing a little uniform. When someone scored a run or made a good play in the field, everyone would rise from the bench to slap hands with that player as he re-entered the dugout. Max would stand in line with the rest of them, and the returning player inevitably would lift Max in the air like a trophy, making him giggle. He remembered Dad returning through the gauntlet of congratulations and simply giving Max five as though he was just another member of the team. It was one of Max's favorite memories.

Still, Max couldn't remember much about his father as a player. He got a few hits that week, but no homers or anything exceptional. He made some plays in the outfield, but nothing that stuck with Max. There was one guy there, though, a shortstop named Flip Haley, who made a point of telling Max what a stellar center field his father played. "He's a genius out there," Haley said. "Like the Einstein or something of catching fly balls." Men were always telling Max stuff like that.

A kid brought a water bottle to Donnie. The water tasted exceptionally good. He was sucking air, sweating profusely, but giddy. The announcer spoke.

"And now, ladies and gentlemen, we have a real treat for you. A hitting exhibition to whet our appetite for the finals to come. I know a lot of you have been looking forward to this. Our next batter played big-league ball for fourteen seasons. During his career, he appeared in more than fifteen hundred games and two league championship series. And we should note, considering the setting, that he retired with one-hundred-and-fifty-two career big-league home runs. A former star at Deep Creek and the current owner of the Woodson Baseball Academy, Richmond's own Stubs Woodson."

Donnie felt his heart clutch. Stubs came strolling out from the dugout, a bat lifted in greeting to the crowd. He took off his cap and waved it rapidly, then put it back on his head. The people responded with waves of adulation. He swirled the bat in blurred circles. Then Stubs looked right out at Donnie and pointed his bat at him. Donnie could see the flash of white teeth, the unmistakable grin. The crowd cheered.

Donnie scanned the infield area for his brother. He spotted him near the third-base dugout. In fact, Joe was already looking right at him, as though he'd been waiting for Donnie to realize what was happening. Joe held out his arms in mock supplication. Then he made a fist and shook it in encouragement. It was, right down to the slight crouch he fell into, the exact way their father had silently urged them on when they were playing.

Donnie felt a kick like he hadn't felt in a long time. It was several levels stronger than the buzz that had sent him rushing after these fly balls. It was an angry thing, but—unlike the anger that might send him rushing at an umpire—it was thrilling, too. He felt in control of it. He tossed the water bottle back to the kid. He jumped as high as he could four times, lifting his knees to his chest. Then he churned his feet, running in place.

Stubs watched the first pitch, measuring it, making sure he had his timing right before he took a swing. Donnie could see that his old friend's stance was more upright than it used to be.

Moments before the second pitch, Donnie realized what Stubs would do, and he knew it was too late to react. He saw the subtle shuffle of the feet as Stubs closed his stance and pointed his front shoulder toward right field. Sure enough, the ball arrived and Stubs whipped his bat through the zone. The ball shot into the air toward right field, far away from Donnie or any of the kids.

Donnie didn't budge, unwilling to give Stubs the satisfaction of seeing him fooled. Instead, he leaned forward, placed his hands on his knees and stared at Stubs. Several of the kids chasing balls sprinted into right field, as though Stubs would be launching more that way. Donnie knew better.

Stubs looked out toward him and gestured with his bat toward his last hit, as if to say, "Go get it." The crowd was laughing. Donnie could play to the crowd himself—offer a shrug, maybe gesture with his hand to bring it on—but he had no interest in that. He simply stared.

Stubs put his hands on his hips and squinted toward Donnie, acting with a cartoonish anger. Donnie spit in the grass, keeping his gaze on him. He knew he was acting ridiculous, offering up an easy target to be mocked. He didn't care, though. He just wanted to play.

As Stubs settled back into the batter's box, he pointed his bat toward Donnie one more time. The first time had felt like a joke, Stubs playing to the crowd. He didn't smile for this one, though, and Donnie knew the intention was different. He wanted Donnie to know he wasn't messing around.

The pitch arrived, and Stubs slammed a long, high homer fifteen steps to Donnie's right. Donnie caught it easily, flipped the ball back over, and returned to his spot. Stubs didn't respond to the crowd's applause this time. He returned to his stance and waited for the next pitch.

The homers continued, one after the other, broken up by the occasional line drive or long fly ball that died near the fence. Balls to his left and right, balls over his head, ripped liners, soft flies that seemed destined to stay pinned against the sky and never drop. Donnie got great jumps against every hitter, but against Stubs they were unnatural. It was as if the two of them were attached by a giant rope, and each ball simply traveled along the rope from Stubs' bat to Donnie's glove on an unalterable path.

Donnie knew no one better. They had begun to play ball together in seventh grade. By the summer after eighth, they were practicing together constantly, playing one-on-one whiffle ball games and throwing to each other in the cage. On weekends, Donnie's father would toss batting practice to them and Joe on the Deep Creek field for hours. Donnie would stand in center field while Stubs hit. Joe stayed entrenched at third base. Some guys in that position, especially on the hottest summer days, would just lazily catch up to the balls within easy reach and get them back into the infield, waiting it out until it was their turn to hit. However, Donnie challenged himself to catch every single ball that left the bat. Many were unreachable, but anything in the air he chased furiously no matter how futile it seemed. To get as many balls as possible—to catch a fly ball in left field when he was playing center—he needed to start running early. Soon he felt as though he knew where Stubs would hit the ball when it was still traveling toward the plate. He didn't know how he knew, but he did.

Donnie could tell Stubs was frustrated. He was hitting homers at a steady pace, but he looked edgy and short-tempered at home plate. Donnie could hear his grunts from the outfield. When his longest drive yet—far longer than any of the contestants had hit—was snared by Donnie over his left shoulder with relative ease, Stubs slammed his bat into the ground.

Stubs hit everything with the fat part of the bat. As a guy who had never figured hitting out, Max felt an overwhelming envy watching the way he whipped the bat at the ball. It seemed effortless and so certain. Ball after ball sailed over the fence, and ball after ball Dad tracked down. If Stubs hit a mere line drive or high fly ball that didn't cross the fence, Dad wouldn't flinch from his spot, as though he knew immediately. It was uncanny.

When Stubs stepped out of the batter's box for a moment to sip from a water bottle, the announcer spoke. "A special thank you today to Donnie Wilson. Donnie, who y'all might remember from his days at Deep Creek and Clemson, is that man out there catching everything that clears the fence. You can see why he's known as Donnie Baseball. Some of you know Stubs and Donnie brought a state title to Deep Creek once upon a time ago."

Some in the crowd clapped politely. Stubs didn't lift his head.

The man next to Max said with a big grin on his face, "Donnie Baseball. Of course." He leaned down again for the kids. "Boys, I played high school ball against that man catching all those homers. He was the best player in the city."

"Is he famous?" one of the kids asked. The boy had ketchup streaks on his cheeks, and he was bouncing up and down in place, full of more energy than he knew what to do with.

The man laughed. "Not really," he said. He folded his arms on the top of the fence. "Only to some of us, I guess."

After Stubs' brief break, Dad began to show off. For the next homer he saw, he slapped his glove repeatedly on his thigh as the ball descended, then swung his glove in a rapid, snapping circle into the air, snagging the ball out of the air audaciously.

Several in the crowd noticed the catch, and Max picked up on laughter and stray comments nearby.

"Did you see that, boys?" the man next to him said. "Did you see that catch?"

The next homer Dad again tracked easily, taking a few steps to his left and stopping. This time he never even lifted his glove, putting his hands on his hips, as though bored. His glove jutted behind his back, turned upward. He didn't budge as the ball zeroed in on him, as though it was pursuing him instead of he it. Max expected to see the ball smack his father in the chest or go bouncing on the ground behind him, but instead it simply disappeared over his head. Then, Dad, after remaining still for a dramatic moment, pulled his glove in front of him, held the ball aloft for the world to see and tossed it back over the fence.

The crowd ate it up. People laughed and broke into loud cheers. Max scanned the crowd and saw nothing but grinning faces looking out toward his father. He felt his anxiety building.

Stubs smashed the next pitch on a curling line away from Dad, toward the third-base line. Max felt the crowd holding its breath. It seemed finally to be too much for the old man—a ball too fast and far. However, his graceful pursuit had a look of assurance about it. As his path crossed with the ball's, he again declined to lift his glove. Instead, he stuck out his bare right hand and caught the ball on a dead run as casually as if he was plucking a tomato off a vine. He slowed into a trot, turned, crow hopped toward the field, and rifled a throw of eerie accuracy and velocity all the way to the pitcher, who caught it at chest level without moving. It was an astonishing thing to witness.

At this the crowd exploded with applause. A few people stood to cheer. Even Stubs laughed and stepped out of the box to give Donnie his moment. The announcer, sensing the turn things had taken, put on his best showman's voice and boomed, "Donnie Wilson, everybody!" And the crowd cheered some more. One woman nearby said, "He's fantastic."

Max didn't feel any stirring of pride. Dad didn't acknowledge the cheering, as if he was disinterested in the attention. And yet he'd just been clowning around for the crowd, openly craving this very moment they were giving him.

The man who had recognized Dad was cheering his ass off, clapping fanatically like something was wrong with him. Not for the first time of late, Max envisioned a punch—a swift, clean roundhouse to the jaw.

Stubs launched back-to-back fly balls well short of the fence. Cans of corn. Max thought Donnie looked irritated as he slammed his fist into his mitt, eager for more of a challenge.

Then Stubs smacked a long drive toward Donnie. Max watched as he drifted easily to his left until the ball was headed right for him. Then he turned his back to the field, dropped to his knees and cupped his glove with both hands, raising it above his head like a congregant taking the communion wafer. The ball dropped into the glove as if divined.

The bleachers shook. Stubs dropped his bat, held his hands aloft, and clapped over his head. The cheers sounded so loud to Max that they seemed to have come from somewhere inside him. The man leaning on the fence near him seemed about to say something, but he paused and looked at Max. He smiled and shook his head. "Holy shit, he's something else."

The PA announcer bumped in.

"Five more swings for Stubs Woodson and then we'll return to our main event: the derby finals between Stoke Kelly and Bobby Laird. We'll see if Stubs can find a way to get one ball past Donnie Wilson out there. Did you know, by the way, that it was Donnie that won the state player of the year when he and Stubs were seniors?"

Donnie saw Stubs' head jerk toward the press box at the mention of the state award. The guy found slights everywhere he could. Together, they'd once spurred each other on, searching out and collecting scraps and meals of disrespect and feeding them to each other as they lifted weights or ran stairs side by side. It was the sustenance they needed. Stubs had never said it, but Donnie knew playing in his shadow in high school had been a special fuel for Stubs, probably stronger than any of the others.

Donnie thought he had understood the extent of that resentment the evening Stubs visited Donnie's backyard to drink beers and tell him he was opening WBA. The guy already had the career and the fame that they'd both wanted, and now he'd decided to come home and take the one thing that Donnie had managed to build in the ashes of his own career. Donnie had been making enough money with his gig that he and Amy had begun planning for the possibility of him opening his own physical facility in a few years.

He'd told Stubs that, but Stubs had only offered him a job as an instructor, just to turn the screw, Donnie figured.

"It's something *I* want to do," Stubs had said, fiddling with a bat. Donnie had rarely hated someone so much in a single, concentrated moment. "It's not about you at all. You've been thinking that way since we were kids. People aren't out there in the world thinking about Donnie Wilson all the time."

That's when Donnie had thrown the beer at him. He still regretted not hiding his intentions better, as the way Stubs had simply knocked the beer away with the bat was a final humiliation.

The next homer was a monster to left field, and Donnie was running at full speed within a step of departing his spot. The ball was hit directly over his head, the most difficult kind of drive to track. He ran with his back completely to home plate, facing away from the crowd and Stubs and the rest of the world. He could hear himself breathe. It was just him and the ball and the empty sky.

For the first time that day, Donnie was uncertain if he'd get there in time. There'd been urgent chases, but he'd always deep down known he'd be there. This was better, though, this weightless unknowing, this worried emptiness in his stomach, this tingly fear. These catches—when you made them—were the ones that meant something, the ones you and others remembered.

As the ball descended, Donnie saw that one desperate sprawl may get him there, outstretched at full speed, fully extended, if everything went just right. He could imagine it happening, the slight but firm weight of the ball striking his palm.

A step before he leapt, though, he remembered the fence, remembered his steps, and he knew he'd screwed up badly.

And then things went black.

Donnie slowly returned to the world on his back with two little kids in little league uniforms leaning over him. He pulled himself up onto his elbows. A small crowd was rushing toward him. He felt acutely nauseous.

He began to stand. He strained and worked to get his feet under him, but they wouldn't catch. He grabbed the fence and heaved himself up.

Joe arrived at his side and gripped him, holding him up by the elbows just in time as he started to wobble. Still, Donnie pushed Joe away, reaching out to hold the top of the fence for independence.

"Get the hell off me," he said. "I'm fine."

Joe crossed his arms and looked at him with the frustrated face of a parent. "I don't know how you could be."

Greg Hall was alongside Joe, watching with a wide grin. "Yeah," he said. "That was about the worst car wreck I've ever seen."

Donnie didn't care about that, though. He cared about the ball. But when he opened his glove, there was nothing there.

Chapter Sixteen

Post 125 split its two games the weekend immediately following the derby. After it won its Saturday contest, 10-9, with a wild late-inning rally, Donnie felt buoyant, thinking the boys had found themselves and their purpose as a team. He realized he was even attached to them, forgiving and warmhearted, as they celebrated in a boisterous pile at home plate. But it was a false spring. On Sunday, they got squashed, dropping a dreary 15-3 affair that seemed even worse than the score. His players caved when they fell behind and moved in slow motion the rest of the afternoon, performing with an infuriating disinterest that made Donnie despise them all over again. On top of that, he had a gnarly black eye and a headache that couldn't be solved no matter how much Advil he took.

Despite the carnage, Donnie walked off the field feeling a glimmer of optimism, knowing that Eddie Barnes had a start coming up in the week ahead. He couldn't wait for the game and the revelation to the world of the kid's true level of talent. There was something special there.

On Monday morning, Donnie had to weed and edge the baseball field—work he didn't care for. He didn't rush out there first thing. Instead, he sat on a folding chair in the shop with his feet propped on a stool and watched Otis and Ricky as they went after each other. Esau, a gray-bearded man with a high voice who had worked on the crew since Donnie was a kid, sat on a nearby ripped leather sofa alongside Tippie, his son, who had joined the crew four weeks before. They were playing cards and laughing along with Donnie.

Otis was scanning through the newspaper, while Ricky fiddled with a push mower that had been acting up. Even though he was overseeing the inside facilities these days, Ricky still came down to help with repairs. He had a knack for them.

Otis was enraged again at Ricky's wife, his nemesis.

"Can you tell her not to answer the phone when she sees my number?" Otis said. "I don't want to hear her goddamned voice at this point. I think she answers just to tell me you're not around, even if you're standing right next to her."

"You always think it's some lying thing," Ricky said, shaking his head while he crouched and tinkered with the mower's motor. Ricky turned his cell phone off on the weekends, which drove Otis mad. It didn't help that Ava, who had lived with Otis for two years, had recently left him with only a harsh note and a missing TV. "I really was at the hardware store. I swear it."

"Yeah? And you think she plain forgot to give you my message?"

"Of course. And, like I said, I wouldn't have been able to hit up that movie Saturday night anyway. We were doing something."

"Doing what?"

Ricky grew a mischievous grin and shrugged. "Something."

Otis dropped the paper in his lap and held his hand up. "Nope. Hell, no."
Ricky laughed.

Otis looked repulsed. "I don't want to hear about that nasty woman."

Tippie looked up in surprise. "You're going to let him say that about your lady, Rick? For real?"

"He's said worse," Ricky said.

Esau nodded and cackled, "Much worse."

Tippie looked to Donnie, who was smiling, and then back at Ricky. "And you cool with that?"

"I don't give a shit. It's his issue, not mine. He just don't like that I'm happy."

"You're happy because she tells you you're happy," Otis said. "If she tells you you're a goat tonight, you'll come in tomorrow on all fours eating grass."

"You're always saying stuff like that," Ricky said. "Maybe you're not the best expert in this particular area?"

Otis' face reddened in anger. "Asshole." He stood and walked briskly toward the privacy of his office. He slammed the door behind him. Donnie and Esau exchanged knowing looks. The fights usually ended like this: Otis turning petulant and walking away in childish silence. He gave much more comfortably than he got.

Ricky returned to his work on the mower, clearly agitated. "The guy can't keep a woman, so he hates mine. If you can't make your shit work, maybe blame yourself and leave the folks that got it figured out alone."

The door of Otis's office swung open, and all eyes turned to Otis as he strode directly toward Tippie, ignoring everyone else. "Hey Tippie, you know Ricky and I played ball together growing up? Basketball for Deep Creek?"

"No shit?" Tippie said.

"Ah, shit," Esau said, putting down his cards and rubbing his eyes.

"C'mon, Otis," Donnie said, watching Ricky, who had dropped his hands and had a sunken look on his face. "Give it a rest."

"Nah, Tippie should hear about this," Otis said. He turned his attention back to Tippie. "We were good, man. We could ball. Our senior year we went to the state semis. I played point, and Ricky was sort of an undersized forward type. Rebounding, setting picks, playing hard-ass D. The unglamorous stuff."

"A glue guy," Tippie said, helpfully. "Draymond Green."

"That's right, Tippie. A glue guy. Point is he wasn't out shooting three-pointers, you understand? That wasn't his place."

"Good lord," Ricky said. Donnie hated when this story came up, and he could see Esau was every bit as uncomfortable as he was. This pair of best friends could be hell to be around when things turned sour.

"I'll give you one guess who took a three-pointer in the final seconds of the semis when we were down three, even though he hadn't hit one all year."

Tippie looked at Ricky with a big smile, ready to tease him, but then he saw the look of anguish on Ricky's face and he kept his mouth shut.

"That's right," Otis said. "Ricky."

"I had to," Ricky said. "There wasn't any time left."

Otis shook his head and continued to focus his speech on Tippie. "He always says there wasn't any time left, but there was four seconds still to go. That sound like enough time to pass?"

"I don't know, man," said Tippie, who seemed to understand he was now stuck in the middle of something. "I wasn't there. Maybe nobody else was open."

"A good guess," Otis said. "But not the right answer. I was there, ten feet away, hollering for the ball, not a jersey on me, wide open three. The kind of clear shot you dream about growing up. And the difference was I could shoot a little. Heck, I could shoot a lot."

"I didn't see you," Ricky said.

"Of course, he didn't see me. He only saw the basket."

"Give it a rest," Donnie said. "It's been a hell of a lot of time."

"Hard to forget something like that," Otis said. "I knew Ricky wasn't going to pass, too. You know why, Tippie?"

Esau groaned and got up, heading for the bathroom. Donnie wondered why Ricky didn't leave, too. They'd all heard this many times before, and Ricky never budged. He always sat there and took it, as though he thought he deserved the punishment.

"Because Ricky had made a couple of threes that week fooling around before practice. I could see him getting convinced that meant something all week. The ball didn't go to him on purpose, you see? The play was set up for me, and I was coming around a pick and the pass got deflected and fell to Ricky. He coulda just passed it on to me. He knew where I was. He knew I was supposed to get that shot. And he just went up with it. Brick. No state title game. I think about it every day."

Ricky shook his head. "I do, too."

Otis looked thrown for a moment, his anger paused, but then he steeled again. "Well, you should."

Only then did Ricky rise and walk out of the room. "I can't wait to get you on the mat," he said.

"Shit, you'll be on your back before you know it," Otis shouted. He walked back to his office and slammed the door. Tippie looked at Donnie. "Pretty messed up they're still holding onto that."

"Yeah," Donnie said. "I guess they'll be fighting about it the rest of their lives, especially because Otis will never let it go."

"Makes you wonder what they'd be like if they'd gone all the way. Gave 'em less to think about?"

"Ah, they'd always have something to think about," Donnie said, heading for the door. "Winning a state title doesn't solve all that much."

Donnie parked one of the school's pickup trucks at the baseball field and walked onto the infield with an angled weeder, a small scythe-shaped device with a serrated edge that Ricky had introduced him to. He'd weed with that first and then get out the edger and get the shape right. It had rained overnight, so there would be little give to the roots. He knew Otis would urge him to use the chemicals and spray, be thorough and efficient, but that made him uneasy. Seemed wrong to bring poison onto a baseball field.

It was uncomfortable work, bending down or kneeling or crouching or sitting to tug and dig at weeds—he kept shifting his position to ease a knot here and a strain there—and it was also mindless. He tried to control his thoughts and think of Eddie Barnes and his peppy new fastball, but he kept thinking of Amy instead.

It was difficult now for Donnie to reflect on the months before Amy's death with anything resembling clarity. In retrospect, it was easy enough to see evidence of the upcoming disaster in every recalled moment, every word Amy had uttered that he could now remember. At the time, however, he hadn't been aware of some calamity approaching. Instead, he'd been wrapped up in his dwindling client base, fixated on diminishing Stubs' stranglehold on the area's ambitious young players, and Amy had been busy with her own many distractions. They had crossed paths easily enough in those days, navigating their lives together without fireworks, good or bad, and running a household as half-decent parents. It was true that Donnie was aware of a vague space between them, but to him that only seemed like a function of age and complicated careers. She did seem to be working hard all the time. Exceptionally hard. But wasn't that just what people did? Who wasn't busy all the time?

Donnie was still thinking about Amy when the Post 125 baseball co-chairs snuck up on him. Tom Warner and Bobby Stetson were on the field, crossing the pitcher's mound toward Donnie's burrow near third base, before he noticed them. He stood as they approached, reviewing the possible reasons for an unannounced visit. No good ones came to him.

"Howdy, boys," Donnie said.

The two greeted him with restrained politeness. When Tom stuck out his hand to shake, Donnie lifted his own dirt-encrusted hand and grinned. He kept the weeder gripped in his left.

"Probably you'd rather you didn't."

"Looks good out here," Bobby said. "Infield's smooth enough to eat off."

"I'm a serious craftsman," Donnie said. They seemed uncomfortable, watching each other to see who would get started on the reason for their visit.

Tom smirked at him. "My God, that's a hell of a shiner."

"So, guys, it's nice to see you and all," Donnie said. "You here about a raise? Some new stud want to join the team?"

Bobby squinted toward the outfield. He'd been a year above Donnie at Deep Creek and a decent pitcher, a swing guy who started against the doormats and threw some empty innings in relief of games that were already decided. He'd helped Donnie get the coaching post. He'd put on about fifty pounds and grown bald since high school, though he always covered his dome with a Tredegar Landscapes hat, his landscaping business. Donnie didn't know Tom as well, though Tom had a kid on the team, a bratty, spoiled second baseman who pouted all the time. Tom was wearing a suit and shades, looking intently sophisticated. He was some sort of ambulance-chasing lawyer on Broad Street. Donnie had seen his TV commercial many times, with Tom arguing in court, nodding on the phone with his sleeves rolled up, and sitting at a conference table and nodding tenderly at a devastated old woman.

"Donnie, we appreciate all that you've done for the post and for the ballclub," Bobby said, sounding as if he was reading from a script. "Everybody understands your passion and your knowledge. We know you care about these boys doing well. But we don't think you're a good fit for the program anymore. It's not working out and we're going to have to let you go."

Donnie stared at Bobby, but Bobby only watched him with an even, knowing look.

"What are you talking about?" Donnie said. "You guys think you run the Yankees? We got off to a slow start, but we're going to come around. You should see the adjustments I made with Eddie Barnes. That guy's going to be an ace for us that's going to cut through the league."

Tom exhaled. "Look, Donnie, we know you know your stuff, but it doesn't do a bit of good if the kids don't listen to you. You simply don't have their respect. And you don't have the parents' respect either. That tantrum with the umpire the other day was the last straw. I mean, what the hell was that?"

"I was trying to light a fire in them. They were sleepwalking out there."

Tom laughed and shook his head. "Come on. You lost your temper, guy, and you fell apart. I was there and so was Bobby" —Bobby was nodding at him—

"and it was clear as day that you were in another world. I mean, the ump was giving warnings to the teams. It was a logical thing to do, and you acted like he'd shit in your shoes."

"What kind of example is that for the kids?" Bobby said.

Donnie hated these men more than any he'd ever known. Bobby the scrub from high school now telling him about baseball. Incredible how life could turn out. He dropped the weeder, reached down to the infield, and grabbed some dirt in both hands.

He saw himself on the bases, focused and calm. Bobby and Tom stared at him, waiting, but he ignored them.

Fine, he thought. It's a summer job coaching teenagers. Fine. I'm not going to give these assholes the satisfaction of making a scene.

"OK, men," he said. "It's been a pleasure. Thanks for the opportunity."

Donnie recognized the way the men relaxed, as though they'd been steeled for more.

"That's big of you," Bobby said. "Good luck."

"Yeah, Donnie," Tom said. "Best of luck to you."

"So, who you got to right the ship?" Donnie said. "You promoting Tag?"

"No," Bobby said. "He's a good guy but not quite there yet. We're hiring Pete Scott. You know him?"

Donnie squeezed the dirt in his hands tight. Scott was one of Stubs' toadies, and he worked individually with several of the Post 125 players. "I know him. Works at WBA, awful player at VCU, barely got off the bench. Been scamming rich moms and dads ever since. Yeah, I know the guy."

"He's a great coach," Tom said, looking flustered. "He knows how to make kids better."

Donnie laughed hysterically. He flung the dirt in his hands onto the infield with relish. "He works with your kid, Tom? That's hilarious. I've seen Pete Scott throw tantrums that make mine look like a little shake of the head. The guy emptied a bat rack onto the field at a 13U game two years ago. Could have killed someone. All this bullshit about respect and getting them to listen to you, and this is just because you want to give the job to your kid's tutor."

"That's not the case at all," Bobby said. "He was highly recommended."

Donnie laughed. "By who? Tom's idiot kid?"

Tom put his hands on his hips. "Watch it."

Donnie waved his hand toward the parking lot. "Get off my field."

"Your field?" Tom said, looking amused. "Just because you pull its weeds doesn't make it yours. That's like a janitor saying he owns an office building because he cleans its toilets."

Donnie picked up the angled weeder and pointed it at them. "Off my field."

Bobby and Tom exchanged glances. Tom shrugged. "What're we arguing with him for? Let him get back to his dirt. I gotta meet a client."

Without another look at Donnie, the two men turned and walked away. Donnie watched, the weeder by his side, and waited until they were out of sight to return to his work.

Chapter Seventeen

Donnie felt like swimming. He hadn't been to the pool at all that summer and suddenly that felt like some kind of offense against Amy. He bounded up the stairs, two at a time, and dug his swimsuit out of a basket that sat on the floor of what was now his closet. The closet was a cramped thing, shared with Amy, whose clothes still dominated it. Donnie only had a gray suit and a handful of dress shirts and khaki pants in there. He paused in the closet door, staring at the array of dresses, tops, and skirts that had remained there untouched since Amy's last day. He felt an acute, anxious guilt staring at those clothes. He was still sure there was something he should have done to prevent her death. Paid attention to the meds she was taking or somehow helped her manage her stress better. He'd gone to bed early the night she died. She'd been working at the kitchen table downstairs and told him to go on without her. Instead of encouraging her to get some rest, he'd kissed her on the top of the head and said, "You're a bad-ass machine, honey." She'd kept pounding away on her laptop without looking up, preparing for a presentation she'd never give. Donnie hadn't even stirred when she'd come to bed, never seeing her pop in the fatal pills. Had he mumbled to her in his sleep as she settled onto the bed, as she said he'd done many times before? Had she kissed him on the cheek before closing her eyes for the last time? He'd never know.

Downstairs, in the kitchen, Donnie loaded up a small cooler bag with three cans of Bud Light, dug a koozie out of a drawer, and walked out the door at seven. The pool closed at nine.

The pool had been a refuge for Amy and Max and occasionally Donnie since they'd moved into their house. A small private neighborhood place, built down in a hidden little hollow off the street, surrounded by large trees. You walked down a path to get to it. The place felt comfortably reclusive and removed from the daily concerns of the world. Amy had always thought it was a perfect space for summer, and she would go often with Max. Donnie occasionally joined them on free evenings and never regretted it. It was technically a club, but without the extravagances that suggested. The clubhouse was a single room that Donnie had never stepped foot in. The snack bar—a small kitchen with a sliding window for processing orders—served frozen desserts, popcorn, and toaster oven hot dogs and pizza slices.

When Max was little, and Donnie was off playing ball, Amy would walk him to the pool to meet other neighborhood kids and their mothers on weekends and during the hot evenings. She'd pack a snack and a couple of pool toys—plastic sticks, cloth balls—and they'd spend hours there. Max did not last long in the limits of the baby pool. He clamored for the big pool, and Amy taught him to swim in what seemed like no time at all. Soon, he was on his own, Amy staying close, but Max paddling and kicking ferociously around the shallow end. Amy would recount all this during long phone calls. Max was forever climbing out on the steps, shuffling over to the side, and plunging back into the water with a wide grin on his sterling little face. Amy would sit on the steps, half in the water and half out, chatting with whichever other mothers were around, and consider what an electric little boy she had. Donnie could only imagine the scene, but now it felt as real as anything else from his life.

Max grew older, Amy went to work, and then Donnie was suddenly home for the summers. Amy would bring Max on summer evenings after work when he didn't have a ballgame, and Donnie liked to join them when baseball didn't keep him away. Donnie discovered the pool had a distinctive atmosphere at the end of the day. Men and women would come with their children and a cooler. They'd have pizzas delivered or they'd cook on the grill, eating dinner on picnic tables. And while the kids swam boisterously, the adults would drink cans of beer and plastic cups of wine, lie back on white resin chaise lounges, and talk about whatever occurred to them. For a few years, the Wilsons became regulars of what some called "the dusk crowd."

Donnie walked rather than drove to the pool, which was only four blocks away. He realized he could track the years very simply with the way this little walk had changed. First, Amy had pushed Max there alone in a little stroller, while Donnie played ball somewhere far away. Then, Max had walked alongside Amy, as she'd watched closely and talked firmly to him whenever he veered too far from the curb. Then, Donnie had joined them, and he and Amy had walked with the boy. Max would run out ahead of them, in sight, but too excited to stay back at their pace. And now, finally, Donnie was going alone.

As he descended the well-worn path, he scoured the pool and could see that almost no one was there. A few kids were screaming in the water, and a handful of adults sat on the incline that rose from the pool toward a shelter and picnic area. The incline was covered in chaise lounges and matching chairs.

He checked in with the bored lifeguard at the front gate. As he walked toward the incline, he saw two familiar faces. One of them had raised up on her chaise lounge and was waving.

"Oh, my God. Donnie! Over here."

Donnie grinned. The two women lying out were Heather and Megan, a couple of stalwarts of the dusk crowd. Each had red plastic cups that were surely filled with white wine if history was a reliable guide. Heather was the one on her feet, motioning him over.

Donnie was surprised how happy he was to see them. They were much more Amy's friends than his, but he'd been there for some memorable evenings with them over the years. They exchanged hugs and exaggerated greetings. They hadn't seen each other since the funeral, though no one mentioned that. Each had kids around Max's age, but also younger sons and daughters and Donnie recognized them slapping around in the pool. Heather and Megan were wearing cloth covers over their bathing suits—there was no sun to catch anymore—and both looked a bit bleary eyed, as though they'd had a couple of cups so far. Donnie scanned around, but their husbands, Seth and Roger, weren't around. He liked them both, but he found he was glad. He was excited at the prospect of hanging out with Amy's friends. It was almost like catching a glimpse of her again.

"I've missed you guys," Donnie said, settling onto an empty chaise lounge between the women. He leaned back and groaned with pleasure as he felt his back and legs relax. He kicked off his sneakers with a flourish.

"We missed you too," said Megan, who had spectacular red curly hair and the strong remnants of the accent she'd gotten growing up in New Hampshire. She patted him on the shoulder. "Welcome back. Your poor eye, though. Are you OK?"

"You should see the other guy," Donnie said. He reached down and pulled a beer from the cooler, slid it into a koozie, and popped the top, eliciting a satisfying fizz. He surveyed the pool. Beyond it stood woods of thick, gawky pines. "I forgot how much I like it here. What is it about this that feels so calm? It's just a boring little pool. I feel like I've already wasted half the summer staying away."

Heather, who was on Donnie's right, reached her cup toward him. "Well, don't waste the rest of it."

Donnie smiled, remembering the toast Amy liked to use with these two. He held out his beer. "Live free," he said.

Heather laughed and bumped his beer. "Or die hard," she said.

"Your Amy was so silly," Megan said.

Donnie laughed. "She was *your* Amy, too."

"We agree," Megan said.

"No Max?" Heather asked.

Donnie winced. "He's hanging out with friends. He's old enough now where that seems to be what he's always doing. He's always 'getting together' somewhere with someone. I forget where he's supposed to be most of the time."

"How's he holding up?" Megan said, sitting up and turning to face Donnie.

Heather sat up on the other side and faced him, too. "And how are you holding up?"

Donnie took a long sip. "I've been better. Can I ask you something? What did you guys used to talk about when she was the one sitting in this chair? When I wasn't around?"

103

Megan and Heather smiled, and Megan lay back down.

"All kinds of things," Heather said. "Depended on the night, really. Sometimes, we got deep and talked about serious shit, but mostly we laughed a lot."

"A lot," Megan said. "Amy was funny as hell, wasn't she?"

"She really was," Donnie said. "What kind of serious stuff?"

"A lot about work," Megan said. "She'd talk about her own crap, what she was working on, but she was an incredible listener and she'd let us go on and on about whatever we were dealing with."

"And then give the best advice," Heather said. "She was so smart about that sort of thing."

"Actually, I know you think we were just three drunks hanging out, but most nights we were down here with our laptops working away," Megan said. "Plenty of nights there was no booze at all. You probably thought we were just getting sauced and talking about our husbands." She winked at Donnie. "Mostly, though, we were bouncing ideas off each other, bitching about the assholes we work with, talking through stuff we were trying to figure out. We were getting shit done."

"That's the truth," Heather said. "Amy most of all. That lady was a machine."

Heather was looking at Donnie with a buzzy grin. She was a sweet and egoless woman, eager to do favors and help everyone out. It made you feel better to be around her.

Donnie smiled and resisted the urge to point out that Amy wasn't the machine she thought she was—the machine had broken down. The kids in the pool were giggling. They had buckets and were slapping water at each other, seeming thrilled at every splash. Just then the lights beneath the water in the pool flashed on. Donnie felt a fluttering pleasure at the sight, and he knew he'd need to swim soon.

Listening to the women talking about Amy, he felt almost as though she would materialize before them—as though their memories would summon her. He didn't want it to stop.

"Tell me about her," he said, surprising himself. "Would you do that for me? Just tell me everything you remember."

"Nothing would make us happier," Heather said.

The women told Donnie stories about his wife. Fun stories. Stories he'd never heard. They told him about the time she got drunk at Fourth of July and did a belly flop off the diving board to the chants of a cheering mob. And the time she stole Megan's towel, bathing suit, and change of clothes from the hook in the women's shower room when Megan insisted she had to leave the pool to meet a different friend for happy hour somewhere. Megan had screamed until Amy relented and handed over the clothes while laughing through tears. There was also the time a guy had shown up with his family as part of a visitor's pass and loudly complained about the "shitty pool" and the "sad" snack bar with nothing worth eating, and Amy had walked up to his wife and asked in a loud voice, "What's it like being with a man with a micro-penis?"

And Megan told Donnie about how Amy had called her every year on June 4, the day Megan's sister had died of cancer, and how much Megan had missed that call this summer—how much harder the day had been without Amy's voice.

"She wasn't a saint," Megan said, her eyes wet. "We fought once or twice, and she had an edge to her—that cleverness could really hurt when she got sharp with you—but I wouldn't have changed a thing about her."

"Me neither," Donnie said, opening a new beer. "She was lucky to have such good friends. And she always knew that."

"We were lucky to have her," Heather said.

Megan raised her cup. "Cheers to that."

Heather squinted at Donnie, as though examining him. "This isn't the first time you've talked to someone about Amy, is it?"

Donnie studied the pool. "Kind of."

"Don't you have friends you could talk to?" Heather said. "Maybe your brother?"

"I don't think so," Donnie said. "Don't get me wrong. They'd try to help. They'd do their best. But it wouldn't feel right."

"You don't know that if you don't try," Megan said, looking very concerned.

"I think I know. Like I said, not their fault. I wouldn't be any better."

"Then you definitely have to come back to the pool," Megan said. "We'll be here."

"How's Max doing?" Heather said. "Does he have someone to talk to?"

Donnie shifted in his seat and considered the pool in front of him. "I know he's taking it hard, but I don't know much more than that. The kid doesn't want to talk to me. He's the wrong age for it. He just squirms and gets uncomfortable and finds any excuse he can to get away from me."

"A teenager," Megan said, nodding.

"And a boy," Heather said.

"It's impossible to know what's going on inside his head. Impossible."

"Amy certainly was proud of him," Heather said. "You, too, Donnie. I hope you know that."

"I do. I never had to worry about that with her, no matter how much I screwed up."

Megan put her hand on Donnie's left shoulder, and Heather did the same on the right. Donnie laughed. "This right here is corny as hell, but Amy would have loved it," he said. "She'd have rolled her eyes and cussed at us and told us we were being idiots, but she'd also have cried while she was complaining."

They held up their drinks.

"Yeah, you know, to Amy," Donnie managed to say. "She was one of a kind, for better and worse. But mostly better." And they all drank.

The conversation steered toward more mundane stuff, and then before Donnie realized it the women were standing there with bags over their shoulders and the kids were out of the pool, dry, and dressed. Heather and Megan hugged Donnie and drew out promises to meet again. "Don't forget," Heather said. "You love it here."

Donnie watched their backs as they passed through the gate, and then he stood and pulled off his T-shirt. He reached in Amy's bag and grabbed a pair of her goggles. He walked toward the placid, glowing pool.

The two lifeguards had started to climb down from their stands, but they paused and returned to their seats when they saw Donnie approach. He smiled apologetically at the one closest to him, a floppy-haired blonde kid who would have looked at home on a California beach. The kid smiled back, as if to say, "No problem." Donnie walked to the deep end, feeling the three beers in his blood. He hadn't eaten anything yet. He felt light and unbalanced. He pulled on the goggles, tightening them around his eyes to make sure they were sealed, and curled his toes over the edge of the pool. Then he dove in.

The water was bracing, cooler than he expected. He propelled himself forward in an unrushed breaststroke, reaching and pulling and kicking, the water disrupting and reorganizing around him, and then switched to freestyle for a couple of laps. He'd gotten into swimming for exercise on the advice of a coach one spring training in Florida, an eccentric guy with odd ideas. He found himself diving to the bottom of the deep end, dropping down the full twelve feet. His ears ached but the remote calm down there was relaxation at its finest. He stood on the bottom, waving his hands upward to stay anchored, and looked up. What a great way to see the world, he thought. Hazy and at a distance. It was undisturbed, unworried, uncomplicated. His brain seemed blissfully empty, aware only of the space around him. He wished he could hook his feet into straps and stay there, but he started to want to breathe again, first vaguely and then desperately, and he kicked himself back up to the surface. When he broke through, sucking in big breaths, he saw that the floppy-haired lifeguard had climbed down from his stand and seemed poised to dive in. Donnie waved at him. "Sorry," he said, stripping off his goggles. "I'll stay up here where it's safe now." And he turned onto his back and floated idly on the surface, his head refilling with everything he had too briefly forgotten.

Chapter Eighteen

Donnie sat at his kitchen table and wrote about baserunning. He started with simple guidance on taking a lead (slide steps, never cross your feet), reading a pitcher (watch the front knee), how the foot should hit the bag when rounding a base (inside corner, not the top), and the various slides (if you go headfirst into first base, you're an idiot). However, when he began to write about knowing the right situations for taking a risk as a runner—when to chance a bang-bang play by trying to take an extra base—he started writing almost unwittingly about The Play at Clemson, the one where he scored from first on a single to win his team a national title. The play still showed up every year at some point during the College World Series broadcast. Donnie would get texts and phone calls from old teammates letting him know they'd shown it again.

Donnie wrote about his big lead, breaking for second on the pitcher's move and the way he kept moving when the ball hit the bat. He wrote about his perfect path through second and then hitting third and running through the stop sign his coach—a bumpkin savant named Sonny Brown—was showing him.

I think about that moment of pushing past third. I think about my helmet floating away, my feet digging down the line, and this kind of exciting fear that I was feeling. I thought I could feel the entire ballpark hold its breath as I ran toward home. The lights seemed brighter all of a sudden. I knew everyone was rising from their seats and getting that little surge you get in your chest when something like this happens in sports and you're watching something crazy and important and you don't know what the hell is about to happen. Being safe was great and the celebration and all the stuff that came after. But the best part was right there between third and home when everything was up in the air and it felt like the whole world was watching me to see what happened next. Once you feel that it's kind of hard for anything else to measure up.

Donnie sat at the table and ran his fingers along the grooves in the table. He was surprised to realize he was breathing hard, as though he'd been running. He felt exhausted and kind of stupid. He hated writing. Not only was it difficult sledding every time he sat down and picked up the pen, but there was a loss of control that could feel almost incapacitating. He stumbled from the table to the sofa in the den and crashed asleep.

He slept for two hours, then rushed out the door to Max's game. He still felt drowsy as he stood in his customary spot down the third-base line and watched Max's final warmup pitches on the mound. Donnie liked the composure of Max's delivery and guessed the boy had done his dry drills. He looked connected and sharp, his windup a smooth, effortless-looking motion that consisted not of multiple components but of only a single, unified piece.

When the first batter dug into the box, Max tugged twice on his cap, checked the front of his belt, lifted his glove into place in front of him—relaxed and just above the waist—and studied his catcher. He looked intent and purposeful, but comfortable, and Donnie was pleased. The boy had found some confidence somewhere.

Max picked up two quick strikes on fastballs away to the leadoff hitter— the second pitch a soft foul ball down the right field line. "Bust him in," Donnie muttered. "Tie him up." He saw the catcher slide away. "Dammit, not outside again," Donnie said, a bit louder. "He's got that one measured."

The next pitch was a slow, tumbling thing with a sharp break and lovely, abrupt arc. Donnie's breath caught. The batter flailed helplessly at the pitch, which dove into the dirt alongside the outer part of the plate. Strike three.

Donnie's ears rang with cheers. He thought he saw Max glance his way with a mischievous look.

The boy had a curveball.

As though to confirm what he'd done, Max's first pitch to the next batter was another beautiful, looping wonder. This one froze the hitter for a called first strike.

Donnie sagged, uncrossing his arms, and wishing he had a place to sit. He felt his fatigue deepen. He leaned over and scooped dirt into both hands. He squeezed tight.

The peach fuzz on the boy's face seemed thick, shining a bit in the sun, and Donnie wondered if the boy would be shaving soon. Would Donnie get to have a role in that, showing Max how to lather right and move the razor in steady, deliberate strokes, or would it be another lesson the boy learned outside of his father's sight?

Max rocked into his delivery and spun another beauty of a curve. The hitter swung and missed. Donnie released the dirt in his hands, wiped his hands on his shorts. It wasn't just any curve—it was the knuckle curve, specialty pitch of WBA. His hands formed into fists.

After the first curve, Max felt like a giant. Chuck was catching and he nodded vigorously and pointed at him, "More of THAT, Max! More of that!" Max couldn't believe the power he felt, the difference it made in his relationship with each hitter. The balance had shifted utterly. He was the one in control again.

Each of the first two hitters went down on the knuckle curve, and he wondered if anyone would ever get another hit off him. He was eager to throw this magical pitch again and again. He couldn't believe what it did for him. When he called upon the pitch, it behaved exactly as he wanted it to. There'd been no transition, no struggle to adapt. It was instantly a piece of him, and he could summon it in its perfect form whenever he liked.

As he circled the mound after the second strikeout and waited for the infielders to throw the ball around the horn, he looked toward his father in search of a reaction. He was surprised to feel that he was hoping for him to be smiling, clapping, maybe pumping his fist for him the way he used to. Now that he'd seen what the knuckle curve could do for Max maybe he would relax about it, stop fighting it. But Dad was just staring at him, his hands in fists at his sides.

Max couldn't focus and flung the first pitch to the next batter sharply into the dirt, but the break on the curve was so dramatic that the hitter still swung at it. Max took Chuck's return throw and resolved to ignore his father. If the old man was upset, that was his problem. He ascended back to the top of the mound and looked at the catcher and took a deep breath. Two more curves, and he had another strikeout.

Max slapped five with all his teammates as he entered the dugout, pleased to be back in their good graces. By the time he found a seat on the bench and looked back toward his father, he was stunned to see that old Donnie Baseball was gone. Max had never known him to leave one of his games early. He imagined Dad wanted him to feel wounded, but he didn't feel that at all. He was just angry.

Donnie didn't drive straight home. Instead, he drove to his warehouse. The building looked solitary and forbidding on the empty, unpeopled block. No sign of life in either direction down the street, not even a passing vehicle. He emerged from his car and walked to the open window and checked inside.

He listened for the sound of popping catcher's mitts and panging bats in the empty space. Enthusiastic voices, cussing. He swore he could pick up the rude smell of sweat. It was real to him. He saw Max and Cole McGuire and Eddie Barnes with their gloves on, working through their bullpen sessions on homemade clay mounds. He saw himself standing nearby, his arms crossed and his hat pulled down low over his eyes, missing nothing as he hollered and praised and scolded. Right on that floor it could happen. He knew this was not the major leagues. He knew this was not fame. But this is what he wanted. He leaned on the windowsill and considered how small his dreams had become and yet how maddeningly elusive they remained.

Now Max was throwing a knuckle curve, a pitch that had been spreading fast among the young pitchers of the Greater Richmond area. Donnie knew that large building on Broad Street was where these boys were learning the pitch.

Donnie thought about Cole, who was gone, and about Max, who had tuned him out. Then there was Barnes, the newest project and possibly the most talented. It bugged him to think Barnes might not stick with what he'd taught him—that he might slip into old habits and Donnie wouldn't be there to correct him, to say the right thing that would guide him back on track.

Donnie drove home. He turned on the laptop computer in Amy's old office where he had painstakingly typed up parts of his book. He printed his chapters on "Mound Mechanics," "Drills for Pitchers," "Fitness for Pitchers," and "Pitch Location," and slid them into a manila envelope. Then he pulled the contact sheet he still had for his team and drove to Barnes' house, an unassuming ranch with a screened-in porch. Rather than knock, he left the envelope propped against the front door.

Chapter Nineteen

Fletcher lived on the other side of the golf course from Lucas, a few convenient and well-struck drivers away. Fletcher's parents were out for a few hours at a big party to raise money for sick kids or a museum or something. Max and Lucas met Fletcher on his backyard terrace by the pool. Liz, Caroline, and Whitney were already there, sprawled on patio furniture apart from Fletcher, looking loose-limbed and languorous and without a care in the world. It was dusk. Lit gas lamps circled the terrace. The kids drank dark liquid from classy glasses.

"Pull up a chair and fix yourself a refreshment," Fletcher said. "We're chillin'."

A couple of liter Coke bottles were on the wrought iron table next to him, along with two glasses and a small cooler.

"Chillin' with Coke?" Lucas said.

Fletcher grinned. "I see what's going on. You think we've just got chips." He casually reached to the terrace behind him. He pulled up a bottle of Jim Beam and placed it next to the Coke bottles. "But we've got chips *and* dip."

Max felt a simmering panic, a faltering resolve. He'd never tried hard liquor before. Beer was still a challenge for him. He could feel Caroline watching him.

"Awesome," Lucas said, stepping forward and filling the glasses with ice from the cooler. "This is the right way to celebrate. My boy here struck out twelve today."

"Damn," Fletcher said, holding up his hand. Max slapped it sheepishly, embarrassed at the staginess of the attention.

"Is that a lot?" Liz said, giggling.

"Nah," Whitney said. "I bet I could strike out thirteen easy."

She stood and pretended to spit in her hand. She bent toward an imaginary catcher convincingly—she was tall and athletic, a star serve-and-volley tennis player—and Max could almost hear his father complimenting her relaxed, calm starting position. Then, she stepped back and entered into a confusing windup of flailing arms and legs. As she fired her imaginary pitch, her front foot slid—too long a stride, Max noted—and she wiped out hard onto the brick terrace.

"Oh, my God," Caroline said.

Caroline and Liz rushed to Whitney, who was lying on the ground motionless. Max could see the night headed for a quick end. By the time they reached her, however, she was laughing maniacally. She didn't seem hurt or embarrassed at all. Caroline and Liz tried to help her up, pulling on her shoulders, but Whitney slumped bonelessly to the terrace and kept laughing. Caroline held up her hands in surrender, smiling but a bit uncertain. "You're such a klutz," she said, returning to her chair. "Oh, my God."

"Whit's on her third already," Fletcher said, confiding to Max and Lucas. "I'm thinking it better be her last, too."

Lucas handed Max a drink. He studied it, looked to Fletcher and Lucas, who were both watching him, and took a sip. Coke with a bit of caramel to it.

"It's alright," Max said. He squinted at his glass as though analyzing its contents. "Not bad at all."

"It shouldn't be too strong," Lucas said. "I went easy with the booze."

Fletcher stood and held out his glass. "Confusion to our enemies," he said. Max and Lucas laughed and clinked glasses with him. They all drank.

"What enemies?" Max said.

"I don't know," Fletcher said. "Some Southern thing. My Dad always says it."

Max could feel Caroline stealing glances at him, the same way he kept looking her way without lingering. It was one thing to think about her, and another to see her. She looked beautiful in an almost painful way—her black hair and deep summer tan and sharp blue eyes seeming all warm and vivid to him. She was wearing a white top with thin straps on the shoulders and a thigh-high navy skirt. He was preoccupied by her while talking with Fletcher and Lucas, participating abstractly in the conversation while the bulk of his attention went across the way. The three girls were huddled together around Whitney's phone as she texted with someone. At one point, Max and Caroline locked eyes. She grinned and tucked her chin into her chest, returning her gaze to Whitney's phone without losing the radiance in her expression. Max felt a thrill like he couldn't ever remember before.

Fletcher looked at complete ease as he sat with his docksiders propped on a nearby chair, as though he did this all the time. Max felt exposed cradling his drink and trying to look nonchalant next to his more experienced friends. "So how long til your parents get back?" Max asked.

"Hours and hours," Fletcher said. "They called a car service, which means they're going to stay out super late and get good and lit." He seemed to consider this prospect and shook his head. "Drunk parents are a pain in the ass. Dad gets pissed at stupid stuff. I never know what it's going to be, only that it's going to be something. And Mom gets all loving and mumbly. Like real emotional stuff about when I was little and how I'm growing up so fast."

"You really are, Monkey," Lucas said, using the nickname they'd heard Fletcher's mother drop occasionally, often with a glare from Fletcher. "You're such a big boy now."

Fletcher tossed a bottle cap at Lucas. "What about Foster and Susan? I know they booze it up."

Lucas nodded, taking a big sip. Max was surprised to see his buddy was almost already finished a first drink. Max was less than a quarter into his.

"Sure, they have a good time," Lucas said. "Dad sort of gets rambunctious, and Mom thinks everything is funny. When they get home, she rushes to bed to pass out and he comes down to the basement to watch TV with me and talk. His mouth doesn't stop running. How he was better at this and that than I'll ever be. Talks a bunch of shit about me the whole time."

Fletcher laughed. "About you? What's he got to complain about? You being the best athlete in the grade or you being the best student in the grade?"

"What're you assholes talking about?" Whitney said, slurring her words. Suddenly, she and Liz were standing there. Whitney seemed to lean on Liz.

"Don't worry about it," Fletcher said. "Hey Whit, I think you better switch to water now."

"I think you better kiss my ass," she said, pointing her finger at him purposefully but hurting her cause with the unsteady way she kept to her feet.

Liz, who was short with compact power evident in her legs and arms, grabbed onto Whitney's elbow. They made a funny pair. "I was thinking we maybe could get some food?" Liz said. She widened her eyes and nodded discreetly toward Whitney. "You know?"

Fletcher pulled to his feet. "Good idea." He slapped Lucas on the back. "How about it, Lucas? You want a snack?"

Lucas shot to his feet. "Absolutely. See you in a bit, Max. I know you're good." And the four of them climbed the brick stairs toward the house, as if in collusion with Max's unspoken wishes.

When they were gone, and it was just him and Caroline, Max stood from his chair, stretched with aplomb, and crossed the terrace toward her. She sat dreamy eyed with a helpless grin and watched him. Her flawless legs were crossed, and she leaned forward and held her drink over her perfect knees. She was perched on the side of a chaise lounge. He dropped into a chair facing her. Their feet were almost touching. She seemed nervous but pleased.

"Hey," he said.

"Hey," she said.

"I was hoping you'd say that," he said. She laughed. He wondered what he was supposed to do next. He was thankful for the bourbon, because even in his confusion he felt relaxed and comfortable, feeling confident things were going well. Then she uncrossed her legs, put her drink on a small nearby table, and folded her hands in her lap, as if waiting for something. He stood, put his drink on the table, and sat next to her. Then, without any more hesitation, he kissed her, and she kissed back, at first leaning back on her hands to receive it and then finally rising upright to provide more pressure in return.

Max didn't know he knew how to kiss, but he performed adeptly, as far as he could tell. They sort of went at it, their mouths open and searching and their tongues doing wonderful things. He was stunned it was real. She was eager and assured, and Max felt her hands gently gripping the neckline of his T-shirt, her fingers alternately pulling and relaxing. Those little tugs made him unspeakably happy.

He didn't know how long it went on. It seemed like both forever and no time at all. Eventually, though, they heard Fletcher yell from the backdoor of the house, "Here we come. Y'all got your clothes on?" And they stopped, though not abruptly but with a slow break, her biting his lip a bit in the act of detachment. She laughed, bowed her head, and wiped at her lips.

He stood, returned to his chair. She picked her glass back up. They looked at each other and beamed. She was flushed, and he was sure he must be, too.

He grabbed his glass and drank deeply. The bourbon tasted better than before, because now it tasted like her. Her lips, her mouth had held that exquisite flavor, and now here it was again and suddenly bourbon was something richer, more complex, and more wonderful.

The others came trudging down the brick stairs, looking sloppy and dull. They had dumb grins on their faces, as if they were all in on the same joke. Fletcher was in the lead. The rest of the group trailed him, holding bags of chips and popcorn.

"Y'all OK without us?" Fletcher said.

Caroline giggled.

Max smiled and drained his glass.

Chapter Twenty

Donnie sat at his kitchen table, scribbling at paper yet again in search of inspiration, but instead only settling into the same struggle that had been haunting this project. He wanted to write about the curveball and the way it could infect a young pitcher, ruin him from ever being what he was truly capable of, but he didn't think he was making his point the right way.

Yes, it's the danger to the arm. The curveball motion can hurt young arms, I'm sure of it. But that's only part of it. An important part, but I don't want people thinking the danger is only some kind of physical disaster. It's also maturation if that makes sense. Look, the best four pitches in baseball are a good fastball, a good fastball, a good fastball, and a good fastball. We can argue about what's fifth. And the big problem with throwing a curveball when you're a kid is that nobody knows how to hit it yet. The damned silly thing works. And the fastball becomes the pitch you throw between curveballs, instead of the other way around, and you don't learn to throw it to spots and you don't learn to throw different types of fastballs and to be subtle with it. The smartest pitchers in the world are the ones that know this. They know that even if they don't throw hard their best pitch is a fastball in the right spot. That's why the knuckle curve without the strain on the arm is still a problem for me.

So, kids, throw your fastball for years. OK? Throw it inside and outside, up and down. Throw a two-seamer and a four-seamer, hit your catcher's glove. Learn to apply pressure in different ways to make it move a bit differently. Learn to vary the speed so that a hitter never gets too comfortable. That's being in command in a way that uses your brain in a way just tricking them with the curve won't do. You'll feel like a goddamned magician, trust me. And when you're 15 and you start throwing that curve for real, it's going to be that much better because you know how to pitch.

I get it, though, patience is hard. You want to win now, and you also want to get better. Why can't you do both? Because you can't. Nobody likes losing. I get that. I wish I could prove to you that I'm right. But remember this: losing is learning. That means you got to lose now if you're ever going to win big later.

What the hell? Donnie thought. He thought of Andy Liu, the publisher at Bailiwick, reading this and shaking his head. The man had called him earlier that day to check on him, see how things were going. "The idea's growing on me more and more," Liu had said. "You reach out to a partner yet? I see a potential market with a known name attached." Donnie had said he was looking into some possibilities.

But what kind of instructional book was this? He was spending all this time writing and revising and acting like he was producing something important, but did any of it add up to anything really? It seemed to him that every time he sat down, he wrote something disconcertingly different from the time before. It was as though he produced chapters to different books instead of the same one. One page he's writing some convoluted, technical thing about catching fly balls, and the next he's going on meandering rants. This one, he understood, was directly addressed to Max. How much was he really going to teach anybody if he wrote so half-cocked? He felt not for the first time since Amy's death that he was letting her down. She'd believed he had enough to say to fill a book—he needed to "share his knowledge with the world," she kept saying—but who would want to read this?

Christ, he missed her.

Donnie stood and stretched his shoulders, feeling the right one grind and crack. The newspaper was folded, still unread, on the kitchen counter. He flipped it open and pulled out the Sports page. On the front, at the top of an article that ran down the left side, a headline read, "McGuire to make pro debut in Lynchburg."

"Sure," Donnie said aloud. "Terrific."

He looked around the floor for Baxter, but he wasn't around—he probably had put himself to bed on Amy's pillows upstairs, as he did most nights. Max was at the Tennysons, and Donnie wasn't sure he wanted to see him anyway. He felt antsy and trapped. He stepped onto the back terrace. It was a lovely summer evening, and he felt as though he was missing something great by not engaging with it. Going back indoors to the kitchen to write seemed impossible. He decided to go for a drive.

He rolled down the window and found himself heading for school. He effortlessly retrieved the same sense memory he always did when driving on a summer evening. He remembered as a kind of perfect place of mind the satisfying trips home late at night after games when he was a teenager playing Legion ball, the windows down on the family station wagon, the radio blaring, his body cashed in and caked in sweat and dirt. A good, hard day behind him, the night's action still fresh, and something undeniably great ahead. He'd felt a rush in those days playing under the lights, even on listless summer nights that otherwise seemed anything but consequential. The games started in the early evening, when the sun was still around and the light was indistinct and shared from one place to the next, and then night arrived gradually and the light drew tight, closing around their scene, narrowing its focus to the dimensions of the field until it felt to Donnie as though their lights were the only ones on anywhere in the world.

In recent years, Donnie had spent many summer nights like this one with Amy. They had a small TV in the kitchen, and he'd turn it to a game with the sound off so she could focus on her work. She was always working. He'd bring her a beer, crack himself one. And they'd sit in silence, doing their thing. Donnie kept his notebook open on the table and would occasionally jot down something from the game that struck him, often as it related to one of his pupils. Max might pass through, grabbing some ice cream or lingering to watch a couple of innings with

Donnie. Amy would look up from her work to ask about something or to chit chat about nothing to give her brain a break. She'd stand up, stretch her back, and drink from her beer. He always thought she seemed content those nights. She loved her work, but he thought she'd also loved being with him, nothing happening in their world as they comfortably inhabited each other's lives.

When Donnie's ballgame was over on those nights, he'd stand and take the empty beer bottles or cans to the recycling bin, and that would be Amy's cue that her night was through. She'd shut down the computer, pile her papers into her bag, and together they'd tell Max good night—he was inevitably lying on the sofa in the den, watching TV—and head upstairs to bed. They almost always went to bed together. The night she died had felt strange at the time. Her stress had seemed elevated, and she'd been curt with him when he'd try to talk earlier in the evening. He'd brought up a summer they'd lived in Frederick, Maryland together early in his career—before her own career and before Max—and the tiny apartment where they'd lived and been very, very happy.

"I need space to think tonight, Donnie, OK?" she'd said. "I'm sorry but tomorrow's a big day."

Donnie had retreated to the living room and the larger TV. He remembered feeling wounded by her, but he'd thanked himself every day since then that he hadn't said anything—hadn't started some kind of fight out of petulance that he'd have regretted. The quick kiss he'd given her had been a reminder to her that he loved her—that she was loved. Somewhere in there that night, she'd understood that.

Donnie was surprised to find the lights on and the door open at the maintenance shop at Deep Creek. Inside, Otis was drinking a beer on the sofa and watching baseball highlights on TV while sifting through a *Tennis* magazine. He looked at Donnie as though he'd been expecting him.

"Pull up a pew, chum," he said. "Just looking for some tips on the old serve. How's the eye?"

"Better." Donnie fell onto the other end of the sofa.

"You should hit a bar or two. See how it plays with the ladies."

"Not well, I imagine."

"I bet they'd eat it up."

"Shit."

"I'm right as radar on that. They're out there just waiting for you. No disrespect to Amy, of course."

Donnie hated the thought of being one of those guys, getting dressed up, socializing at bars, going on dates, working through the etiquettes and protocols. Maybe getting dumped. None of them would ever measure up anyway.

"What're you doing here?" Donnie said. "Don't you have a home?"

117

"Don't you?" Otis removed a cigarette from the pack on the sofa next to him and lit it. He looked haggard and unrested, his eyes cloudy and glum. He seemed to be considering the question more. "Honestly, I'm a tad lonely these days," he said. "Somehow feels less lonely here than at home. Don't know the math on that one. I miss Ava. It's rough right after they leave you, you know?" He stopped, sipped his beer. "I guess I shouldn't be complaining to you about it, huh?"

"Can't seem to get my head straight about it," Donnie said. "I'd been with Amy since we were just about kids. I never been serious with anyone else in my life. A couple of girlfriends in high school, but that was always easy. I always had one eye elsewhere."

"Lemme ask you something."

"Oh, lord."

"Say go to hell if you got to. But be honest, all those years on the road you ever step outside the, uh, boundaries of marriage?"

"Nope. Not a once."

"Come on, it's me here. You were like a baseball monk? Months and months without your wife, new women in every city, and you didn't wander a bit? Stray here and there?"

"Didn't even consider it. I wasn't always the most attentive husband when I was gone, but I was never one of those guys. I don't even remember being tempted."

"Were there many like you? The loyal type?"

"Nah, they're almost all dogs. Worse than you can imagine."

"I don't blame 'em."

"I expect you wouldn't."

Otis lifted his beer in acknowledgement and drank from it. "I make a big deal about hating my exes, I know. I guess you've heard me say some terrible things about them over the years."

Donnie grunted an assent.

"Fact is I say that stuff because I can't get over them. Not one of them." He frowned at his cigarette, thinking it over. "I don't seem to put any of them behind me. And then when one of them goes away, I sit here and think about all of them, not just the last one. I can't get the nice times from playing over and over again. It hurts like hell."

"Oof."

"You got that right."

"At least you'll always have Ricky."

"I do love that man," Otis said. He shook his head. "I wish he was prettier."

Donnie laughed.

"I keep thinking about the things I didn't appreciate or notice about Amy." Otis studied him. "Yeah? Like what?"

"Like her career. I think it surprised me, and I don't know why. She kicked ass in school and had awesome grades, and she was always working, too. She loved working. Hell, she had two jobs most of the time we were at Clemson, and she still had damn near a 4.0. But that was just Amy to me. I never thought how impressive it was. When she got into PR and started killing it, I know I told her I was proud of her or whatever, but I never actually thought about it. I never actually cared what she did at work—what she was so good at and so passionate about. I never asked her about it. No details. We talked baseball all the time. We never talked about whatever it was she really did. I still don't really know. I was always too wrapped up in my own shit."

Otis gave a sympathetic nod. "It probably just all seems like missed opportunities now, right? Wouldn't have mattered what you did when she was alive? Nobody's that good a husband or friend or whatever that they don't regret all kinds of shit when someone's gone. And I know this is going to sound worse than I mean it to, but at least you and Amy never fell out of love. At least you've got that."

Donnie thought about that for a moment but then he shook his head. "I'm going to be honest with you, Otis. Right now, that don't feel like enough. I want it to, but it just don't. You got any more beers?"

Otis tilted his head toward the shop fridge, and Donnie went looking for a can of something cold.

Chapter Twenty-One

Max felt drunk. He didn't know if it was the bourbon-and-cokes or the making out with Caroline or the combination of the two, but in his various sipping experiments with alcohol this was the most pleasantly buzzy he'd felt yet. His brain was floating, his words seemed strange, as though they were not really his, and his steps as he half-skated across the shaved fairways of the moonlit rolling golf course were curiously uncertain and irregular—faster than he meant, then slower, as if he wasn't coordinated enough to pace himself right. He imagined lying down in this same grass with Caroline, looking up at the vast, starred sky and talking about anything and everything. He'd explain Liszt's Liebestraum No. 3 to her, and she'd understand exactly what he meant. Then, offhandedly, he would mention its other name, "Love Dream."

Max had stopped at two drinks out of caution, taking an hour to work his way through his second one. He and Caroline had barely spoken again the rest of the night, but everything had felt so charged between them that it didn't really matter to him. That kiss seemed to linger and settle somehow. She couldn't stop smiling, and neither could he. He only wished he could have been alone with her one more time before the girls rushed off in a hurry, having realized they were late. She waved at him and mouthed, "Bye," rolling her eyes comically as Whitney pulled her away in a panic.

Lucas had downed three drinks over the course of the night, but he didn't act much inhibited. He walked with his hands in his pockets and his face cast to the ground, apparently stuck on a thought. Mr. Tennyson never liked it when Lucas walked this way, saying he looked weak and spacey. "Stop checking for land mines," he'd say. "Get your head up and about for the snipers. They're the ones who'll get ya."

Max didn't appreciate Lucas's solemnity. It was biting into his giddy vibe.

"Ping pong showdown when we get back?" Max said. "Two out of three, winner takes nothing."

"Sure. That'll work," Lucas said without enthusiasm. "Hey, you really think I'll hit OK again?"

"Is that seriously what you're thinking about right now?"

"It's bugging me."

"You'll come around," Max said, full of new confidence. "It's only a matter of time. Look at what happened to me today. Don't even think about it."

A deep sand trap loomed ahead. Lucas walked around it, but Max got a notion and plunged through it, running with his arms spread open like an airplane, whining, "Wheeeeeeeeeee." On the other side, breathing heavily and happily, he looked at Lucas, but his friend's dour appearance had not changed.

"Maybe I better go see your dad again," Lucas said. "I didn't like working with Stubs that much. I feel like your dad gets me better."

Max shook the sand from his sandals and then hustled to catch up with Lucas, who had not paused for him. "My Dad doesn't really *get* anybody," Max said. "He hasn't helped you at all, has he? And look at what Stubs did for me in like two minutes. I went from being a scrub to mowing guys down in a couple of days."

"Your Dad coulda done that for you, though. He just didn't want you throwing that pitch. It's not like he doesn't know how to throw a knuckle curve. He was doing what he thought was best."

"Clearly he was wrong," Max said. "So, screw him."

They climbed the slope to the fourteenth green in silence, then crossed the green.

"Your dad ever tell you your head's not right?" Lucas said. "That you got mental problems?"

Max chuckled. "Whatever, dude."

They climbed over the fence to Lucas's backyard and approached the house.

"Seriously," Lucas said. "Has he ever said something like that to you?"

"Uh, no. He's gotten on me for being dumb on the field, not thinking stuff through, blah, blah, blah, but he never said I was defective or something."

"Dad wants me to see a shrink. Says this hitting thing is a mental weakness, and I'm just being soft in the head. Says I'm afraid of success. I'm supposed to make varsity in the spring. Tennysons don't play JV."

"Damn."

"I know."

Max suddenly stopped in the backyard and put his hands in his pockets. He felt the urge to share something, and he wasn't sure if it was the alcohol or the kiss or a combination of the two. Lucas stopped and looked at him. "Dad keeps trying to talk to me about mom, and I can't do it," Max said. "Like, I physically can't do it. I feel like I'm going to explode listening to him try to talk about her like he's some therapist or something. I just want to run away from him as fast as I can."

Lucas nodded and seemed to consider what Max was saying. "That sucks. Probably sucks for him, too, though."

Max didn't want to think about that. "I doubt it." He shook his head and resumed walking. "Nah."

Inside the basement, they went straight to the ping pong table and returned to the comfort of their eternal battle—one with no stakes or observers.

Chapter Twenty-Two

Max was dressed in his uniform, glove in hand, talking on the phone with Caroline and wishing he could skip his game. She wanted him to meet her for lunch at this place called Pete's that Max had heard some of the country club kids mention casually—limeades and club sandwiches and milkshakes—and then walk down the block to watch a romantic comedy she was dying to see. They'd yet to hang out together solo, though they'd managed a couple of long phone calls. He thought a meal and a movie with her—just the two of them—sounded "awesome," he kept saying, but he had a game.

"Can't you just skip?" she said. "You don't have to go to every game, do you?"

"I kinda do," he said. He was perched on a kitchen chair near the window, watching for his father to arrive to pick him up. "At least, I'm supposed to be at all of them."

"Is that because you're the star?" she asked. Her voice was playful and teasing. "Would the team suck without you?"

Max loved the intimate way she already talked to him, as though they'd been together for some time. "Nah, they wouldn't know I was gone, especially because I'm not even pitching today. I don't hit as well as I pitch."

"Is that what your dad did? Pitch?"

Max was surprised by the question. He wouldn't have guessed she knew he'd been a ballplayer. "He did both, though he didn't pitch once he was in the pros. He coaches a lot of pitchers now"—he realized as he spoke the casual exaggeration of "a lot" — "and he's really pretty much nutso about it. I think he wishes he'd kept pitching instead of just playing outfield. Maybe then he would have made the majors."

"Oh, yeah?" she said, sounding distracted.

"Not that he's ever said anything like that."

"Just skip, come on. Skip, skip," she said. "Please, please, please."

"I can't skip," he said.

"I'll make sure it's worth it," she said.

He felt a cool and wonderful shock. He could picture her on the other end of the line with that flirtatious smile on her face, delighted at her own charms. "Well, then," he said. Through the window, he saw his father's battered sedan lunge into the driveway. "Shit, Dad's here. I gotta go. Look, I'll call you after, OK?"

"Fine," she said, her voice suddenly serious and firm, that wondrous playfulness gone.

"I'm sorry," he said. "Are you mad?"

"Just play your game. I've gotta go, too. See ya."

She hung up before Max could reply. He felt sick. He was tempted to call her right back and say he'd do anything she asked.

Outside, his father honked.

Beyond muttered greetings, the drive to the field was silent. Max wanted his father to know he wasn't happy with him, but he couldn't tell if Dad even cared. Dad didn't talk, didn't ask him questions about whether he was doing his drills or anything. The sun seemed to bother him more than usual, and he couldn't find his sunglasses. He squinted his tired eyes and frowned as he drove. Max could see that the shiner from the home run derby was dimming. He had expected a tirade about the knuckle curve and the ways he was endangering his future, but instead he got nothing. No energy, no life. He seemed preoccupied.

The game was uneventful. Max started at first base and hit sixth in the lineup. He was startled when he jogged out to his position in the first inning to notice that his father was missing from his standard spot down the third base line, and he wondered if his dad—his ride today—had left again. But then he saw him sitting in the upper right corner of the stands, safely apart from the rest of the crowd. He looked relaxed, unconcerned, and he had an open notebook in his lap. He was writing, his eyes on the paper instead of the field.

Max struck out his first two times up, swinging almost petulantly at curves in the dirt on both strikeouts, but then roped a double down the left field line in the sixth inning. It was a better day than Lucas had. He didn't get the ball out of the infield in three times at the plate. He also fumbled a ground ball straight at him. Still, their team won 6-3.

Dad told Max, "Nice game," when they met at the car, but did not expand on it. He was quiet again as they pulled from the parking lot. He turned on the radio. Classic rock again. Dad rock, which he knew Max despised. It was another aggravation.

Max was disappointed Caroline had gotten so quickly bored on the subject of his father, especially since she had brought it up. He wanted to talk about him with her. He'd never thought about his father's love of pitching and was surprised that he'd said anything about it. He had no idea if he was right that Dad believed he could have made the majors if he'd stayed on the mound. It made some sense. He was consumed with pitching and with Max doing everything just right, according to plan, with no missteps. Still, who really knew? Dad's past seemed such an unsettled thing. It had happened, it was finished, and he never spoke about it, yet somehow it seemed everywhere all the time.

Max didn't appreciate his father's silence. That was stealing Max's play, his plan for showing his displeasure with the man. Max didn't have the patience for the long game, especially with this music jabbing at him. He wanted a reaction. He knew this was all about the knuckle curve.

He put his glove on and pounded it with his pitching hand. "Coach says I'm pitching again on Friday this week. He says he thinks I've got the best breaking ball in the league already. It just clicked with me right away."

Dad scratched at the days-old stubble on his face. "Was it fun for you to throw that thing?"

Max laughed. "It was amazing. It felt like I was just toying with them. I couldn't believe the way the ball moved."

"Enjoy it while you can," Dad said. "Because it's not going to last." He reached over and turned up the music.

Max felt a jab. Dad had been many difficult things to him before, but never cold, never distant. The man next to him seemed capable of forgetting that Max existed.

When Max stepped out of the car, Dad said, "Take care," in a distracted, automatic way, as though he was speaking to someone on the street. He didn't elaborate on where he was going. Max said, "See ya," in return. He heard the car backing up as he headed up the sidewalk, Dad not even waiting to make sure he got in OK. It was gone by the time Max put the key in the door. Inside, he dropped his glove, sat straight down on the floor, and began to cry. It was a steep, jagged cry that overtook him fully. After a few minutes, he gathered himself, feeling stupid and furious. He drank a glass of water in the kitchen, wiped his face with a towel, and spoke aloud, "Testing, hello, hello, testing," to make sure nothing sounded shaky. Then he grabbed the phone and dialed Caroline, eager to hear her voice again.

Chapter Twenty-Three

C alvin Falwell Field in Lynchburg was the kind of unpretentious and ancient minor league ballpark Donnie had loved when he first started pro ball. It was difficult not to feel lucky when you were wearing a uniform, loosening up on a summer evening, and a cozy place like this one was sleepily filling in with fans. However, when you'd done it hundreds of times over the course of more years than you'd planned, a ballpark like this one felt exactly like purgatory—a realm between one place and another, in a nowhere city, among nobody people—and the games felt like they repeated themselves. This game like that one, this at bat like the one before it, going on and on without any end in sight.

It was a switch, of course, to be one of those settling into the stands and considering the scene from that vantage point, and Donnie felt a sickening all-over regret as he took his seat before the game between the Lynchburg Hillcats and the Winston-Salem Warthogs. He and Joe were sitting in general admission in the grandstand, well up under a swooping World War II-era roof that protected them from the early evening sun. Donnie hoped that Cole McGuire's family and supporters wouldn't spot them from wherever they were. Donnie had agreed to attend the game only if they could be as inconspicuous as possible.

Donnie had a cool hot dog with mustard and relish and a tepid, sweating beer, while Joe drank bottled water and picked from a baggie of granola he had snuck in. They both flipped through a flimsy program, though it was out of date and didn't even include Cole on the roster yet, and took in their surroundings. In the distance beyond the outfield fence was the gray outline of a set of Blue Ridge foothills. The crowd was sparse, and it was clear there would be nothing close to a full house when the first pitch was thrown.

"There he is," Joe said. "Seems a tad nervous to me."

Donnie scoured the field and found Cole. He was walking toward the bullpen down the right field line. He wore a shiny club warmup jacket and carried his glove in his left hand. He was tall and top heavy, with wide shoulders and the same lean, toothpick legs Donnie used to tease him about. Joe was right. As Cole strode through the grass, which was striped with the fresh diagonal path of the lawnmower, his gait did seem off. It was uncertain and halting and he was looking around a lot, as though he wasn't sure he was doing the right thing. The brim of his hat was unfolded and flat across. Donnie knew it was the way he wore his hats, but the impression it made was of someone who had at that moment grabbed a hat out of a store and shoved it onto his head. He looked like a big, lumbering child out of place among the pros.

A pocket of cheers rose in the box seats behind the first base dugout and Donnie recognized Cole's parents standing in a group of at least thirty, all there to cheer on the first-round pick's pro debut. Cole's father, Mel, who was wearing a Pirates hat, had his arms crossed, and he seemed to be surveying the scene, the long-sought moment, with a menacing intensity. It was the way he had stood and watched every single practice session Cole had ever had with Donnie. It had always struck Donnie as a stance of ownership—of possession—as though he was watching a prized thoroughbred working out on the track. In the wildness of its enthusiasm, the group seemed out of place, as if at a different game.

Cole seemed emboldened by his cheering section, and his walk gained purpose.

Donnie wished he hadn't come. Joe had said he should be there to see what all his hard work had produced, but that was not what Donnie felt. He only felt the loss of Cole, the absence of recognition and appreciation for what he had done for the boy to transform him from an oaf with an arm into a polished pitching talent. He should have been down in the box seats with the rest of the supporters, basking in a big coaching success. He scanned the group for Stubs but didn't find him. He was glad, at least, of that.

Donnie took the last bite of his hot dog, wiped his hands with a paper napkin and placed his beer by his feet. He leaned back. On the field, Cole dropped his glove and jacket by the bullpen and jogged in the outfield grass toward centerfield. Donnie leaned forward, resting his elbows on his knees. He recognized the beginning of the pregame routine he had helped Cole develop years before. Simple stuff, but Donnie had stressed the importance of getting ready for every game the exact same way, of honing your preparations into a straightforward, focused, and repeatable series of actions that transported you from the regular world to something narrower and harder, locking you into the task at hand as though hypnotizing you. Ads for chain restaurants and local retail stores loomed behind Cole on double-decker panels on the outfield walls as he ran. Cole bounced his left hand on his left hip in a steady beat. Donnie clasped his hands tightly together. This was a signal Donnie guessed only he deciphered. It meant Cole was thinking about making sure he got his body closed on his leg lift. Donnie had suggested that reminder.

Cole stopped in center field.

Donnie knew he was about to start rolling his shoulders.

Sure enough, he did.

Joe suddenly slapped Donnie on the back. "You OK, man?"

Donnie pulled his gaze away and eyed his brother warily. "Yeah."

"How's he look to you?"

Donnie released his hands, embarrassed. He picked his beer up off the concrete near his feet. "The same. Pretty much exactly the same."

"I gotta take a leak. You want anything?"

Donnie held up his nearly empty beer.

Joe slapped him on the back yet again and walked past the open row of seats to the steps. Joe kept with this backslapping, as though he was checking on him—as though he was worried about him and wanted to reassure him. Donnie hated it.

Donnie perused the stands and thought he could pick out the wives and girlfriends with the prime seats behind home plate. Amy hadn't made it long in those seats, and Donnie was glad. He'd felt guilty to see her sitting there night after night, letting her life pass as a spectator. He hadn't lied to Otis. He'd stayed faithful to Amy. Some ballplayers he knew would send notes to women in the stands through grounds crew members and batboys and then meet them after the game. Donnie shared an apartment one season with a married player who spent no more than a handful of nights in his own bed. He'd always appreciated Amy's trust in those years, her patience with him, her steady encouragement. She'd never once complained to him, never once suggested he quit and come home.

He felt a solid slap on the back.

"Dammit, Joe," he said, jerking his shoulder in.

Two legs climbed over the row behind him and slid into a chair two seats to his left.

It was Stubs with a huge grin on his face. "This is the least impressive VIP section I ever saw."

Stubs laughed. Donnie didn't smile. He realized it had been stupid to think he could be invisible in a ballpark this small.

"What do you want?" Donnie asked.

Stubs laughed again, though less convincingly. He was wearing a plain gray T-shirt, gym shorts, and running shoes. He wore a WBA ballcap. "Give me a break, man," he said. "I only wanted to hang out at a ballgame. Shoot the shit. That was a heck of a show we put on together the other night, huh? I tried to catch up with you after. I guess you must have bolted."

Donnie felt a familiar crawling, spreading anger turning him twitchy. His jaw tightened. "Joe called you. Unbelievable."

Stubs swiped at something invisible on his shorts. "He thought it'd mean something for us to watch Cole's big debut together. He's our guy, isn't he? We got him here."

"That's not what I read in the paper."

Stubs waved his hand at Donnie. "You should know better than to believe that shit."

"Right."

"For what it's worth, I told that writer dude you deserved most of the credit, but he said Mel told him I was being generous to an old friend—that you hadn't done squat. I asked Mel about it, and he said—and I quote— 'To hell with Donnie.' What'd you do to that family anyway?"

Donnie took off his hat and scratched his head. He took a final pull off his beer, now as warm as the seat beneath him. "What do you care? You got a client out of it."

"I'm curious how you screwed it up."

Donnie wanted to keep quiet about it, keep from sharing anything with Stubs, but he also wanted Stubs to know it wasn't Donnie's fault. "You know how Mel lurks around every practice session, staring at you and acting like he's judging every word out of your mouth?"

"That's half the population at WBA on any given weekend."

Donnie nodded. "Well, a few years of Mel doing that wore on me. Especially because he'd never said a goddamned word about what I'd done for Cole. You don't know what that kid was like when I first saw him. Raw and awkward as you can get. Just a big arm on a big body with no idea about anything. But Mel still acted like I didn't know what I was talking about or something."

"That's the Mel I know."

"Plus, I'd gotten to like Cole. He's a good kid, you know?"

"Real good kid. Polite and listens to everything you say, always yes-siring you, but he also breathes fire if you ask for it."

Donnie was nodding again, recognizing his thoughts uttered by someone else. "One day Cole's struggling a bit with his changeup during a winter bullpen. We were in the gym at Deep Creek. Short workout, thirty pitches. Cole's front leg was swinging wildly, and he was opening up early. So, he leaves a couple of changes up, belt high, and Mel starts muttering and marching around and I told him to take a walk outside and cool off."

Stubs whistled. "You ask him or tell him?"

"Told him."

"No shit?"

"No shit. He didn't say a word. He grabbed Cole, took a walk outside and never came back. Haven't talked to him or Cole since."

"That sucks, man. Truly."

Donnie and Stubs stared at the field as a microphone was set up behind home plate. They had sat together in the stands at too many games to count, though every one of them had been when they were kids. The players had drifted off the field and were joking around near the dugouts, ready to play. Joe still wasn't back, and Donnie's irritation was growing.

"What're you doing up here, Stubs?" Donnie said. "Why don't you go down with Cole's crew? You belong with them."

Stubs looked pained. "Dude, let's just watch the game."

The Hillcats players ran to their positions on the field. Cole jogged out last. He climbed the mound and began kicking in the dirt, manicuring it around the rubber and at his landing spot to his liking.

A color guard marched onto the field and the PA announcer asked the crowd to rise. A small girl in a summer dress stepped up to a microphone stand that had been lowered to her height. An organ began, and she started to sing the National Anthem. Her voice was beautiful, seeming to reach out wonderfully over the outfield fence toward those distant foothills.

When the anthem finished and the crowd had mustered a weak applause, Donnie and Stubs dropped back into their seats. Joe arrived promptly, holding beers in each hand. Donnie tried to shoot him a hard look, but Joe wouldn't meet his eyes. Joe passed one beer to Stubs and one to Donnie. He sat two seats to Donnie's right. Donnie felt hemmed in—his childhood best friend to one side, his brother to the other.

Cole made quick work of the first batter, striking him out on three fastballs—the last one a rising chin-high gasser that the hitter looked ridiculous chasing with a hacking, helpless swing. The second batter flew weakly to shallow right field. And the third popped up to the catcher.

"A nice start to his career," Stubs said. "It's all in front of him now. Wouldn't mind being in his place."

Donnie looked at Stubs with the most disdainful smirk he could manage and shook his head slowly.

Stubs shifted in his seat, took off his hat, fiddled with the brim, and put it back on. "I'm serious," he said. "I hate watching games now. Hate it. All those bastards out there don't know what it's like to be done—for it all to be over. They don't know how lucky they are. I would trade places with every single one of 'em."

"You always got coaching."

"Coaching sucks."

"Then don't do it," Donnie said. "You're rich. Go sit on your ass somewhere."

"That's not me," Stubs said.

"Then find something else to complain about." Donnie shook his head. "You played in two All-Star games, and you're bitching to me? Give me a break.

The Warthogs pitcher was a short lefty with a herky-jerky, high-effort delivery that Donnie didn't like the looks of. He seemed doomed to persistent wildness and fatigue.

Stubs said, "I really would do it over. Start at the very beginning. Little League. Go from there and see what happens. I can't sit around watching other people have all the fun."

"You might not be so lucky the second time around."

"I doubt that, dude. What about you? You start over if you could?"

Donnie grunted. "You're the dumbest genie I ever heard of."

Stubs shifted uncomfortably in his seat. "I really wish I could go back to one at bat at least and do it all over again. Maybe that would be enough for me. Just one at bat that I think about every morning I wake up. Seventh game of the NLCS against the Cardinals. Winner goes to the World Series. Ninth inning, down a run, I'm up with a guy on third and one out. 2-0 count. A frigging fly ball and we're into extra innings. I get a waist-high fastball over the heart of the plate. Everything I could ever want, everything I could ever dream of. And what do I do with it? Sawed off to the second baseman. Just jammed to hell. Next guy strikes out, and that's it. I was that close to playing in a World Series and I fucked it up." He shook his head. "I'll never get another chance, and I still don't understand what the hell happened. It was exactly the pitch I was hoping for. I can see the seams of that ball right now as clearly as I can see you."

A Hillcats batter launched a long home run to left field and the ballpark awoke with gusto. Fans stood and applauded. Joe was among them, but Donnie and Stubs remained in their seats and glared at the field.

After a walk, the Hillcats were retired on a slick double play. The Warthogs second baseman, a short block of a guy, managed a tricky, ballsy pivot over the bag to avoid the charging baserunner and get off a strong throw to first. He jawed at the baserunner after the play, shouting at him with his chest out. Some nearby twentysomething guys sprung to life, yelling at the player and booing him with everything they had. Stubs laughed. "I like that guy."

Donnie couldn't help but grin. A ballplayer like that—a ballplayer made in Stubs' image—made you happy to be around the game. His enthusiasm was contagious. That was the effect Stubs had always had on people. Donnie saw that Stubs was avidly following the second baseman's determined run back into the visiting dugout.

Cole threw two more perfect innings with three more strikeouts. With each out, his personal cheering section came to exuberant life, giving the sleeping stadium a momentary shake. Stubs, Donnie, and Joe talked little while Cole was on the mound. They were absorbed by the performance, studying every one of his movements on the mound.

Cole's traveling fan club gave him a standing ovation as he strolled off the field at the end of the third, knowing his day was done. He had a pitch count, and the Pirates organization would be watching it closely for the rest of the summer, monitoring their prized prospect in everything they did.

With Cole gone, Stubs started talking again, commenting on everything he saw on the field and elsewhere. Occasionally, Donnie argued with him, debating a point or correcting a memory. Joe kept his mouth shut, except to laugh frequently. He twice fetched Donnie and Stubs more beers.

During the seventh-inning stretch, a man approached them. He held a pen and program out to Stubs. "Would you mind signing this, Mr. Woodson? I'm sorry to bother you."

Stubs looked embarrassed, glancing at Donnie. "No problem," Stubs said. As he signed, the fan, who appeared to be about the same age as Stubs and Donnie, stole a studying look at Donnie. It was an expression Donnie believed he recognized. The guy thought Donnie seemed familiar, but he couldn't decide if he was looking at a man who was somebody or not. When he got the scorecard and his pen back, he said, "Thanks. Enjoy the game," and glanced once more at Donnie. "That's a hell of a shiner," he said, before returning to his seat.

Donnie stewed silently in his seat. He felt Joe studying him.

"You know how Dad would drop his little pet sayings at us every day of the week?" Joe said. "How sick we got of them?"

"He had a way of nailing you with one right when you didn't want to hear it," Stubs said.

"You ever think about them now?" Joe said.

"All the time," Stubs said, shaking his head in disbelief. "They come up all of the time. The other day one of my guys was complaining about some blister he had on his thumb and without thinking, I said, 'Well, major, I guess things are tough all over.'"

Donnie and Joe shook their heads and smiled in recognition.

"There's something about saying that to someone that makes them feel naked and stupid," Stubs said. "Just guilty as hell for whining."

"That was one of his better ones," Joe said. "It pops in my head at work all the time, but it almost seems too toxic to use there. Like I'd never be forgiven for it. Whining is holy in an office. It's like a form of prayer."

"Glad I'm not in any office, I guess," Donnie said.

"Amen to that," Stubs said.

Joe ignored them. "How about what Dad would say when we wouldn't let something go? Like if you had a bad at bat or a bad game and you were sulking around about it. You remember that one?"

Stubs and Donnie looked at each other, shook their heads. "Nah," Donnie said. "I guess I didn't have enough bad games."

Stubs laughed, "There you go."

Joe nodded, allowing himself a brief, patient smile. "I had my share," he said.

"Well," Donnie said. "What the hell did he say?"

"It's one his father had used," Joe said. "Remember Grandpa Wilson was a big quail hunter? Loved shooting those little things. He used to tell Dad, when Dad was moaning over some mistake or something, 'Leave it alone. That bird is good and gone.' And so Dad used to say that to me all the time in high school when I was freaking out over every goddamned thing. A bad test, a bad game, forgetting something I was supposed to do."

"So pretty much every day," Stubs said.

"Pretty much. He'd see me pouting around and say, 'Ah, Joe, leave it alone. That bird is good and gone. You ain't getting it now. Get the next one.' Crazy as it sounds to say, it helped. Is it as big a cliche as the rest of them? I guess. But that was the only one that I never got sick of. I started using it on myself, like I'd prescribe it when I'd feel things getting away from me again. I used to get paralyzed with going over every angle of some way I'd done less than I should have, some fresh failure. I couldn't think about anything else. But I'd close my eyes and take a deep breath and say out loud, 'That bird is good and gone.' Understand I'd actually stop and picture that bird flying away, over some woods, pines mostly, away from this empty field where I was standing with a shotgun in my hands. I'd close my eyes and I'd watch that bird getting smaller and smaller, turning into this vague dot, until it was completely out of sight. I had to be sure it was really gone. And when it had disappeared, I'd open my eyes again and I'd be ready to move on."

Donnie was trying to remember Joe more clearly in high school. In those days, Donnie had never wondered why Joe would get so angry, or why he was so worked up about everything he took on. It was just the way he was. Donnie used to hear him muttering angrily by himself in his room, and he'd think it was funny. Good athlete, top student, extracurriculars Donnie gladly ignored. He was more well-rounded than Donnie or Stubs, but he could never do what they could do on a baseball field, as hard as he tried.

"You're trying to teach us something, aren't you, Joe?" Stubs said. "This some kind of a lesson?" He seemed serious, not like he was screwing with Joe.

"Just something I felt like saying. I don't know if you're like this, but my brother is. Always looking for some secret, like if you could figure this one thing out then things would fall into place for you. I'm just telling you one thing that's helped me a bit get over things and move on because it seems like maybe you two are having trouble with that."

Donnie felt stung but Stubs seemed fine. He beamed at Joe. "Now what makes you think that? Because we been acting too much like things are tough all over?"

"I mean it, man. I don't know any lessons," Joe said. "Yeah, this little Zen gimmick of mine helps me get past some crap, but I still wonder why things didn't work out with my marriage and I'm sure now there's never going to be another one. No bird trick works there. I'm pretty good at my job, but it bores the hell out of me so who cares? You know anybody you actually think deep down is happy beyond anything else? I don't. Everyone I know thinks more about the stuff that bothers them at least five to one—the stuff they could have done better, the opportunities they missed, the mistakes they made. You don't know how to grow up, and Donnie can't let go of the fact that he never got to the majors or whatever. I get that, but, I mean, shit take a number."

Donnie felt himself go hot. "Good lord, Joe. What're you so worked up about?"

Joe spoke forcefully, intent on getting his point across. "Because you seem to think that even your misery is special. This goes back to before you lost Amy, Donnie. Goes back years you've been stewing about what you didn't get. You think because I didn't have your talent I was OK with being a plugger, an average guy? Don't get me wrong. I was always happy for you and proud as hell, but we had the same Mom and Dad, right? It was hard for me not to wish I was the one with speed and coordination and goddamned gracefulness. I wanted to play pro ball. I wanted to be that guy who made people suck in their breath and say, 'Holy shit.'"

"Ah, nobody did that," Donnie said.

"Yeah, they did," Stubs said. "Everyone did."

Donnie looked at Stubs in surprise. His old friend seemed fidgety and embarrassed. On his other side, Joe tapped mindlessly on the empty seat back ahead of him. They both seemed to be waiting for him to speak, but he didn't say anything else. He leaned back and turned his attention to the game.

In the bottom of the eighth, Joe left for a final piss before the long drive home. With Joe gone, Stubs exhaled significantly, as though he'd been waiting for the moment.

"Look, Donnie, I'm sorry about the knuckle curve," he said. "I don't know what the hell I was thinking. I couldn't help myself."

"It was a dick thing to do," Donnie said.

"Agreed."

Donnie wondered where the anger was, why he wasn't pressing the point and bringing up everything else, why he wasn't unloading on him about WBA and the ways it had ruined what he had in Richmond, but it's not what he felt right then and there. He felt something closer to relief. When Stubs talked to him, it wasn't with the superiority Donnie always imagined his old friend felt for him. Instead, it was light and natural and easy, as though the recent years hadn't come between them at all. There wasn't anyone else in the world like this for Donnie—not Joe, not Amy, not Max. They'd dreamed together when they were young, strived for something more, and they understood each other like no one else could. Wilson and Woodson, Woodson and Wilson. Now here they were, under the lights in another ballpark, wanting the same thing again—to be young with all their successes and failures in front of them. He thought of Amy's persistent urging for him to imagine the miseries of other people, and he felt Stubs' frustration as though it was his own. The guy was still despondent over a single at bat. Donnie could relate to that. Suddenly, for the first time since the prospect had been raised, Donnie could see the appeal of working for the guy.

"That home run derby the other day?" Donnie said. "That was the most fun I've had in a long, long time."

Stubs seemed caught off guard, and he looked at Donnie with a searching expression. He nodded and his shoulders dropped, releasing some subtle tension that Donnie was only now seeing. He leaned forward on his knees and shook his head. "Me, too, dude," Stubs said. "That was a blast."

They returned their attention to the game. The new Hillcats reliever was a submarine pitcher, nearly scraping the dirt with his sweeping delivery. His first pitch was a slider away.

"I'm sorry about Amy," Stubs said. "I really am. I wanted to help. It killed me to think of what you were going through. I guess I was a coward about it."

Donnie sucked in a large breath and fought a surprising rush of emotion. "That's OK, man. I was the asshole, not you."

Donnie didn't like the pitcher's release point, and he wished he could have five minutes with him. He knew he could help.

Joe didn't speak when they got into the car in the ballpark parking lot, and Donnie didn't say a word either. They drove through the hilly countryside outside of Lynchburg, heading for the interstate with the windows open to the humid summer night, and Donnie thought about what his brother had done and why he had done it. He had to have guessed Donnie's reaction to Stubs' arrival and Joe's role in it would be some kind of tantrum, but he'd done it anyway—stuck his neck out for him, wasted a day driving him hours away to a ballgame he didn't care about.

Donnie reached over and slapped Joe hard on the back, as his brother had done to him so incessantly in recent days. Joe flinched, as though bracing himself.

"You're a piece of shit," Donnie said.

Then Donnie slumped in his seat, looked out the window, and replayed Cole's pitches, one by one, as though they were his.

Chapter Twenty-Four

Max showered when he woke near noon, inhaled two quick bowls of cereal, and dragged his bicycle out of the back shed. It had been a while since he had used the thing—since back when Mom was still alive—and he was annoyed to have to sort through piles of junk to locate the air pump. When he'd finally found it and reanimated the bike's slack tires, he brushed the dust off the seat and took off. Satisfyingly, he was on his own.

It was a hot day, and he was sweating after twenty minutes of pedaling when he reached Mrs. Davenport's house. She opened the door with her customary smile—there was something sly in it, as though she and Max were in on some joke together—and welcomed him in with a wave of the hand, "To the kitchen, Max, as fast as you can. To the kitchen."

While Max sat at the table drinking lemonade and letting the ceiling fan cool him down, Mrs. Davenport stood by the sink and watched him. "So, to what do I owe the pleasure?"

Max had not thought through this trip. He'd just known this is where he wanted to be. He wanted to see Mrs. Davenport, settle in at the piano, and spend time with Liszt.

"You think I could practice here a bit?" he said, watching his glass sweat rather than meet Mrs. Davenport's eyes. "I don't need a lesson. It'd just be fun to play for a bit."

"Of course," she said. She joined him at the table. "It's got you good, doesn't it?"

"I guess." Max looked up. He felt embarrassed but pleased she seemed to understand. No one else seemed to get it. "I've been thinking about it a lot."

"You're lucky," she said. "That's when it's the most fun."

His mother had loved that he played the piano. Baseball was fine and all, but her smile somehow was unique when she heard him play music. Sometimes, at home, she'd sneak in and sit behind him and secretly listen. When he stopped, she'd applaud as though at a recital, startling Max. He hadn't reflected on those moments at all when she was alive, but now he thought about them every day.

While Max played, Mrs. Davenport sat on the sofa in the living room with a book. With his back to her, Max couldn't tell how closely she was paying attention, but he liked knowing she was there, a witness to his work. From the outset, it was the best he had ever played the Liebestraum, or anything else, and it was not only a single performance but a series of them. One time after another he played the piece straight through, pausing only as long as it took the final note to die and then

135

diving back into it with no more than a slight shift on the bench, eager to tour through it again. He felt no fatigue, no hesitancy. It was as though all the imagining of the piece, all the envisioning of it played just right, had seeped into the moment. The playing of it required his two hands to behave independently and precisely, at times to play as though he was playing two different works, and it demanded that he understood not just the proper rhythm and technique but the right pace of the quiet, of the pauses. There was so much patience involved, so much restraint, even as the striking of the keys could spill into almost furiously fast movements. He knew, of course, that it wasn't perfect—that any decent concert pianist would feel humiliated at such a performance—but to him it rang as cleanly as a piece of music could. Still, no matter how many times he played it correctly, it never felt quite real. It felt cold. He was playing it well, but there was an unbridgeable space between him and the notes. He felt as though he was chasing something that could not be caught.

He'd told his mother a few months before she died that he wanted to give up piano. He'd completely stopped playing at home, and he pleaded with her to let him quit his lessons. He'd bitched at her, whined, complained, even insulted her. One time, he remembered, he'd told her that she only made him play piano because she wasn't good at anything herself. He didn't know where that one had come from or if there was any truth to it, but he'd seen in her face that it had somehow drawn blood. She wouldn't let him quit, though, no matter how shitty he behaved.

As he performed for Mrs. Davenport, his thoughts kept turning to Mom. He could never fix what he'd said now. Eventually, he understood that it was time to stop playing, and he did, slumping on the bench and letting his hands rest on his lap. He waited to hear from Mrs. Davenport. When she said nothing, he turned on the bench. Her book was closed on the sofa beside her. She had been crying and had a crumpled tissue in her hands.

"I cannot wait for you to play that at the recital," she said.

Max smiled. "Anything I should work on?"

"Don't change a thing," she said. "I doubt Liszt could have played it better."

Max felt a flash of disappointment. There it was again. He loved working with Mrs. Davenport, loved coming to her house and learning not only about the music but about the composers and their lives. He had been seeing her once a week since he was six and she was still his favorite teacher in any subject. Yet her tendency to overpraise him drove him nuts. He recognized when she said more than she could truly believe. All it did was make him doubt all the other nice things she said. When adults spoke, he had begun to wonder, how did you know when to believe them?

Max became absorbed by his fingernails. "I'm guessing Liszt could have played it better when he was, what, nine? I can't imagine how good he was when he was fourteen."

Mrs. Davenport rose from the sofa and walked to the piano. Max turned and slid over, and she sat beside him on the bench, facing the keys. "Do you think you must play as well as Franz Liszt or the piece is not a success?" she said.

"I'm not saying that."

"Because that is not a reasonable expectation to place on yourself, you understand? It must be you and the music. That's what you can control. That's enough. You cannot decide you are competing against everyone else in the world, too. OK? You cannot do that to yourself."

Max cracked his knuckles idly. "When Liszt was my age, he was a big star already," he said. "He knew he was great and that he would be great his whole life. That's got to be a pretty good feeling." He struck a few keys. "He knew, since he was a little kid, without any doubts, I'm amazing at this."

Mrs. Davenport sighed. "Just because he was a prodigy doesn't mean it was as easy as all of that. It doesn't mean he didn't have the same doubts, the same questions the rest of us have."

"Yeah, right."

"In fact, he did," she said sternly, her hands clenching each other in her lap. "Yes, he was famous at a very young age, but that's a small slice of his life. We haven't talked about when he was a teenager, for instance. When he was your age. Sometime around fourteen or fifteen, his father died. He lost him. And his father had been his greatest teacher, his greatest advocate. He had pushed him hard, certainly, but he was not just a hard man. He also loved his son and wanted him to succeed for the boy's sake and not for his own. You understand the difference?"

"Yeah," Max said, with the sullen tone he favored for his father these days. Then he caught himself, "Yes, ma'am."

Mrs. Davenport smiled and patted Max on the shoulder. "When his dad died, Liszt was devastated. He stopped touring, stopped composing, and started earning money giving lessons to kids as though he was some silly old lady" —she paused and smiled at her joke, but Max did not respond. She nodded, apparently understanding he was in no mood for it. "His forward momentum, you see, that had made everything seem so inevitable halted completely. That doubt you think he never had suddenly ruled him. It was everything. He had seen his work and his art as being all wrapped up with his father, as though they were linked and necessary to each other—without one, the other would crumble on its own. So, he stopped because he did not believe he was a great pianist and composer without his father, and also because he did not *want* to be a great pianist and composer without him. The one had driven the other. Does that make sense?" Max stared at the keys

137

without a response. "Life had been one way for him, and it took him several years to understand life could be other ways, too. Some people never understand, of course. Something bad and inconvenient happens and that's it for them. They never recover. But he did, eventually. In his twenties, he was inspired to push himself without someone else's hand on his back. And then, when determination came, it came from within and so it was very powerful. Much more powerful than before. This time, he was in charge of it."

Max jerked his hands toward the keys and then removed them in embarrassment. He was surprised to feel a fresh jolt of adrenaline.

Mrs. Davenport carefully folded the tissue in her hands. "That's why you can sit here and play the Liebestraum, which was written many years later, when he was an adult and very much his own man. You think the terrific sadness in that piece, the terrific and beautiful melancholy, is a product of an easy life? Think if he'd never picked things up again and instead had folded shop forever when his dad died. Think what we'd be missing."

She patted Max on the knee. He took a breath. They sat in silence, staring at the keys. Then she stood and returned to the sofa. Behind him, she broke into applause. Max turned and stared at her in confusion. She sat upright—rod-straight and profoundly attentive. She lifted her eyebrows and nodded. Max felt a mysterious swelling in his chest.

He stood and bowed to her extravagantly, then turned and sat on the bench. It seemed to him that Liszt was right there in the room with them, waiting and watching, an expression of rapt curiosity on his teenage face. He felt an exquisite sense of calm. He examined the piano. The keys seemed to vibrate with possibility. The world was quiet and still—and, best of all, simple. It was him and the Liebestraum. That was all. He placed his fingers on the keys and began to play.

Chapter Twenty-Five

Once Joe let Stubs know Donnie had been working on an instructional video and book, it was only a matter of time before Donnie showed them to his old friend. The guy was relentless, and Donnie found that after a couple of conversations with Stubs about the work he had done, he had shifted from protective of the projects to eager to share them with him. Amy's vision for him—in which he and Stubs collaborated on the work—made sense to him in a way it never had before. Stubs had a way of making you believe.

Stubs had set up a time to stop by the house after Donnie got off work to check out what existed already of the video. Donnie had cautioned him that it was just him experimenting, using Max as his model as he taught the basics of pitching to a camera. In fact, there had been no one to shoot the video, and he had left the camera running on a tripod. It was only a test.

Donnie found the disk in one of several cardboard boxes around his bedroom. Stubs hammered on the door as Donnie descended the steps. He opened the door.

"Alright, Spielberg, let's see this thing," Stubs said.

They moved into the den, a wood-paneled room with a flat-screen TV. Donnie wished he'd had time to review the video before he showed it to Stubs.

As he slid the disk into the DVD player, he laid the case next to the TV. Stubs grabbed it and held it up, pointing the label toward Donnie. "Snowstorm?" he said. "That some kind of code?"

"There was some old family stuff on the disk that I recorded over. We've got hours of that stuff."

Donnie suddenly filled the frame, slightly out of focus. He was looking into the camera. He wore a uniform—Donnie had forgotten the outfit—complete with white baseball pants, stirrups, and a gray T-shirt with "Coach" across the front of it. He wore a plain black cap. His shirt was tucked in.

Donnie felt a sharp sense of disappointment. This might be embarrassing.

"I gotta get me one of those 'Coach' shirts," Stubs said. "That's awesome."

Donnie talked to the camera, awkwardly using his hands to express himself. He introduced himself— "College World Series MVP and fifteen years in professional baseball"—and the purpose of the video— "to teach you the keys to pitching mechanics." Donnie figured Stubs must have been amused by his efforts to establish his bona fides for viewers.

At the end of the introduction, Donnie clapped his hands once and then spoke, "So keep watching as we teach you"—he paused and thrust a finger at the camera— "to pitch to win."

"Whoa," Stubs said. "I'm fired up."

Donnie stepped aside offscreen and suddenly Max was standing atop the rubber on the mound on the field at Deep Creek. He looked nervous as he glanced between the camera and his shoes. Donnie re-entered the screen from the right side. Max seemed almost startled to see him. "OK," Donnie said. "Let's get started."

Using Max as his model, he took viewers through the basics of the pitching delivery. Max handled the role fine at first, dutifully moving as Donnie directed him. Donnie talked too much. Way too much. As he watched in the den, he remembered the babbling and started to remember the filming better. He hadn't trusted himself, hadn't believed he was getting his point across adequately, so he kept talking, kept massaging the message and restating it however many ways it occurred to him in the moment. At times, Max simply looked bored as Donnie prattled on about balance and leg lifts and hip rotation. As the video played, Donnie found he paid less attention to his words and lessons and more to the state of his son. He'd remembered the video shoot as being something fun they had done together. It had been a fond memory for him, but now, as he watched it, Max looked like some kind of prisoner, following the orders of a strict, humorless, long-winded man in a silly uniform.

Then came an incident. Donnie was explaining the key to being able to balance over the rubber during the leg lift. The ideal position at the top of the lift, he said, was "with your risen leg in a squared position with your chest and back leg. In other words, the lift leg shouldn't be kicked too far backward, crossing the rubber and corkscrewing your body away from its target, or left too far forward, leaving your body open and prematurely sliding toward the plate. Either way, your timing would be off." The explanation sounded convoluted and confusing even to Donnie as he sat in the den, but the real problem occurred when one of Max's recurring bugaboos materialized during his demonstration of the proper leg lift. He swung his lift leg too strongly and too far backward, twisting his body and leading to a rushed, ugly push toward home. The first time it happened the Donnie stared at Max and said, "Let's try that again."

When Max repeated the mistake, Donnie shook his head and said, "Dammit, Max, no. Stop swinging your leg so far back."

Max's face showed anguish as Donnie paced in a circle, shaking his head. He stopped, looked at his son and said, "Alright, let's see it. Easy lift. Get it right."

Max swallowed and stood on the rubber. He looked at his target offscreen—Donnie had set up a screen at the plate for Max to pitch toward—and began his delivery. That leg lifted and crossed too far back again.

Donnie begged the version of him on the screen to keep it together, but it did not. Instead, it kicked dirt and said, "Is it that hard?" Stubs exhaled loudly and

Donnie reached for the remote and pushed pause as he grabbed Max around the shoulders on the screen. Donnie remembered what was next: He would stand next to Max as he started his pitching motion yet again and catch his front leg as he lifted it and hold it in place. He'd then talk at him some more about where the leg goes and doesn't go. He'd long forgotten the camera by that point.

Donnie wondered what Stubs was thinking. "Sorry about this," Donnie said. "We got a bit sidetracked."

"It happens," Stubs said. "Look, there's a lot of good stuff here. It's a solid start for planning."

"You serious?"

"Yeah, man. I like you on the screen. I just don't like you winging it all the time. You need a script."

Donnie watched himself and his son. The man he saw was frozen with a look of frustrated derision. Max looked terrified. That was who he was to his son. When the temper ignited and he became what he liked to call "demanding," this is what he looked like to Max and the rest of the world.

"C'mon," Stubs said. "Let's see the rest."

Donnie pushed the skip button and suddenly they were no longer on Deep Creek Field. It was still Donnie and Max on the screen, but they were younger and there was thick snow blanketing their front yard. Max was puffed up in a parka-like jacket with snow pants and boots and a warm stocking cap. He wore colorful knit mittens. Donnie guessed the boy on the screen was about seven. Donnie was sitting next to him on a shelf of snow that had formed in their front yard—probably Donnie had shoveled it that way. Max was laughing and so was Donnie. They both looked at the camera, or rather above the camera, at Amy, who was speaking to them. They sat as casually as if they were on a park bench.

"Well, boys, what do you think of this snow?" Amy asked.

"It's awesome," Max said.

Donnie only showed a mischievous grin to the camera. He surreptitiously reached behind his son and dug at the snow that was beneath the boy with his hand. The camera shook, and Donnie heard Amy chuckle.

Max was bouncing on his seat in the snow, his grin wide and beautiful, unaware of his father's scheme. Donnie dug diligently beneath him, scooping away snow in handfuls. Then, the snow suddenly shifted and the shelf collapsed under Max, and he fell backwards, his legs shooting into the air as he dropped with a splash into the snow. The camera shook violently up and down, and Donnie and Amy laughed uproariously. Donnie and Stubs laughed in the den, too. As the camera steadied itself and stopped bouncing, Donnie lifted his padded son from the snow and placed him on his feet in front of the camera. He brushed at the snow on the boy's clothes. Max looked dazed and unsteady. His face was serious as he looked between his guffawing father and mother.

"There you are," Donnie said, patting the boy on the back. He leaned toward Max and whispered into his ear. Max got a sly smile on his face, and they both dug into the snow beneath them. "What are you doing?" Amy said, her voice sounding concerned. "Boys? Boys!" Max and Donnie lifted snowballs in their respective right hands and faced the camera.

"Count it, Max," Donnie said.

"No, Max," Amy said, the camera moving backward as she moved away from danger. The crunching sound of her steps in the snow was audible. "Don't count anything."

Max cocked his arm back and faced his mother. "One," he said. He and Donnie followed the retreating camera. "Two," he said, giggling now. "No!" Amy said. "Don't do it."

"Three!!" Max yelled with glee, and Donnie and Max fired snowballs directly at the camera. The screen went black to the sound of Amy's half-delighted scream.

Donnie sat stunned, a smile stuck on his face, and felt an ache fill him unbearably. This felt like pain beyond what he was capable of handling. He remembered that day in the snow as though it had just happened, as though Amy and Max were still in the front yard with him at that moment. And yet he hadn't thought of it in years.

Stubs was chuckling and rubbing his hands together. He shifted in his seat. "That was funny as shit. Look, I'm going to hire someone, a real pro, bring them in to map this whole thing out for us. We'll start with the pitching, but it'll be a series. Hitting, baserunning, fielding. Game strategy, maybe. Training. It'll be great. I want us to work together on this, OK? You've got to take a central role or I'm not doing it. Deal?"

Donnie was barely listening. He was thinking about Max and the cruel way he'd left his last game without a word, all because the kid had thrown a knuckle curve. What kind of a man was he anyway?

"OK," Donnie said.

"No joking," Stubs said, standing up and slapping him on the back. "We good?"

"Yeah, we're good."

"I'm going to jet," Stubs said. "But I'm calling you tomorrow. We're doing this." He started to leave and then paused in the den doorway. "We make a great team, Donnie."

Donnie didn't look up, keeping his eyes on the blank screen. Stubs had now offered him the simple next step, and no doubt the right one.

"These videos, the book, they could be a complete WBA production," Stubs said.

When the front door closed, Donnie walked into the kitchen. Then he sat at the table and thought about how unhappy he'd allowed himself to be during what could have been the happiest years of his life. He'd returned from his baseball career to a wife and a kid he'd loved, and he'd never thought to appreciate them the way he should have. Instead, he'd been absorbed with his failures and what he couldn't have. His chance at a successful life—at climbing to the top of the heap—had passed him by, and there was nothing for him to do about it. That was what was important. He'd never really lost the frustration that had consumed him since he'd first injured his knee. Everything after that was about some cosmic injustice. Now, he'd lost Amy and there would never be another quite like her, no matter how lucky he got. And he was losing Max. He reviewed every piece of his relationship with him, every bullpen session in recent time he could remember. Could he blame the kid for ignoring him and turning to the knuckle curve? He needed to speak with him, but he couldn't figure what it was he should say.

Donnie opened Amy's address book by the landline. He knew Max would ignore it if he called his cell. He should have the Tennysons' number memorized by now, but he had to look it up every time. Beneath the address book was a calendar that Amy had kept. She was a planner, and even six months after her death there were still events marked on the calendar. Curious, Donnie took a look. He was surprised to see a marking for today. "Max Recital, 7 p.m., First Baptist." The kid had told him about the recital, told him how much it meant to him, and Donnie was going to miss it. Probably Max had gotten a ride with the Tennysons, his new family. Donnie grabbed his keys and rushed out the door.

Donnie reached First Baptist twenty minutes after seven. He figured they were still working through the younger kids and he was there in plenty of time for Max, who likely would be the closer based on what he'd heard. He walked to the parish hall, where he'd remembered it being held before, but instead of children, parents, and a piano, he found senior citizens at work on arts and crafts. He approached the first table. A woman with thick glasses was making a collage with pictures cut from a magazine.

"Isn't there supposed to be a kids' piano recital here?" he asked.

The woman looked up impatiently. "They moved that to the choir room," she said. She waved her hand toward the door he'd entered. "Down that hall and the stairs on your left."

Donnie rushed down the hall and flew down the stairs two at a time. The double doors of the choir room were closed. He stopped, caught his breath, and opened one slowly. He stood there, dumbfounded to realize that he was standing in front, not behind, the seated crowd that had gathered for the occasion, and a young child was playing the piano to his right with Mrs. Davenport sitting next to him. The crowd facing him glared at him. A couple of the mothers, in particular, looked appalled. Donnie walked as quietly as possible while the child, a tiny boy in a red bowtie, haltingly played his piece. Donnie slipped through the first few rows of seats and found an open one on the edge of the aisle.

The boy finished his piece with a neat little flourish, and the crowd applauded with genuine enthusiasm, Donnie included. His moment of embarrassment dissipating, he scanned the room. He realized Max was nowhere to be seen. His panic returned.

A girl, slightly bigger than the boy, approached the piano bench in her flowered dress, bowed to the crowd hurriedly, and then fell onto the bench and played in a rush, as though she wanted to finish as fast as she could. Donnie watched with a creeping anxiety.

One child after another approached the piano, played with progressively higher skill and sophistication, and bowed to earnest applause. Donnie's attention was trained on the double doors at the front, trying to will them to open.

At the conclusion, though, after the last kid, a long-haired boy with an almost sickly thin frame, played his final note, Mrs. Davenport stood and faced the crowd. She smiled with pride and kindness and spoke of the wonderful playing of the children. "I appreciate their hard work and effort," she said. "I hope you do, too." Then she pointed to a table that had been set up to the side of the chairs. "Please enjoy some refreshments." As the crowd stood, she caught Donnie's eye and motioned him over.

"Did I miss something?" Donnie said.

"I'm sorry but there must have been a misunderstanding. Max decided not to participate."

"But why? I thought he was gunning for this thing."

"He was, but he came over to my house the other day and played the piece over and over again. It was beautiful. Just beautiful. I was mesmerized. After he was done, he told me that he never wanted to play it again. He'd had his moment with it, and he was ready to move on. And it really was a wonderful moment."

Donnie understood that he didn't get to be part of the moment—Max had reserved it for Mrs. Davenport. The boy never would have done that if his mother was alive. "I wished he'd told me."

Mrs. Davenport's expression was one of clear compassion. "I know it's difficult, Donnie. He's having a hard time, and it's difficult enough to figure them out when they're this age and things are easy." She smiled. "Please take comfort, though, in knowing that he found something in this music. Something that meant a lot to him. Something that helped."

Donnie nodded. "That does help, thanks."

A young girl approached with her mother, and Mrs. Davenport turned her attention to the girl and gave her a hug. "Wonderful, dear," she said. "Just wonderful." Donnie slid through the crowd and out the doors.

Chapter Twenty-Six

Donnie called Max twice from the church parking lot, but only got his voice mail. So, he tried Stubs next. He wanted to see WBA—wanted to walk inside. Stubs was up for it. They met at the front door of the WBA facility twenty minutes later. It was locked and dark. Stubs seemed almost nervous.

Inside, Stubs showed him the lobby with its rows of photos of WBA players. He paused long enough at a section dedicated to pictures from his own playing days to point out Donnie in the background of a shot from high school that showed Stubs celebrating with a mob of teammates. Donnie remembered the game, which had ended when Stubs had scored on Donnie's clutch double. He showed him the snack bar, pointed at the menu— "we've actually got a real solid hot dog you can get here"—and Donnie found he felt guilty to see his old friend talking with such polish and restraint, earnestly explaining himself and his facility instead of just boasting about it like an authentic Stubs truly would. Donnie knew he was the reason for this unnatural behavior.

They walked through the door into the open gym area, and Stubs flipped on a series of light switches. Donnie was stunned at what lay ahead of him. He'd had a picture in his mind of a dark gym with a few cages and pitching mounds, but this place had large windows that would allow in extensive sunlight, the centerpiece practice field was beautiful and welcoming, and the surrounding rows of cages and mounds were impressive in their number and orderliness, instead of the battered things he'd imagined. The nets were taut and without rips, the mounds were impeccably formed and raked. They were begging for action. There was no sign of loose balls or a single piece of equipment out of place. It was, as Donnie's Dad used to like to say, "all squared away." They wandered around the gym. Stubs chattered away about this feature and that one, but Donnie largely ignored him. He was studying everything through his own filter. He felt a kind of panic to see what his friend had pulled off in just a few years, while Donnie struggled away in his backyard. What must Stubs have thought of him all this time?

Stubs didn't seem aware of where Donnie's head was. "It can be a madhouse in here with a million voices going at once and bats pinging and gloves popping and baseballs just flying all over." Stubs looked at Donnie directly for the first time since he'd arrived. "You'd love it."

They stopped at a cage in the back. A pitching machine was at the far end of the cage, so that Donnie could look down its barrel from where he stood.

Stubs had grabbed a bat as they headed out, and he now held it on the barrel and flipped it casually from hand to hand. "So what do you think?"

Donnie nodded, his hands on his hips as he scanned around the place. "This is something else. Miles better than the piddly little thing I was going to do. This is plain fancy."

Stubs stopped flipping the bat, probably wondering if it was a dig. "I know one thing," he said. "It'd have been great to have something like this when we were kids. You can only get better in a place like this."

"I don't know," Donnie said. "You're always working with coaches here and it's all formal and stuff, with lessons and set times and shit. Maybe it was better the way we did it. Running out on the field with a bag of baseballs and just knocking around for hours."

Stubs laughed. "Yeah, there's something to that, but I'll never admit it to anyone else. I don't want this place empty. Though I guess we had your pops as our coach, didn't we?"

They laughed at that. He'd be out there any time they asked him and never with a cross word about it. He'd pitch to them, catch them, hit fungoed ground balls and fly balls at them. And yet it was never as though he was in charge. If they wanted to do something, he'd do it. If they were ready to stop, he'd stop. He never made them do anything. And he wasn't some coach yapping at them, centering on their screwups. It was all encouragement— "thataboys" and "there you gos." He was short but sturdy, and he'd wear a T-shirt, gray sweatpants, and a Red Sox hat that covered his bald head. A lefthander, he had a compact delivery and remarkable control well into his forties.

"You remember how he'd mess with us sometimes by dropping in a curve or a change when we weren't looking for it?" Stubs said.

"Man, he loved that," Donnie said. "He'd be laughing his ass off and I'd want to rush the mound with my bat half the time I was so pissed. The guy had good stuff."

"That he did," Stubs said.

Donnie realized they were talking about the past again, reminiscing like they'd done at the ballpark. It seemed to be the easiest way they could communicate—going back to that time when they were still friends. Stubs had finally relaxed.

"Look, I know you don't want to work here," Stubs said. "I know you got your reasons, and it drives me crazy. There's nothing more I'd like than for the two of us to be in here working together every day, but I get it."

"I appreciate that. I just can't."

"So, here's what I'm thinking. Joe told me about that little space you've been looking at in the city."

"Man, what a gossip that guy is."

"He's just looking out for you. What I'm thinking is that I buy that space for you under the WBA umbrella. We call it WBA East. I'll pay for all the equipment, whatever, get it on our books, but you run the place however you see fit. You run the lessons, you develop the kids however you like. It's your space, just like you've been wanting."

Donnie was taken aback, and he turned and took a few steps away from Stubs. "I don't know, man. It sounds like charity."

"It's not. It's an investment. I know you, and I know the way you can teach. I know this spot will work. It'll be more convenient for some kids. Some of them will prefer the atmosphere. The margins will be great. This thing's going to make money, and I'll make you an equal partner in it. Fifty-fifty. Trust me."

"I could just keep working in the backyard for myself. And at Deep Creek."

"What about late fall to early spring? What about when it rains? That's a ton of income you're giving up because you don't want to work with me. Like I said, too, this way you've got your own place, your own deal. I just want to visit and hang out every once in a while."

Stubs handed him the bat, and Donnie took it. He felt a smile taking over his face. Stubs was smiling back at him.

"You shoulda been in sales or something," Donnie said.

Stubs clapped. "Old Donnie Baseball."

Donnie bounced the bat on the floor. "Give me a break with that Donnie Baseball stuff, OK?"

"Why? You always loved it."

"Yeah, when I was a kid I loved it. But it was Mattingly's nickname first, right? There could never really be a second Donnie Baseball. I figured it was just something people would call me when I was a kid. I'd grow up, get to the majors, and people would call me something else." Donnie tossed the bat back to Stubs. "And when they say it now, it's always with this little smile. You can see it in their eyes. It's like the name's another way to needle me about the way things went for me. Shit, the fact people still call me that is a punch in the nuts."

"Man, I think people just like the name. That's what makes them smile." Stubs shook his head. "Good lord, getting old sucks."

Chapter Twenty-Seven

Max's wish had come true. He and Lucas were back at Fletcher's, and the girls, including Caroline, were there, too. Fletcher had some more of that bourbon and Coke, and the six of them lounged again around the terrace by the pool. It was as though Max, after daydreaming with gratitude and desire of the first time they had joined together at Fletcher's house, had been able to reach back into the past and pluck that night into the present so he could relive it.

The summer night had that same surreal atmosphere as before—the dreamy half-light of the gas lamps, the calming, still water of the pool, the buzzy influence of the bourbon. Max and Caroline hadn't gotten their time in private yet, but they had broken from the group, moving from the terrace chairs to the far end of the pool, where they sat on the edge of the pool and dangled their feet in the water. They talked about inconsequential things—favorite sodas, toenail polish, overnight thunderstorms—and Caroline laughed at his lame jokes. She looked beautiful and happy.

The decision to skip the piano recital kept surfacing for him. In particular, he wanted to know if his father had showed up and found him missing. Max seriously doubted it, but the prospect of it pleased him.

"Don't look serious," Caroline said. She playfully brushed his foot underwater with one of her own. "I don't like it."

He smiled. "As you wish."

She leaned into him with her shoulder and laughed.

Lucas was grinning in his direction. He and Fletcher, Liz, and Whitney were sitting in a cluster of chairs, and Fletcher seemed to be holding court, his voice an incessant, blustery bassline. Lucas held his glass toward Max, as though toasting him. Max held his glass up in return and drank. He still hadn't finished his first glass, but he was close and he wasn't so worried about starting his second this time.

Then they heard the men. Loud, emphatic voices bellowed at each other at the house. A door jerked open, and the voices moved down the walk toward the pool. Max recognized the sight and sound of Mr. Tennyson and knew that the other man must be Fletcher's father. Fletcher stood from his chair and slid the bottle and his glass to the base of the hedge that surrounded the terrace. Max grabbed Caroline's glass and pulled himself from the pool to stuff their glasses behind a potted plant. The other kids made similar arrangements.

Everything was safely out of sight when the men arrived on the pool deck. Mr. Kelly and Mr. Tennyson were shirtless and wearing bathing suits and they carried glasses of dark liquid. Max wondered if it was some of that same bourbon he and the rest had been testing.

"What the hell is this mess?" Mr. Kelly said, his head faintly wavering and bouncing as he spoke, as though his neck was a coil of springs. He turned in a slow circle to take in the whole scene. "It's like a daycare around here sometimes."

Mr. Tennyson strode straight to his son, who was sitting in an unconvincingly relaxed pose on a deck chair. "Lucas, my boy, you better not be getting into trouble." His voice was loud and assured. He patted Lucas on the cheek. "I'm kidding. Look at this handsome devil." He smiled at Liz and Whitney, who were sitting upright and alert. "Isn't he a beautiful kid?"

Whitney laughed. "Oh, yes, Mr. Tennyson. Quite handsome," she said, her tone honeyed and enthusiastic. "He drives all the girls crazy."

Mr. Tennyson patted his son's cheek again. "Damn right he does. He looks like his mother. That was a good break." He removed his hand and continued to study his son. "Too bad that wasn't all he got from her." Max noticed the way Lucas dropped his head sullenly at that.

Mr. Kelly stood on the edge of the pool and looked off vaguely into the night. He was a skinny man except for a protruding belly that seemed almost childlike to Max. He had very little chest hair, furthering the impression. Now that the men were close, Max could see that the bathing suits they wore were identical. Mr. Tennyson must have borrowed one from his host. Both men were drunk. That wasn't hard to see.

Mr. Kelly stepped slowly down the steps into the pool. He lowered himself into the water and then backed into the steps and sat down with a deep sigh. He sipped from his drink with a blank expression on his face.

Mr. Tennyson's gaze shifted across the pool and Max knew he'd been recognized.

"Max, my boy!" Mr. Tennyson thrust his broad chest forward and walked with swift steps around the side of the pool until he stood above Max and Caroline. "Didn't see you over here with this lovely young woman." He tipped a pretend cap. "Ma'am." Caroline laughed.

Mr. Tennyson set his drink on the edge of the pool alongside Max, took three steps back, and ran forward yelling "Tsunami!" He leapt in the air high above the pool. Before Max or Caroline could react, his powerful body plunged into the water in the practiced form of a perfect can opener. A large eruption of water rose and washed over them, and Caroline gasped and leaned into Max. He was thrilled at her instinctive move.

Mr. Tennyson rose to the surface, shot a spurt of water from his mouth, and rubbed his eyes. He grinned at the sight of Max and Caroline assessing their wet clothes and hair. "Gotta be alert, guys," he said. He kicked to the edge of the pool, retrieved his dark drink from alongside Max, and swam on his side, holding his drink above the water, to the other end of the pool. He began to walk in circles, pushing through the water in a steady lap around the shallow end, as though he couldn't stand still.

"You think we interrupted some kind of party here, Kelly?" he said. "I hate to break up the kids' fun."

"Maybe they're breaking up my fun," Mr. Kelly said. "Didja think of that?"

"It doesn't have to be that way," Mr. Tennyson said. "Children, if you've got refreshments around here that you're drinking to stay hydrated on this warm night, you don't have to quit on account of us. Ain't that right, Kelly?"

"I don't give a shit."

Fletcher rose hesitantly from his chair, eyeing Lucas, who was staring at the ground. Fletcher looked back at the girls, who were grinning. Fletcher shrugged, walked to the hedge, and grabbed his drink. He dropped back into his chair.

"There ya go," Mr. Tennyson said.

Caroline whispered into Max's ear, "Should we get ours?" Max felt conflicted. He didn't think it was a trap, but he didn't like that Lucas hadn't budged. "Sure," he said.

She rose, retrieved their drinks from behind the potted plant, and sat back beside him, closer this time, so their legs were pressed together.

On the other side of the pool, the girls had found their drinks and planted themselves back into their chairs. They'd loosened back up, too, and were laughing about something Fletcher had said.

"What about you, Lucas?" Mr. Tennyson leaned over the edge of the pool nearest his son. "Nothing for you?"

"I'm good," Lucas said. His eyes did not leave the ground.

Mr. Tennyson nodded, as though he'd expected that answer, and resumed his slow, methodical pacing around the shallow end. "Have I told you about my daughter, Kelly? What she's been up to?"

"Nah, haven't seen her in ages. I always liked her. Quick wit. What's she doing anyhow?"

"Two words: art school."

"Oh, God."

Caroline giggled.

"Two more words," Mr. Tennyson said. "Nose ring."

"Ah, hell."

"Exactly." Mr. Tennyson paced around the shallow end in unhurried, mesmerizing circles. Everyone there watched his easy, meandering path, unable to take their eyes off him—except for Lucas, who inspected his palms. Mr. Tennyson held his drink in front of him like a flashlight in the dark as he moseyed through the water. "I'll tell you a story my mother always told me about kids. She grew up on a farm, and they had a springer spaniel bitch they would breed occasionally. The bitch had two litters—two good, healthy litters that looked exactly like her, same kind of black and tan markings—and she was a wonderful mother, nurturing them to an age when they could be sold. Then they bred her again and she had a third litter. Now these puppies didn't look like the first two, didn't look like this beautiful bitch. I don't know who the father was or anything, but they must have looked like him. I think their coats were lighter and their ears were shorter or something. You get the idea. One morning, a day or two after the puppies were born, my mother came down early to check on them and she found all the puppies, all five of them, dead. Their little bodies were these sad tiny heaps. Mom was devastated, obviously, and couldn't stop crying. She couldn't understand it and was blaming herself. Her dad sat her down and told her what must have happened. Sometimes, he told her, when dogs don't recognize the puppies they have—when they seem like little aliens to them—they sort of methodically sit on each little puppy until they expire, one by one. All because they're a bit foreign. And that's what this bitch had done."

"Holy shit," Fletcher said.

Mr. Kelly chuckled into his drink. Caroline laughed loudly, much to Max's surprise. Max had been feeling something like his guts being scooped out, and he'd never have guessed the owner of that smooth leg pressed to his could be having such a different reaction.

"That's so messed up," she whispered to him. She still sounded amused.

Max didn't reply.

Mr. Tennyson was whirling around the pool, following the lead of his drink, allowing his story to sink in. "I think about that story quite a bit," he said. "I think about that bitch not recognizing herself in those puppies and taking them out and ending the whole charade before it gets started."

Max hadn't thought about the purpose of the story, only the horror of it, but he got it now. He imagined everyone else thought Mr. Tennyson was talking about his daughter. Max understood the other angle, and he looked at Lucas as he sat, slumped in his chair, his arms shut tight, and his legs kicked out long in front of him. As he looked at his friend, Max felt something snap.

Max placed his drink down next to him. Mr. Tennyson kept with his perpetual pacing, silently moving and moving. He was hairy and muscular with a large, imposing chest. Max knew the man understood the figure he cut, the way he drew everyone's attention to him. Everything he did had a point, even when he was soused.

"He's so funny," Caroline said softly to him. She brushed her fingers lightly along Max's forearm. It felt grotesque to him, and he reflexively moved his arm away from her and then scratched at his cheek in confusion.

"I gotta take a leak," he said. She pecked him on the cheek. He stood and walked back into the magnolia trees that were beyond the pool. He unzipped and peed. He finished and headed for the pool but stopped when Lucas appeared coming his way.

"I think I'm done here," Lucas said.

"Yeah," Max said. "Let's jet."

They slogged straight through the trees away from the pool. They slipped through the gate that bordered the golf course and headed home. They didn't speak. When they reached the Tennysons' backyard, Lucas stopped and looked at the house. Every light appeared to be turned on in the place.

"I don't want to go in there," Lucas said.

Max understood. Neither did he. "You want to sleep over at my house?"

"You think your dad will be cool with it?"

"Who cares?"

Chapter Twenty-Eight

Lucas and Max arrived at Max's house after a twenty-minute walk. Their route took them across the University of Richmond's quiet campus and around its still, dark lake and then through dark, eerily slumbering suburban streets laid out among patches of woods. At one point, they stumbled upon a family of three deer, snacking by the side of the road. They were disappointed when the startled deer promptly dashed away. After Caroline's second call, Max put his phone on silent. He hated the thought of even hearing her voice. He didn't understand why, but something about her laughter during Mr. Tennyson's story gnawed at him. The houses in Max's neighborhood were in a different weight class than those where the Tennysons lived—comfortable but much more modest. Max wasn't sure whether he needed to be worried about the reliability of his living arrangements. He knew the family's money had come from his mom's career rather than whatever Dad could collect from a dwindling handful of lessons and what he brought home from the grounds crew. Max tried not to think about it.

His father's car was gone, and he and Lucas raided the kitchen for cold fried chicken and sodas as soon as they walked in the door.

"Does your dad ever cook or anything?" Lucas said. "I can't picture him fixing you dinner in the kitchen."

"Why do you think I like staying at your house so much?"

Max got a bone for Baxter, who was quietly whining, and brought it out back for him. When he gave it to him, Baxter gently took it and dropped immediately on the terrace to go to work. The three of them snacked together with the backyard spotlight on.

"You want to do some hitting?" Lucas said, licking his fingers clean of a second drumstick. "Fire up the machine?"

Max checked his phone. It was nearly eleven o'clock. "Nah, we're not supposed to run it past nine. The neighbors are OK with the noise as long as we keep decent hours."

"That sucks," Lucas said, standing up and pacing. He grabbed a bat that was propped against the cage and rolled it in his hands. "I really want to hit right now. Just crush some shit."

"I get it." Max leaned back in an Adirondack chair and yawned.

Lucas got into his stance and stared at an imaginary pitcher. "I've been thinking about something recently. Do you even like baseball anymore? I can't decide if I do."

Max was surprised at the question, and he realized he didn't have a clear answer. "I guess I like it. I loved it the other day when I started throwing that knuckle curve. But it hadn't been fun for a while before then. This year mostly has been trash."

"Right," Lucas pointed at him with the bat. "It's fun if you're doing well and it sucks if you're not. And if it sucks, it really, really sucks. I don't remember it being like that before. I used to just like playing, period. Now it's a whole thing."

"That's for sure."

"I don't play now without feeling my dad staring at me. He doesn't even have to be around. He can be on a frigging business trip on the other side of the country."

"Yeah, I'm always thinking about what I'm doing instead of just doing it." Max paused and let out a loud burp. He crushed his empty Coke can in his hand. "Every pitch I throw I can hear Dad, like, commenting on it. Telling me what I did wrong, even if I'm just throwing a bullpen."

"Can't we hit for a few minutes?" Lucas asked. "Your neighbors probably won't even notice." He was still pacing, as if he couldn't stay still.

Max smirked at him. "I thought baseball wasn't fun. Make up your mind."

"I don't know. I just feel like doing something. I've got to get this figured out or I'm going to lose it."

The doorbell rang, and Baxter gave a quick, shrill, perfunctory bark before returning to his bone. Max looked at Lucas. "Man, it's late as hell for someone to be showing up here."

"Where is your dad anyway?"

"I don't know. Probably out drinking with the grounds crew. Keep an eye on Baxter. I'll circle around front."

Max walked to the back gate and started to open it but stopped when he saw an older kid approaching. He recognized him as Eddie Barnes, a pitcher from Dad's Legion team. Max had been to a game earlier in the summer when the guy had melted down on the mound and started yelling at the visiting team's dugout. Tonight, he was wearing gray uniform pants and a T-shirt with Post 125 on it. He'd clearly just come from a game.

Eddie held up his hand. "Hey, man, how you doing? I saw the lights and thought I'd just come around here. You're Donnie Baseball's kid, right?"

"Yeah, I'm Max." He pointed behind him. "This is Lucas. Sorry, my dad's not here."

"That's a bummer," Eddie said. "I really wanted to talk to him."

Max leaned on the fence. "Didn't he get fired from that team?"

Eddie laughed. "In a big old blaze of glory."

"That sounds right."

"But before he did, he figured something out with my delivery, man, and it's changed my life. Not exaggerating. I hit ninety-three on the gun tonight."

"Holy shit," Max said.

"That's a major league arm," Lucas said, shaking his head. "I want one of those."

"Talk to Donnie. I'd never gone higher than eighty-eight before. I struck out fifteen in seven innings tonight. I was dealing like I never thought I'd deal in my life. After the game, a pro scout introduced himself. He didn't know I existed before tonight."

"Damn, what the hell did Dad do?" Max said.

"Here, I'll show you." Eddie walked the rest of the way to the gate, and Max opened it for him, glancing back to make sure Baxter was still focused on his bone.

Eddie walked in and surveyed the yard. "This is a nice setup. Must be cool to have a dad who's a coach."

"Only if you want to be coached all the time," Max said. "The batting cage is alright, I guess."

"Well, my dad's a deadbeat," Eddie said. "Haven't seen him in five years, so, tough luck and all that."

Max and Lucas exchanged looks.

Eddie smiled. "Does that pitching machine work?"

When Donnie got home, he saw the spotlights were on out back. Then he heard the ping of an aluminum bat. "Goddammit, Max." He walked quickly through the yard toward the back gate. When he got there, he was surprised at what he saw. Not that his son was feeding a ball into the pitching machine while Lucas waited with his rigid stance to hit, but that Eddie Barnes watched outside the cage, leaning on the netting as he peered at Lucas. "Right back up the middle, Lucas," Eddie said. "You got this."

Donnie opened the gate and was met by a leaping Baxter. He knelt and dutifully greeted the dog, rubbing under his chin, but looked toward Max and gave him a cutting motion to turn the machine off. Max complied. Donnie waited for the whirring machine to stop. "Fellas, it's way too late to be hitting. Max knows better."

"Sorry, Coach, that's on me," Eddie said. "I wanted to see if I could help Lucas with something."

Donnie stood and considered the three boys all looking at him. He noted how grim Max and Lucas seemed, while Eddie was practically vibrating with excitement.

"Tag called and told me about your night, Eddie. Nice job."

Eddie walked toward him, grinning. "It was incredible, Coach. Incredible. I wish you'd seen it. It was like I was a different guy. I read and reread and reread those pages you brought by, too. What are those? I've practically got them memorized already."

Donnie was embarrassed, and he was aware of his son watching him with curiosity. He'd forgotten the pages. "I'm kinda trying to write a book."

"Awesome," Eddie said. "I want to read all of it. I'll do whatever you say now. You want me to set myself on fire, I'll do it after tonight. I can't believe what that felt like out there. I owned those guys."

Donnie smiled. He knew exactly what Eddie meant.

"I tell you what," Donnie said. "I'll draw you up a schedule that's built around your pitching days. Workouts, drills, throwing, the whole shit and shebang. If you're serious, you'll stick to it. Some of it will involve coming over to school to work with me a couple of times a week."

Eddie looked uncomfortable. "Coach, I don't have that kind of dough."

Donnie waved him off. "I don't want anything from you."

Eddie shook his head. "I can't believe this, Coach. I can't believe this is happening. I wanted this so bad."

"Yeah, yeah, we all do. There's a few million guys out there who wished they had your arm. I hope you don't ever get used to it."

Eddie blinked quickly. "I won't."

Donnie stuck out his hand, and Eddie shook it. "OK, fine, fine, now please just go home. It's late as hell."

Eddie nodded. "I doubt I'm falling asleep anytime soon. I'm amped." He turned to Max and Lucas and waved. "See ya, guys."

After he'd left, Donnie turned to Max and Lucas. "You kids get it figured out or what?"

Lucas lifted the net and came out beneath it. "I can't take this anymore. It doesn't matter how hard I work or what I do—I can't hit a single line drive anymore. Period. But that guy gets to throw ninety-three because you shortened his stride? It doesn't make any sense."

"You'll be a lot better off if you stop thinking things are going to ever make any kind of sense," Donnie said. "What happened to Eddie was a fluke. I could take a thousand over-striders and fix them like I did him, and I bet there wouldn't be one of them that would gain more than a couple miles an hour. Not a one. He's a fluke, a goddamned beautiful lucky-ass fluke, and you don't want to waste your time wishing you were one of those. That's like wishing your right arm was magic."

Donnie thought both Max and Lucas seemed brooding and edgy, unreceptive to whatever was coming out of his mouth. No fun dealing with kids when they were like that. "Come in, get some ice cream or something, OK?" he said. "We'll take another shot at it tomorrow."

157

Lucas dropped the bat and nodded. Donnie patted him on the back as he passed. Max approached from his end of the cage, and Donnie grabbed him on the shoulder. "You got to show me how you're throwing that knuckle curve tomorrow, OK? Stubs don't know as much about pitching as he thinks he does."

"He knows plenty. Eddie's not the only one killing it." Max smirked. "So, you're writing a book? Seems like a stretch."

Donnie grimaced. "Don't I know it. But it's something your mom really wanted. She egged me on, kept telling me I should do this and share what I know. The video, too. And I ignored her when she was around. Said they weren't for me." He paused. "I know it sounds stupid, but I feel like it's something I can still do for her."

Max's smirk disappeared. He scratched at his nose as though it irritated him. Then he took a deep breath and nodded. "I think that's why I'm playing the piano so much." He started to walk inside but stopped, half inside and half out, and spoke again without looking up. "I didn't have to be such a dick about taking lessons. I knew how she felt about all that."

Donnie's throat caught on a response as he watched his son head for the kitchen. He considered his yard, the equipment scattered about, balls lying in the grass throughout the inside of the cage, and Baxter asleep on the terrace. He gave Baxter a gentle scratch on the back, and the dog opened his eyes, looked at Donnie, rose, shook, stretched, and ambled through the sliding back door to see what was happening in the kitchen. Donnie turned off the spotlight and followed him inside. Max and Lucas were considering the ice cream options. Baxter sat attentively to watch, while Donnie headed upstairs to write.

Chapter Twenty-Nine

Donnie arrived at Deep Creek on the morning of the triathlon. He brought a travel mug of coffee. Otis and Ricky were already at the shop, as was a small gathering of lively and familiar faces. A keg rested in the middle of the room, though a blanket was half-draped over it in case the wrong person walked in the door. It pained Donnie to stick to coffee, but he had a lesson with Lucas, and he was determined to get it right this time. The boy's problems had bothered him for months, and it seemed like a great failure on his part. It wasn't only Lucas, of course. He also wanted to be at his best for Max.

The mood in the shop was jovial. Esau was settled on the sofa with a red plastic cup of beer in his hand, and Tippie was sitting next to him, armed in the same fashion. Several former and current maintenance workers, a bunch of the teachers and coaches, and a few in-the-know alumni were there.

On the west side of the shop, Otis was working his way through his warm-up routine. Much to Donnie's amusement, he was jumping rope, looking as intense as a prizefighter, if not as quick.

Stubs had arrived, too. He stood on the east side of the shop and bawled at Ricky, who was stretching his calves. Ricky likely couldn't hear all the shit he was getting, since he wore earbuds and was bouncing his head to whatever private concert he was using to get in the mood. He made eye contact with Donnie, but there was no flicker of recognition.

"C'mon, you fat old man," Stubs yelled at Ricky. "Get your ass in gear."

Stubs spotted Donnie and approached him. "I got fifty on Ricky and I'm starting to consider it gone. He looks tubbier than I remembered." Stubs hadn't been to the triathlon in years.

"I wouldn't worry about that," Donnie said. "I saw him rip off a bunch of pushups a few weeks ago, and I know for a fact he's been off booze for like a week in preparation for this. I definitely can't say the same for Otis."

"Otis'll never go off booze," Stubs said. "That's like asking a bird to go off flying or Picasso to go off painting." He pointed at Donnie's coffee. "What's going on here?"

"Max's coming by with Lucas," he said. "I'm going to give Lucas a lesson."

If Stubs was bothered a client was going elsewhere, he didn't show it. In fact, he seemed pleased. "That kid. That goddamned kid. He's got some juice in that bat, but I cannot figure out how to get it out."

At nine, Esau, who served as a sort of emcee, brought Otis and Ricky together in the center of the shop. The place grew quiet as the men faced off nearly nose to nose and glowered at each other, surrounded by the small crowd. It was

159

silent. Stubs was so excited he was bouncing from one foot to the next, unable to stay still. Joe, who had arrived moments before, stood with them and took his first sip of beer.

"This is a best-of-three series of athletic superiority," Esau said solemnly. "One man wins, one man loses. There is nothing in the goddamned world simpler than that. The winner gets to pick his job for a year. The loser does not. Do you agree to these terms?"

"We do," Otis and Ricky said in unison. Then they turned together and walked in lockstep out the front door. The gathered mass clapped and shouted, cheering on whoever they had money on— "Kick his ass, Otis," "You the man, Ricky"—and fell in behind them.

Stubs walked alongside Donnie. He held up his arm. "Look, I've got goosebumps," he said.

The 400-meter run at the track was racing at its nip-and-tuck best. In years past, Ricky had thrived in the event, but he stumbled after 100 meters and seemed to panic, failing to trust his pace and rushing too hard to catch up. He had nothing left at the end, and Otis shuffled across the finish line first.

However, the tennis match turned into an upset, too. Otis was the annual favorite, but his stiff, one-handed backhand betrayed him to a degree that was awkward to watch. He sprayed his returns everywhere except between the white lines. He hit some wicked forehand winners and his serve was far more accomplished than Ricky's, but all Ricky had to do was steer the ball over to his opponent's backhand side and Otis was doomed. Ricky took the pro-set, 8-5, meaning the title, as every spectator there had hoped, would come down to the wrestling match.

Donnie, Joe, and Stubs were sitting in the wrestling gym stands with the rest of the crowd, awaiting the entrance of the stars for the day's main event, when Max and Lucas appeared in the doorway. Both boys were carrying their equipment bags and were dressed to play ball in shorts and T-shirts. Donnie rose and made his way to them.

"Hey, guys," he said. He could feel himself beaming. "You don't mind watching Otis and Ricky tear each other apart before we do some hitting, do you, Lucas?"

"Definitely not."

"I saved a couple of seats for you up by Joe," Donnie said, motioning with his thumb toward his brother. "Real primo spots."

The boys worked their way through the crowd to where Stubs and Joe were in the middle of the stands. Soon, the speakers blared to life with the sounds of AC/DC, and the impassioned crowd whooped and hollered.

Donnie returned to the stands and took a seat next to Max. On the mat, Ricky and Otis were working the crowd, and never were they more in their element. Ricky wore a pink feather boa, green wraparound shades, and copious amounts of glitter, while Otis had donned the cape of a vampire and greased the front of his hair into a remarkable point. Both wore maroon wrestling singlets with "Eagles" across the front that they had swiped from the school's supplies, and the varsity wrestling coach was standing on the mat in a ref's outfit with a whistle in his mouth. Ricky kept doing minor gymnastic stunts—a somersault, a running jump—and acting amazed at the results, pleading with the crowd for recognition, while Otis strutted coldly around the outside of the mat and watched him, as though sizing up his prey. "You're both embarrassing," Joe yelled.

Max laughed along with the rolling, thundering crowd. Donnie felt a tremendous relief that Max appeared to be enjoying himself. Then someone somewhere turned off the music, and the pals stopped their performance, ripped off the costume elements of their outfits, and prepared themselves for battle in earnest.

Ricky scored with a two-legged takedown in the first period, and Stubs erupted from the stands, "That's it, Ricky. You're a bad mother. Beat on that drunk like he deserves." Lucas and Max giggled.

The match was brutal and exhilarating. Ricky nearly managed a pin in the first, while Otis was on the verge of getting his counterpart's shoulders stuck to the mat in the second. In both instances, however, the subdued made desperate escapes to the sound of roars from the stands and the match continued. The third period was an epic confrontation. The wrestling was neither well-executed nor strategically sound, but it was hog-wild and headlong and that was better. Ricky and Otis slammed into each other over and over again, tossing each other to the mat with astounding emphasis. Donnie could see the exhaustion hitting them as they struggled with each other, their arms trembling and slick with sweat as they wrapped each other up and fought for position. Otis held a narrow lead until the match's final seconds, when Ricky managed a hair-raising takedown, flinging his buddy to the mat with a resounding thud to score two points and tie the score. Time expired, and the ref refused to allow the match to continue, citing the age and condition of the two participants, despite pleas from each of them. For the first time in the proud history of the triathlon, there was a tie.

Otis and Ricky hugged each other and then lay down separately on their backs on the mats. The crowd booed at first, but then Stubs started a chant of "U-S-A" that soon filled the room. Otis and Ricky rose to their feet, clasped hands, and held them together skyward. The place went crazy.

Donnie joined in, but he found himself unable to shake a thought that had snuck up on him. For the moment, all the boys and men in this raucous room were deliriously happy. Every single one of them. They were witnesses to a kind of triumph. Soon this performance would be over, though, and who knows what self-inflicted misery awaited them then—who knows where their thoughts would turn. Perhaps to old knee injuries, fat fastballs, and missed jump shots.

When things finally died down, Max and Lucas gathered their bags, slung them over their shoulders, and started for the door. Joe dropped from the stands behind Donnie.

"You joining us?" Donnie asked.

"Nah, I wouldn't be any help. I'm going to check on our fallen heroes." He glanced at Stubs, who was still in the stands, dancing from foot to foot. "That jackass could be useful."

Joe walked away, beer in hand, to tend to Otis and Ricky.

Stubs shuffled down the stands toward Donnie.

"You want to take another look at Lucas' swing?" Donnie said.

Stubs seemed surprised. "You sure?"

"Of course."

"Then hell yeah." He took two steps and jumped off the stands. He caught up to Lucas and wrapped an arm around his shoulders. "You, my friend, are a badass." They walked through the door together. Max and Donnie trailed them.

Outside, the sun was straight above without a cloud to bother it, and the day was hot, humid, and harsh. Donnie thought Max seemed taller somehow.

At the field, Donnie threw with Max to loosen up his arm, while Stubs supervised Lucas as he hit off the tee. Before they moved to the cage, Max approached Donnie and said, outside of Lucas' hearing, "You think you can help him?"

Donnie shook his head. "I don't know, man. Maybe, maybe not."

"He just wants to do better," Max said. He paused. "Badly."

"Yeah, yeah, don't we all."

Batting practice went about as poorly as Max had suspected it might. Lucas was still blocking every pitch, keeping his hips from ever releasing, so that ball after ball sliced harmlessly toward the right side of the pitching cage. Stubs remained quiet, deferring to Dad, and the atmosphere was tense and uneasy. Dad kept emphasizing relaxation, telling Lucas to loosen his fingers as completely as he could while resting the bat on his shoulder. No stride. As little movement as possible, a short swing that went from point A to point B. But nothing worked.

Lucas looked enraged, on the verge of tears, and after he failed to catch up with an inside fastball and missed it completely, he screamed, "Dammit," and slammed the bat on the ground. "Sorry," he said. "Sorry." He got back into his determined and rigid stance.

"Let's take a five-minute break," Dad said, dropping a ball from his hand into the plastic bucket at his feet. "Go get some water."

Donnie and Stubs picked up baseballs, while Lucas and Max crossed the dirt infield toward the dugout, slouching and dragging their feet. Max couldn't think of anything to say to help his friend, at least anything he hadn't already said many times over. Lucas was bouncing his bat on the ground as he walked and muttered curses.

They reached the dugout and Lucas took first turn at the water fountain. He sipped, rose, and wiped at his mouth, then looked at the bat in his hands with disgust. "I don't understand." He waved the bat back and forth in front of his eyes. "What the hell is wrong with me?"

Max drank from the fountain and sat on the dugout bench. Lucas stood nearby and took furious practice swings, one after the other. Dad was in the batting cage scooping up balls with Stubs, and Max watched him. Max's father was strange and sad and heartsick, and it was hard for Max to be around him without feeling those things, too. Mom had been the one that held them together—the reasonable one, the calm one, the funny one, the responsible one. Dad only understood baseball, and he seemed determined to say and do the wrong thing as often as possible. And yet here he was again, giving a shit about Max, no matter how terrible he was at it. Tomorrow, Max knew, would be no different.

Max thought of his dad trying to write a book, probably scribbling away in some notebook with a pen or typing awkwardly while he looked between the screen and the keyboard. Max couldn't imagine how difficult the work was for his father. Sitting still, reflecting, organizing his thoughts, writing clear sentences. That seemed like torture for the man. But Max also understood why he had to do it anyway.

Max stood from the bench and exited the dugout. He called back to his friend. "Come on, now, Lucas. Next round will be the one. Nothing but frozen ropes and bombs. You'll see."

When Lucas and Max returned, Stubs hopped behind the pitching fence and took a turn throwing. Donnie stood outside the cage on Lucas's open side and watched him slice pitch after pitch, the boy malfunctioning with eerie consistency. Donnie first studied his mechanics but then gave that up and watched the boy. He saw the barely hidden fury and desperation on his face, and he recognized it, knew it intimately, and wished he could wish it away for him. It was the result of wanting something badly, and it could never be solved for good. This boy had it in his mind that he had to get this right—that if he wasn't a superstar, he would be a failure. Max, of course, was in the same boat. All that pushing Donnie did, all of that yelling and cajoling was designed, day upon day, to build that very message. Donnie talked incessantly of the future, of doing X when you're fourteen so that you can be Y

163

when you're eighteen or Z when you were twenty-two. He had constructed something for Max that was specific and crushingly ambitious. Donnie was no different than Mel McGuire nor any of the other of those fathers with their crossed arms and grim faces. He may have known more than they did, but the voice that was in the head of his son—that blunt, commanding voice that followed Max wherever he went—was every bit as insistent on what a successful life looked like. And there was precious little room available there. Donnie knew that better than anyone.

Stubs kept throwing and Lucas kept hammering at the ball, his back shoulder dropping, his body failing him time and time again. Max was on the other side of the cage, sitting in the grass. He looked broken-hearted, and Donnie felt acutely the ways he was letting his son down today and had every day before it. He thought of his own father, who had spent every bit as much time on a baseball field with him as Donnie spent with Max. But not once had Donnie ever felt a heavy hand on his shoulder or an overbearing voice in his head. And Donnie, for all his ultimate personal disappointments, had never once felt like he had let down his father because of something he did or didn't do on a baseball field.

He thought of Dad as he preferred to think of him most clearly: throwing to him behind a pitching fence, his face earnest and focused, and then suddenly without warning, dropping a big curveball on him that made Donnie swing and miss in a furious whirl. Donnie would get all worked up in response, yelling and complaining, but Dad would just cackle at him and tell him to get a grip on himself. That would only make Donnie madder. It occurred to Donnie now that his father hadn't only been screwing with him for his own amusement—he'd also been trying to get him to enjoy himself, to not make every practice and day on a baseball field be about some grand, glorious goal. Every at bat, every swing, didn't need to be about the march to the major leagues. Sometimes it could just be about hitting the ball for the hell of it.

Then Donnie got an idea.

"Stop," Donnie said abruptly. He lifted the net on the batting cage and stepped inside. Lucas was breathing hard, his eyes near tears, the bat clutched tight in his hands. Donnie put his hand on his shoulder. "Are you having fun, Lucas?"

Lucas winced, dropped his eyes. "No, sir."

Donnie realized Lucas thought he was giving him a hard time. He released his hand from the kid's shoulder. He turned to his son. "You and Lucas walk back to the shop. On the floor, right inside Otis' office door, is a blue duffel bag. Grab that and bring it back here."

Max looked at him strangely, but the two kids took off together.

Stubs came out of the cage with Donnie's glove still on. "What're you up to now?"

"You'll see. Want to throw a bit?"

Donnie grabbed Max's glove and they backed up to sixty feet or so and fired back and forth to each other. Stubs had that good snap on his throws, a strong finish to the ball as it sped into Donnie's mitt. There was something gratifying about catching it.

Donnie wanted to ask Stubs a question. When Donnie was in the minors, he had imagined a certain moment playing out on an almost daily basis—a moment that would come with the big leagues. He would imagine the scene happening in different settings in different ways, but no matter the shape of the episode his imagination settled on, it always upset and excited him. He had never asked Stubs about it before because he hadn't wanted to hear about it. He realized he was ready now.

"So," Donnie said. "What was it like when the Reds called you up?"

Stubs was about to throw, but he stopped and held the ball. He looked apprehensive.

Donnie understood. "I'm serious, man. I want to know, and I want to know exactly. Where were you, what were you doing, who was it who told you?"

Stubs nodded and threw the ball to Donnie. They resumed tossing back and forth.

"It was great," he said. "It really was. I was playing for Chattanooga, and we were headed out on a road trip somewhere. The team bus was in the parking lot, and we'd all just piled into it. I was in the back, spread out back there, getting ready for another one of those awful drives. It doesn't take long for those to get old, does it?"

"That's the truth."

"As we're about to leave, Guy Christopher, our manager, comes onto the bus and holds up his arms for everyone to shut up. 'I've got an announcement,' he says. 'Something serious we got to deal with before we can go anywhere.' There were groans and shit, just because. In fact, I probably was one of the loudest. Then he says, 'We're losing one of our teammates today. Stubs Woodson, you have been called up by the Cincinnati Reds and you will report there immediately. You have made the major leagues.'"

Stubs had the ball again, and he stopped and studied it. "I lost it. You have to understand I had no idea I was even close yet. I wasn't sure the Reds even knew who I was. I've never cried in front of ballplayers before or since, but I started sobbing, right then and there. If I hadn't been so happy, I would have been embarrassed. I mean I leaned over and put my face in my hands and cried like I had no control at all. People didn't care, of course. Those guys went crazy, clapping, and yelling and carrying on. They slapped me on the back and gave me shit in all the best ways, and it took me forever to walk down that aisle. Nobody would let

165

me through. I finally got to the end, and Guy was standing there with his hands on his hips. He'd been a pretty good ballplayer, I knew, but he'd never made it higher than Double-A ball. He's got this huge grin on his face, and he says, 'You goddamned lucky bastard.' And he slapped me on the ass as I walked out the door." Stubs flipped the ball up and down in the air, catching it with his bare hand. He wasn't looking at Donnie. "Happiest moment of my life."

He reared back and hummed a throw to Donnie, who felt a sting on his palm when he caught it. He let the ball sit there for a moment and savored the pain it brought him. He then returned the throw, whipping the ball with a bit more juice to try to return the favor, and they resumed playing catch wordlessly, the ball a blur as it sped between them.

Donnie's hand was on fire, but he didn't betray the slightest indication of discomfort. He knew Stubs was feeling the same thing. Lucas and Max returned with the duffel bag and watched them throw. Could they see what was happening? It was a game he and Stubs had played when they were kids. Throw the ball as hard as you could at a short distance until someone flinched, grimaced, groaned or gave up. It was a battle of wills between two men whose stubbornness could be blamed and thanked for everything.

Donnie wanted that small gym, that dark one without the fancy field and the snack bar and the corps of coaches, and he wanted it to be his and only his. He still wanted to etch out his own place. And yet he was tired of fighting without reward. He thought of Amy and what he'd lost. He was always taking the difficult path when something straighter and clearer was right in front of him. He'd assumed Amy had loved that about him. Maybe she'd loved him despite it.

Stubs rifled a throw and Donnie caught it in the palm of his glove. The pain was acute and seemed to spread throughout his body.

"That's a good story, Stubs."

"Thanks, man. That means a lot."

"We should put it in our book."

Donnie enjoyed the stunned look that appeared on his friend's face. He removed his glove and tossed it and the ball aside. Nobody was forcing him to hurt himself.

He walked over to the duffel bag and opened it, revealing the plastic bats and whiffle balls Otis kept around for the pickup games he occasionally organized at lunch.

"We're going to play a game, two on two, me and Stubs against you two, and we're going to kick your ass," Donnie said. "Everybody hits their offhand, so you guys will be lefty and I'll be righty. Two outs an inning, five innings."

"Awesome," Stubs said.

Max crossed his arms. "What about his lesson?"

"I'm tired of lessons."

The boys hit first. Donnie pitched. Max led off the inning with a weak popup that Stubs snagged without a problem. That brought up Lucas.

Donnie almost laughed when Lucas stepped up to the baseball cap they were using for home plate. Lucas stood there in an unfamiliar left-handed stance and looked as relaxed as a person can look with a bat in his hands. The contrast with his normal stance was startling.

Donnie wasn't going to try to get him out, not this time. He served up a medium-speed pitch, straight as something out of a batting machine, belt high, over the dead center of the plate. Lucas uncoiled on the ball explosively, creating a massive popping sound at contact. The ball flew high and far and even Stubs racing after it at full tilt didn't get anywhere close to tracking it down. Lucas stood at the plate and watched the ball in befuddlement before finally breaking into a sprint. He was standing on second base by the time Stubs' throw whistled into the infield.

"Donnie, you're a goddamned genius," Stubs yelled from the outfield.

Donnie held the ball and walked toward the duffel bag they were using for second base. Lucas was breathing hard, watching Donnie as he approached. His eyes were wide with shock.

Donnie was enjoying himself. "So, what did we learn, Lucas?"

"I'm a lefty?"

"No, you're not a goddamned lefty." Donnie paused. "Shit, maybe you are, I don't know. No, the lesson is to stop listening to all of us old idiots. Forget about your arms and your feet and your hips and whatever else we bugged you about. Just hit the ball with the bat."

Lucas smiled. "I thought you were tired of lessons."

Donnie walked back to the pile of whiffle balls he had used to mark the pitcher's spot. Max had picked up the bat to hit again. He was watching Donnie with a massive grin on his face. Donnie winked at him.

"Hey, Stubs," Donnie yelled. "How the hell do you think it's possible I ended up with a son who can't hit for shit?"

"That's an easy one," Stubs said. "Someone else is the father."

Donnie nodded vigorously. "I always suspected as much."

Max looked delighted at the plate, the bat on his shoulder. "Me, too."

Donnie threw the next pitch at his son's head.

Max lurched out of the way in time but was sent spinning in circles away from the plate. Stubs yelled ecstatically from the outfield, "Back him off the dish, Donnie Baseball. Don't let that mope dig in." Lucas feigned outrage from second base, having a blast at last, "That's bush league BS. C'mon, Max. Back up the middle, baby. Knock him from his perch." Max settled back at the plate. He stared at Donnie with theatrical anger, but he was unable to suppress a smile. Donnie licked his fingers and picked another ball up from the ground by his feet.

He fired a fastball in on the hands. Max swung hard but late, jamming the ball off the bat near the grip and sending a short, soft popup toward third base. Donnie was off chasing the ball at contact. He took a few long and swift strides and then dove fully for it as it dropped. He felt it fall neatly into his outstretched hands as he hit the ground.

Stubs howled into the air. Lucas and Max both shook their heads, looking pissed.

Donnie rose and ran in. He grabbed a bat and stepped to the baseball cap to hit. He waited impatiently as Max moved to the makeshift mound area. Max palmed a ball and looked toward his target full of cold intention. Donnie was hitting righthanded, something he hadn't done in decades, and he felt graceless and wooden but eager. Judging by Max's expression, Donnie guessed the boy was going to bring him the best he had.

Max rocked and fired, and the ball seemed headed directly for Donnie's face—a retribution pitch. Donnie jerked backward, falling away hastily from the plate, only to then recognize the spin on the ball. It was a beautiful, arching curveball, and it broke from Donnie's head to fall neatly across the plate at the knees in one swift, devastating action.

Max stuck out his chest and held a single finger in the air.

Strike one.

Lucas and Stubs laughed and shouted.

Donnie shook his head, smiling, and let everyone have their fun. He checked his fingers on the bat, lining up his knuckles just right. It took skill and practice to make a whiffle ball move like that. He planted a foot back into an imaginary batter's box, looked out toward the field ahead of him, and considered the circumstances. There was no one out, no one on base, and this young pitcher he was facing had a hell of a curveball.

Acknowledgements

I cannot thank enough the many people who have provided support during the writing of this novel, including Tom Batten, Jack Boyd, Ryan Cales, Susann Cokal, Thom Didato, Phil Feger, Matt Gentry, Guy Hansen, Adriane Hanson, Kirk Kjeldsen, Carin and Seth Krawitz, Sarah and Christophe Lawrence, Chad Luibl, Stephanie Mack, Clint McCown, Earl McKenzie, Tom Mervenne (including for the fantastic cover design), Seamus Morgan, Shannon O'Neill, Meagan Saunders-Spearman, and David Romhilt. I'd like to particularly thank Tom De Haven for his time and insight—I feel incredibly fortunate to have worked with him throughout this experience. And, most of all, thanks to my family—Mom and Dad, Peyton, and Luke, Elise, and Shannon.

Made in United States
Cleveland, OH
15 June 2025

17760034R00099